145 Men I Met

in *Dubai*

Han Birondo

Is there still a man today who isn't afraid to go deep
into a woman's heart?

My phone's vibration wakes me up. I pick it up, and with one eye I peep at it. It vibrates again and slips from my hand, hitting me hard on the nose.

Fox! I sit up and thumb open my phone. As I am looking at the notifications, I realize that I do not recognize the logo of one of the apps. I click on it.

Tinder? I have matches? How did it…

"Lana!"

I hurt my throat with that sudden outburst.

"Lana!"

She comes out of the bathroom, scantily clad in a towel.

"What happened?"

She's visibly alarm.

"You're heavily dripping."

"I'm taking a shower when I hear you screaming. What happened?"

"This."

I raise my phone in her direction.

"Your phone's not working?"

"Not properly, to my perspective."

I'm still holding the phone in the air with a raised eyebrow.

"Care to explain what you did with my phone last night?"

"I don't understand you, girl. I'm feeling cold. I will continue my shower."

"Lana, I have messages from men I don't know!"

"Oh…"

And she displays that innocent look which I'm sure works with men, but is annoying me by the minute.

"Let me continue with my shower, and I'll explain after. Just give me ten more minutes, girl."

She retreats back into the bathroom.

Naughty Not Nice: Looking hot, babe.

Romantic Leo: How I'd love to have you in my arms.
You make me dreamy.

Goodness heavens!

Lana made a profile for me on an online dating app! I throw my phone onto her bed.

Deal with that.

A moment more and she is out of the bathroom, looking like Betty Boop in a towel. I'm looking at her with obvious annoyance.

"Why did you do that?"

"Hanna, it's been four months since Zaki left. He's not coming back. It's high time you move on. And this is one sure way to start."

"Lana, it's too soon. I'm not ready."

"You'll never be ready if you're not going to start being ready. You're almost 35 years old. You're beautiful. You're smart. You deserve to be loved. Prince Charming will not find you if you don't proactively look for him too."

"Does he have a profile in that app?"

I retort sarcastically, eyeing the ceiling with annoyance.

"Perhaps he does, but how will you know if you don't have an account there as well?"

"Are you getting any commission from that app for recruiting new users?"

I turn my back to her and cover myself with the blanket.

"OMG, girl! This one is really good-looking. He seems smart too. His profile is well-written. He's British. Check him out."

I make no effort to move. British or not, hottie or not, I am not interested. I only turn when I hear the blow dryer switch on.

"Where are you going?"

"I have a lunch date."

"This early?"

"It's 11:30 AM, girl."

It's tempting to confirm the time on my phone. But I do not want to see the messages from those strangers. I feel like I'm betraying the memories of Zaki by doing so. My phone buzzes intermittently on her bedside table.

"Aren't you going to check who those messages might be from?"

"I'm not interested."

I snap at her drily while making a mental plan of how I'll be spending this weekend.

"But they are interested in you, Hanna! Don't be ridiculous."

"I'm not being ridiculous. I just can't do it now, Lana."

"Then when? You need to help yourself move on. It's May now. When are you going to get out of this?"

Does moving on have to be marked on the calendar? Why is this world so obsessed with moving on, even without a clear direction of where to go or what to do next? What if I don't want to move on yet?

"No one can rush your recovery, not even you to yourself. But I just want to remind you that that chapter of your life with Zaki is over. Stop going over it again and again in your mind, hoping for the ending to be different, when you know it will not be."

That stings. I stay silent.

"Hanna, my date is here. I'll see you later. There are scrambled eggs and bread in the kitchen."

I turn to look at what she's wearing.

"I have not seen that dress before."

"I got it the other day. Is it nice on me?"

"Yeah, you look really pretty in it. Thanks for the breakfast."

"Sure. See you later."

I give her a thumbs up, and to the door she goes. The moment I hear the door locked, I force myself to get up. I'm searching for the other pair of my slippers when my phone vibrates again. It startles me. I press on the general button to see what the alert is – or from whom. I have a new match.

Wow. Will it ever stop?

On my way to the bathroom, my phone vibrates again.

My goodness!

As I'm splashing water on my face, a realization seems to be washing in on my consciousness too. I stop and look at myself in the mirror. My eyes bear the sadness I still feel in my heart. I turn my back to the mirror. My own appearance hurts me. I close my eyes to prevent the tears from coming out. It has more power than my lids. In seconds, my cheeks are drenched. It still pains so bad. The past months have done very little to distance me from the separation.

I walk out of the bathroom without looking at the mirror again. I remember the breakfast Lana prepared for me. I pick up the plate from the kitchen countertop and walk to the couch while wiping my tears with the shirt I have on.

I pick up my phone, and in between mouthfuls, I check the messages on Tinder.

Hot&Hung: Wow! That red dress really got me! Mind wearing that on our first night out?

Romantico Italiano: I'm getting hot and heavy here. Would welcome your help, dear.

Oh, glorified cow!

I'm beginning to get irritated, but I am also enticed to continue reading the other messages. They have similar tones, though singing their phrases differently. I become curious as to what photos Lana has used to generate such reactions. I navigate inside the app. I nearly drop the fork from my hand when I see my photos she uploaded.

Holy mother fox!

Second Helping After The Fall

I'm glad that Ashley is back from her vacation. The silence of the apartment while she's away echoed into my consciousness. Hearing her moving about in her room or in the kitchen is comforting for me. Another beating heart reminds me to keep breathing myself despite the pain inside me becoming overwhelming at times.

"So how's your family, babe?"

"All's good. My mom's symptoms don't show any sign of improving despite her proactive role in containing her moods. My dad's tremendous patience is exceptional, though."

"Love. He loves her so much that he's able to bear it all, and whatever else that might come."

"I agree. I wish we could find the same kind of love, babe."

"We will in time. I'm sure of it."

I almost whisper that. I cannot put enough strength into my words, given the weight of my emotions still ravaging me inside.

"So how are you? How have you been while I was away?"

"Just the same, surviving each day as best I could. I squatted on Lana's couch on some days."

"Does it still hurt that much?"

I simply nod.

"I don't know when or how I can get out of this. I'm tired of feeling sad, of crying, of carrying this baggage. Don't get me wrong, babe. You know how much I loved Zaki, and still do, but Lana is right. I have to help myself. I just don't know where I can find the strength to start over."

I'm beginning to crack, tears moistening my eyes. Ashley comes closer to me. Her hug offers a respite.

"Maybe you need to start seeing other men now. You don't need to love again right away. Love when your heart's ready, and I know that you'll know when that will be. For now, learn to enjoy the company of men again. Who knows who you'll meet?"

Will I meet another Zaki?

**

"Babe?"

Ashley tentatively peeks from behind my door.

"Are you awake?"

"Yeah, babe. Come in."

"What are you up to tonight?"

"I have no plans. Though I'm hoping we can go watch a movie or eat out."

"What about going to a bar? My friend Nikki and her friend are planning to go to Barasti. They're inviting me. I want to tag you along."

"Sure. What time are we going?"

"Around 10:00 PM."

"Alright. For now, can we have dinner?"

"Sure. I'll just go get dress."

**

I have not been to any bars or pubs or whatever's here in Dubai in the years that I have been living here. My work has been my primary preoccupation. I sit on my bed contemplating whether to go or not.

I need to help myself heal. I need to start now.

I pace inside my room, taking deep breaths. I pick up my hula hoop and start spinning it around my waist, even without music on. After a few minutes, my heartbeat starts rising, and sweat is beginning to glisten on my forehead. Soft knocks on my door take me out of my mind.

"Yes, babe?"

"All good? You're still up for going?"

"Yes. I'm actually thinking of what to wear. I've never been out to such a place before."

"It's a beach bar, babe, so casual, I guess. I'm going in jeans."

"Do you think going in shorts is okay?"

"Absolutely."

"Alright then. I'll go for a quick shower and should be ready in 20 minutes max."

"I'll go get ready myself, then."

**

My heart's pounding as we enter Barasti. The place has a vibe to it that I immediately embrace. The noises from the blaring speakers everywhere discourage me from thinking. The plethora of people from different countries who are here excites me, though I cannot understand why. We are multi-racial in the office. We also have colleagues from across the globe who visit our office here in Dubai regularly. I should be used to this scene by now, having been with the company for over four years. However, there's just something about this place that thrills me.

Ashley lets go of my hand upon seeing her friends by the bar. The temporary disconnection from the only thing that's familiar to me at that place kinds of root me at my spot. I move with reluctance as she waves at me to come forward. I'm always very shy around new people. I smile tentatively at her friends as she makes the introduction.

"What would you like to drink?"

Nikki asks, leaning in closer to me.

"I don't know, actually. I've only had wine so far. What would you recommend?"

"Would you like to try this?"

She offers me a sip of Stella Artois.

"What options do I have apart from that?"

"Here, babe, try this."

Ashley hands me her bottle of Heineken. I nod in affirmation.

With drinks in our hands, we roam the place. The song that the DJ is playing on the stage by the beach area entices us to dance. We make our way through the crowd, dancing as we go. I cannot compare my experience at this moment to anything else. I allow myself to be taken in by it.

A little past midnight, we thought of resting by the sun loungers close to the water. My three Indian companions are talking in their language. I lie down and look at the moon, trying to calm my breathing as my heart's still racing from hours of dancing. A voice that I do not recognize cuts through my reverie.

"I think it's too early for you to be sleeping, princess."

Startled, I sit up abruptly, causing the beer in my hand to spill. The blueness of his eyes astounds me. It has a hypnotic effect. My tongue's drunk, cannot utter a word.

"Hi! I'm Marcus."

He offers his hand. I place mine in it instead of shaking it. He assists me to stand. I cannot take my eyes off of his. It has a beautiful contrast against the darkness of our surroundings.

"I'm Hanna."

Then a smile parts my lips, a warm glow beginning to grow inside me.

"So you can talk, after all."

My cheeks flush at that remark.

"Your eyes are beautiful."

"You are beautiful."

And he kisses the back of my hand.

"Shall we dance?"

He's already pulling me back toward the crowd. My friends are surprised but make no objections.

By this time, there are more people dancing. We're all vying for spaces. The songs are all upbeat, but we're dancing very close to each other. The feeling of his hands on my waist and his breath on my ear is an intoxicating mix. I have had three bottles of Heineken, but these first minutes with him are giving me stronger punches in the stomach, so to speak.

"Can we go somewhere else, a bit quieter?"

His voice causes a sensation in me. I slightly shiver. He rubs my back reassuringly.

"It's ok if you want us to stay here. It's just that I want to talk to you a bit. But we can just stay here."

His breath is warm against my ear, making me lose focus. He tightens his hold on my waist, pulling me ever closer to him.

"Perhaps you're right. Let's go inside now."

I'm beginning to feel aroused – and confused – by the proximity of our bodies. He nods.

I talk into Ashley's ear, telling her where we're going, prior to snaking through the thick, dense crowd of people that has pooled in around us. As he leads me away from the drunken crowd, I feel like being taken out of my own mind, with my maddening thoughts parting as I pass.

Inside, there are fewer people and, surprisingly, a table for us. He moves his chair closer to mine and asks if I want to order anything.

"I think water would be nice. Thanks."

He gestures to a crew. After he gives him our orders, the barrage of questions begins.

"So, Hanna, where are you from? I've been thinking about it all the while we were out there."

I chuckle at his obvious confusion.

"I'm from the Philippines."

His disbelief is evident, making his blue eyes seemingly more pronounce.

"Why do you seem so surprised?"

"You look different from the Filipinos I've met so far. You sound different too."

I've received the same remark for years now.

"We all sound different from each other, even if we may be from the same country. But we shouldn't be so concerned about that and miss the value of what one is saying."

"And of course, you're smart."

He leans in closer and kisses my left cheek. I'm caught off guard. In an instant, I feel strong currents of electricity run through me, and it settles on my cheeks, causing them to flush.

"I'm sorry. I think I'm making you uncomfortable."

"You don't miss much, do you?"

"I'm afraid that if I don't pay attention, you'll disappear before my eyes."

I hold his gaze. Then he winks. I crack and we laugh at each other.

"Do you have plans tomorrow?"

"Nothing yet. Why?"

"Maybe we can have lunch?"

"Are you asking me or inviting me?"

"I'm asking you, and I'd love for you to accept my invitation."

"What time?"

"Would 1:00 PM be okay?"

"Okay."

He fishes his phone from his jeans pocket and places it in my hand.

"Please."

I saved my number in it. A moment later, my phone's vibrating.

"That's me."

"It's almost 2:00 AM."

"Does Cinderella have a curfew?"

"No. But I wonder where my friends are."

"Do you live with them?"

"With Ashley, yes."

"Which one is Ashley?"

"The one I spoke to before we headed out here."

"She's an Indian, right?"

"Yes."

"Where's your family?"

"Mom and my oldest brother are in the Philippines. Another older brother lives in England. What about yours?"

"My parents are still in Syria. My sisters are in Lebanon."

The mere mention of Syria rings my internal alarm bell.

"How are your parents? Are they safe?"

"Yes. Thank you. They're in Latakia."

"A government-protected area. That's good to hear."

"How do you know that?"

"I follow the news, Marcus."

He laughs, and I'm flustered.

"What's funny?"

"My name is Saad."

"Who is Marcus?"

"I just kind of like the name."

I give him a narrow look, acting upset.

"I'm sorry. I didn't mean anything bad. I was just being playful."

He reaches for my hand and brings it to his lips.

"Trying to charm your way into my pants, huh?"

"A man can dream, Hanna, and he can also wait."

His words stir me inside. I slowly pull my hand away.

"No, princess."

He pulls it back to him.

"I'm not used to the modern ways, Saad. But I'm not offended by yours. I'm just a bit uncomfortable about it."

I give his hand a gentle squeeze. He squeezes it back and places it against his heart.

"I'll remember to go slowly, habibti, from this moment on."

I smile at him.

"It's getting really late. Can we go and find my friends now, please?"

"Sure."

After paying for our orders, he helps me out of my seat. Then we head back to the open beach. People are starting to walk in the opposite direction from us, and amongst them are my friends.

"Babe!"

I wave at Ashley.

"Someone got busy!"

Ashley beams. Then I introduced Saad to them.

"Let me take you both home now. So this beautiful lady will have the energy to see me again later during the day."

He takes my hand and offers his arm to Ashley.

"Wow! First date tomorrow, huh? You're quick, man!"

"I might have to run against time."

Saad squeezes my hand again. I just smile at him. He seems to be joking, but my ears pick up an underlying tone to it and send it directly to my brain for processing.

Once outside our building, the farewell is slightly awkward.

"I cannot convince you to come home with me?"

"Not a chance."

I smile and lean in closer to his face, his blue eyes pleading. I kiss both his cheeks.

"Good night."

I step out of the car the following second.

"I want a blow-by-blow account of what happened, babe."

Ashley immediately presses me for information the moment we get into the elevator.

"All I know is his name and where he's from."

"What? You were with him for over an hour."

"Yeah, but we were dancing, and we had just a little time to talk. It was so noisy there."

"He seems nice, though. Try to get to know him more tomorrow."

"Oh, I intend to."

We disappeared into our respective bedrooms upon reaching our apartment. The pleasant surprise of this evening follows me to bed.

Saad.

I am replaying what happened tonight in my mind when my phone vibrates on the bedside table. It's a WhatsApp message from a number I haven't saved yet in my contacts list.

SAAD: I've reached home some time back, still smiling at the thought of having met you.

ME: Same here.

SAAD: It may seem stupid of me to ask, but are you single?

ME: Yes. I hope you are too.

SAAD: I am. Never been married and no kids – at least none that I know of!

His message is followed by so many laughing emojis. He sure does have a funny streak.

ME: Should I be worried?

SAAD: Little.

And more emoji follows that short response.

SAAD: Seriously, though, I have none. What about you?

ME: My uterus has not been utilized for that purpose.

SAAD: What other parts of you have not been utilized yet?

ME: Good night, Saad.

SAAD: Oh, really…

ME: You must let me sleep now, or you'll be having lunch by yourself later today.

SAAD: Evasive princess. You can't abandon the conversation just as it's starting to heat up.

ME: Precisely the reason why I should. Good night again. It's really nice to have met you tonight.

I put my phone on flight mode without waiting for his response. I'm overindulging myself in his attention. I can hear my heartbeat thundering inside my chest.

Calm down, Hanna.

I close my eyes and concentrate on my breathing. Sleep knocks me down shortly after.

**

My hula hoop is spinning on my waist when Ashley's head peeks from my bedroom door. I stop its rotation and pause my player.

"Someone's getting ready for her date."

"Good morning, babe."

"So, are you excited?"

There's no denying that I am, and neither can Ashley contain hers.

"Yes! But I'm also nervous."

I can feel my cheeks getting redder.

"That's normal, but I'm sure you'll be fine. What time is he coming?"

"He said at 1:00 PM."

"What is it, babe?"

"I can't believe this is happening. We were just talking about this last night."

"Yes, I know. But I think this is a good thing. Just try to enjoy, and don't think too much. Do you know where you two are going?"

"No. He didn't say anything last night, and neither did it occur to me to ask."

"Do you know where he lives?"

"There are many things I was not able to ask him, babe, even the most basic info. I was overwhelmed. Last night we chatted briefly on WhatsApp. I terminated the conversation hastily because I panicked. I'm not used to talking to another guy, apart from Zaki and those in the office."

"Understandable. It will take some time. But, babe, you really need to try harder. I know it's easier said than done, but there really isn't any other way open for you moving forward."

"I know."

But knowing is very different from doing.

"What are you going to wear?"

"Just a simple dress, perhaps. I don't want to look too put together."

My phone vibrates in my hand, startling me. I raise it to show Ashley who is calling.

"Go ahead, answer him."

Then she quietly slips out.

"Hi."

"Hello! Hello there, princess! You left me last night."

"I was really sleepy and tired. It was very late as well."

"You're not used to the nightlife, I think."

"I don't have a nightlife or any other kind, except the one I'm living."

"Are you always like this?"

"Like what?"

"So serious."

"Is that bad?"

"No, not at all. But your reservations make me wonder."

"About what exactly?"

"About your story. There's always a reason why people are the way they are."

"True. However, I'm afraid you might find me boring."

"I don't think so. Serious, yes, but I doubt you're boring. For one, I think you're smart. I think I'll enjoy shedding your layers as we go on. And I'll definitely start today. Are you still up for lunch?"

"Sure. Where are we going?"

"What do you fancy eating? Are you okay with Arabic food?"

"I'm okay with any cuisine, just nothing too spicy."

"Noted, princess. I'll come pick you up at 1:00 PM then."

"Alright. See you."

"Ciao!"

My muscles tense seconds after hanging up.

I'm going out on a date… with another man! Holy dang, what am I going to wear? How short should I go?

I rummage through my cabinet. My dresses are all above the knees and figure-hugging in cuts. I don't want to give the wrong impression. The vibration of my phone on the bedside table interrupts my dilemma. I check the notification.

Smelly crap. Another new match on Tinder. Will it ever stop?

Shortly before 1:00 PM, I thought of going to Ashley's bedroom for some reassurance. I knock gently.

"Babe?"

"Come in, babe."

"Do I look okay?"

I'm wearing a floral summer dress that covers me well on top, but has a very short hemline – five inches above the knee, to be exact.

"Yes. You look pretty and sexy. Approved! But, babe, your cheeks are so red."

"I'm nervous."

Ashley gets up from her bed and embraces me.

"You'll be fine. Try not to think so much. You're not breaking any law or betraying anyone by going out with him, so chill."

She means well, but her words do not offer any aid to pacify my maddening heartbeat.

"Thanks, babe. I'll see you later."

As I wait in my room for Saad's arrival, my anxiousness only grows by the minute. I check myself in the mirror.

Holy fox. I look like a tomato with a face. Then I hear my phone vibrating on the bedside table. Saad is calling.

"Hello."

"Hi. I'm here."

"Okay. I'll go down now."

My chest is heaving because of my rapid breathing. My excitement is mixed with an equal amount of nervousness.

"Hello, pretty girl!"

"Hi!"

I offer my cheeks, but he peppers me with kisses so close to my lips.

"You're crazy."

"Any man would be crazy not to be crazy over you."

"You seem to have stock loads of those cheesy lines."

"And obviously, they don't seem to be working on you. I need to change tactics."

"You only need to be truthful. That'll surely work with me."

"We just met, and I can understand your doubts, but I hope that I don't scare you. I don't bite so hard."

He winks playfully at me.

"Flirt!"

"That, habibti, is what you call nonverbal communication."

I burst out laughing. He certainly is a funny and smart guy.

"Where are we going?"

"I'm kidnapping you."

"I'm a willing victim."

And I wink at him.

"Oh! My, my, my. Someone's copying my style."

I feel the heat on my cheeks intensifying as we continue our banter. The feel of his cold knuckle surprises me.

"You're blushing so much. I hope this is a good thing."

I just smile at him in response. My ribcages, though, can burst any minute now as my heart is doing quadruple beat per second.

Calm down, Hanna. This is just a date.

"Here we are."

"Arz Lebanon. Am I pronouncing it right?"

"Lebanon, yes."

As he leans closer and kisses me on the cheek, all I can do is close my eyes and let the sensation invade me. He's much too quick for me to predict his next moves. The sound of my own heartbeat is thundering in my ears. When he holds my hand as we enter the restaurant, my disorientation grows.

"Are you okay?"

"Yes."

"You seem tense."

He brings my hand to his lips.

"I'm just not used to…"

"Perfection. I can understand. There's only one me in this world, habibti."

"Surely, you're one of a kind."

I fail to stifle my laughter. I can barely talk. I'm still deep in the joke. He has to order for me when the waiter approaches our table.

"Each time you laugh, my confidence is getting stronger."

"You don't look like you need help on that aspect."

"I do – every man does – when with a girl like you."

"A girl like me?"

"Yes, a girl like you."

His blue eyes look straight into my raven pair.

"You're very guarded. What's your story?"

I'm not expecting that. My mind crams for an answer.

"When was the last time you were with a man?"

"Too many questions."

And my brain seems to be sleeping right now when I need it to think!

"We have the whole afternoon, habibti."

Our food is being served, affording me time to compose my thoughts.

"Bon appétit."

"I wouldn't think twice about having you than this."

I almost choke on a piece of fries.

"How many do you have in a week?"

"What? Do you mean French fries?"

"A different one each night seems like an easy feat for you."

"Ouch!"

He jokingly stabs himself in the chest.

"Don't expect me to apologize."

"I'm expecting you to undress."

I cough out a small portion of Tabouleh from my mouth.

"Damn duck! That was deliberate!"

"What? I meant for you to shed your layers, so I can get to know you."

"Flirt!"

"I don't know why you keep accusing me of being that."

Three minutes of silence is his limit.

"You can start now."

"Start what exactly?"

"Tell me your story."

"What makes you think there's one to tell?"

"A girl like you cannot not have one."

"A girl like me."

"You heat up with a mere touch. Don't think I have not noticed. You're smart and can return my banters quickly, but I can tell it's not something you're used to. So, where's Prince Charming? Or what happened to him?"

The French fries clog my throat, blocking the words from coming out of my mouth.

"I can understand if you can't talk about it yet. I just hope it's okay for me to keep seeing you."

"Yes. I think I like that."

"Good. I like you too."

He winks as he chews down his Kebab.

"I worry you might start losing your lashes as you keep doing that."

"I don't need lashes to look at you. I can lose all of it if it means I get to look at you always."

"You seemed to have memorized a book of pick-up lines. Is that something that you guys pass around to each other?"

"I don't trade secrets with my friends."

"No? But you exchange goods with them?"

"All the more no, especially not someone like you."

"Someone like me. I'm beginning to feel like I'm a peculiar kind."

"I think you're special. I always have the knack for the special ones."

"Oh yeah? What happened to your other special ones?"

"You're good. Really good, in fact."

"What?"

"I asked you ten minutes ago about your story. Now you're the one grilling me."

"I'm special, as you said."

And I wink at him flirtatiously.

"How come you've never been married?"

"Some opportunities don't come knocking on people's doors that easily."

"Could it be that you didn't hear them knocking? Your door doesn't seem to be the kind that has a buzzer outside."

"I'm always looking out of my window, though."

"But you don't open up to just about anyone."

"That's a scary thing to do. Strangers can be robbers, or worse, murderers."

"I can't imagine you to be the kind who'll allow herself to be robbed."

"Can you rob someone of love?"

"I'd love to know how that smart mouth of yours tastes like."

"Gross! I'm sure I have Tabouleh between my molars!"

"Actually, you have something on your chin."

He leans closer and gives me a smack on the lips.

"Thief!"

"I'm willing for you to get even with me."

"I don't think I want another serving of Kebab from your mouth."

"Sure? It might taste different."

My laughter reaches the other tables. I'm aware of the eyes that are now on me, but I cannot stop myself.

"I'll have to charge you for this."

He says teasingly.

"How must I pay?"

"Chance. Can we try?"

He reaches for my hand. That silences me for a moment.

"I'm afraid I'm not good at relationships."

"No one is. I don't think we grow smarter in every relationship. We become more cautious, yes, and more mature. But maturity doesn't always equate to being better at love."

"I agree. I can't promise anything. I'm not even sure I'm ready now."

"I don't think we'll ever be at any given time. It's a matter of desire. And I want you so much, Hanna."

"Is this just about sex? There are plenty for you to choose from here."

"Of course not. Don't mistake my jokes—"

"Loaded with sexual innuendoes!"

"Do I offend you with those? I can stop."

"It's alright, really. It's just that I'm not used to it."

"I was right. You're no street girl."

"What does that mean?"

"Never mind that. Going back to what we're talking about, no, it's not just sex that I want from you. Dubai can be a lonely place for those who are here without their families. What do you say we become Air Supply?"

"Air what?"

"Air Supply. Two less lonely people in the world."

I crack out so loud at that. My sides are starting to hurt. It feels so good to be laughing like this again.

"Thank you. It's been a while since I laughed like this."

"Don't thank me yet. There's more to come."

He sure knows his words. But a woman hardened by experience cannot be easily swayed.

"A woman has three ears. The one inside her records everything that it hears. Please be careful with your words."

"Noted, habibti. Do you want anything else from here?"

"No. I'm good. Thanks."

"What about coffee or ice cream?"

"Ice cream. But can we have it at another place?"

"I knew you're a licker."

I swat the back side of his hand.

"You don't lick your ice cream? I do."

I stifle my giggle while he offers to help me get up as we get ready to leave. He holds my hand as we walk out to the car. With each contact, I feel less threatened.

Perhaps it's okay to get used to this.

"Do you know how to swim?"

"Yes. Why?"

"Do you want to swim tomorrow?"

"Sure. Where?"

"Have you been to Kite Beach?'

"Yes, once. I didn't get to swim then, though. We just picked up another friend."

"I'd love to be your first then."

I look at him with one raised eyebrow.

"First *to swim with you* there. You have quite a malicious mind, habibti."

He delivers his jokes so well that it's hard not to laugh, even with the silly ones.

"Those dimples are really cute."

"Thank you. They're gifts from my father."

"How is he?"

"He had died some years back."

"Oh, I'm sorry to hear that."

"No worries at all. He lived a full life."

"What about your mom?"

"She's in the Philippines, with my older brother."

"How many brothers do you have?"

I think the noise last night at Barasti erased his memory of the same conversation we had there.

"Two. How are your parents?"

"They're okay. They'll be here next month."

"Oh, wow! That's nice."

"On that note, I'd like to ask for your help."

"Sure, anything."

"Can you help me arrange my apartment? To get it ready for them. I ordered some furniture from Ikea. It should be delivered next week."

"Okay."

I've never been to any man's apartment, apart from Zaki's, and certainly not when I just met him. But somehow I just can't decline Saad's request.

"Are your friends going to help out too?"

"No."

Aren't guys better at moving furniture in the house? Is this just an excuse to get me to his place?

"Where are we going now?"

He's taking a familiar route, somewhere I'm not sure I want to be at right now.

"I like to sip my coffee while looking out to the sea."

My heartbeat is picking up its pace. As we enter JBR, I'm once again awash with emotions from the past. I close my eyes.

It's over. It's all over.

"We can go somewhere else if you don't want to be here."

We're already in the basement parking. Saad's looking at me intently, his blue eyes reading the emotions on my face.

"It's alright. I'm sorry for my *temporary* relapsed."

I bow my head down, looking at my hands, and missing Zaki's.

"Did you use to come here with him?"

I just nod in response without looking at him, but I can feel his eyes on me.

"Do you want us to go somewhere else?"

"No. It's okay. It's just memories. I'm a dweller. It takes me time."

"How long ago was it?"

"He left four months ago."

"He left?"

"He was transferred to our France office."

"That's why you broke up?"

"No. We cannot be together."

"He's a Muslim?"

I nod again.

"Let's go up now and get some air."

I cannot oppose, as I feel like I'm going to implode inside his car.

JBR is an easy magnet for the crowd. On weekends, it can be bursting with people, and today's no exception despite the heat. Saad's hold on my hand is tight as we walk, reminding me of his presence.

"You come here just for coffee?"

I can't help asking as we enter the Hilton Hotel.

"You'll see why in a moment."

After being seated, I immediately understood why he likes this place. It gives an unobstructed view of the sea, the sky, and the goings-on below.

"You like it?"

"Yes."

The blueness of his eyes matches the sea outstretched before us. I smile at him, conveying how pleased I am with his choice.

"What would you like to have?"

"An ice cream or a milkshake would be perfect right now."

As Saad dictates our orders, I turn my gaze back to the sea. It stretches as far as my eyes can reach. It's glistening from the sun's rays. Speedboats rush past each other in its vast openness. So many people are in the water. The sight reminds me of that afternoon when Zaki and I, along with Lourdes, were here, and he first opened up to me about his feelings. I close my eyes, meaning to shut the memory too. My heart is struggling to ignore the feelings the place is evoking in me. Saad's touch liberates me from the prison of my own mind.

"Be here with me, Hanna."

I squeeze his hand back.

"Come closer to me."

He does so, and I bury my face on his neck.

"You would need patience with me. My heart needs help."

"I have nowhere else to go for now."

He kisses me on the forehead. It feels different than Zaki's, but it's just as good.

I close my eyes again. My heart finds a new refuge.

"I don't want to press you, but I really want to know what happened. Just a little bit, if you can. So I can understand."

"We're colleagues. Our families were against the relationship. We mutually agreed to separate."

"Do you still love him?"

I feel a tug inside me. *Have I ever stopped loving Zaki? Could I ever stop?*

"It's not an on and off button, Saad."

"I know. But do you know why we use a period in a sentence? Because at some point it has to end."

That word always feels like a stab when I hear it. *End.* Lana sure does say it to me a lot. However, hearing it from a man, from this man in particular, the word kind of has a different effect.

Our orders come on time. My throat needs some liquid to open it up, so to speak. Saad is quiet. I know he's waiting for my answer.

"Are you upset with me right now?"

I look at him with worried eyes.

"No, Hanna. I'm more concern for you, for your heart. It seems to me that it got beaten quite badly."

That's an understatement, I almost want to say aloud.

"It was painful."

"As most separations are, I suppose."

"Why would life make us meet someone only to be separated from that person again? I don't understand what the chance was for."

"The wind doesn't stay in one place too. But don't we appreciate it when it passes us by?"

"I don't want it to just pass me by. I want it to stay."

"I'll buy you an electric fan, and you can have it on steady mode. Then you'll have a manufactured wind always blowing at you."

I cannot keep a straight face after hearing him say that.

"What are you, a stand-up comedian?"

"Some nights, yes. During the day, I'm an engineer."

"And on the weekends?"

"I'm the ultimate man of your dreams."

He leans for a quick smack on my lips.

"You're developing a habit of stealing kisses from me. Don't cry out loud if my teeth catch your lips one time."

"Then I must keep kissing you so you can score too."

"How many lips do you steal kisses from?"

"In a day?"

My eyes grow big in surprise.

"Come on, habibti, I'm just joking."

"Can you kiss without feelings?"

"Yes, and even more."

Hearing that is like a period for me, stopping me from continuing.

"Did you two have sex?"

I shake my head to mean no.

"What?"

"We almost did, but he stopped."

"He stopped? How could he have stopped himself when I feel like ravishing you since last night!"

"Your voice is getting too loud, Saad. You don't want others to know that you're a pervert, right? So keep it low."

"Pervert, huh?"

He runs his fingers along my knee. I shiver, causing my drink to spill out of my mouth onto my dress.

"Saad!"

"Let me help you clean that."

He kisses me full on the lips. The gesture is like an ambush, forcing me to surrender. It's just a few seconds, and yet I feel like being unglued. When I open my eyes, his are staring at me, piercing blue, testing the resolve of my raven pair. I playfully slap him.

"Thief."

"And I intend to keep stealing until the vaults open."

"That might take a while."

"I'm a patient man."

He caresses the tip of my nose with his. The hour passes quietly on a romantic note since then.

"Do you fancy a movie?"

"Sure. Let's check what's showing down there at Roxy."

Just as we are leaving, a call comes from one of my male colleagues.

"I have to get this."

Eli needs to go to Iran at the last minute. He's requesting for tickets. I hastily work on it so I can return my attention to Saad.

"Thank you. I'm all yours now."

"Are you, really?"

I know he's teasing me, but his question reverberates deep inside me.

Can I ever really give myself completely again to another man?

"Patience. Some good things don't come as easily."

As I clasp his hand, I give it a gentle squeeze.

"Every investor expects an ROI. Do you know what that is?"

I nod.

"I don't expect it to be immediate, but I'm hoping that it will come."

I nod again. His words are like soft knocks at the door of my heart. It took me time to open up to Zaki. I cannot just let a stranger in.

"Penny for your thoughts?"

"My thoughts are worth more than that."

"I'm sure. What would it take for me to know what they are?"

"Time. I'm a Scorpio. I'm not easily lured out of the sands. I come out on my own."

We're outside of the cinema, standing face to face, his beautiful piercing blue eyes challenging my dark pair. I have to look away after a minute, scared of what he might see if I let him look longer.

"Pain is one thing, and hope is another. I've never seen both in anyone's eyes before."

His words cage me in.

"Hanna, some things when they end, that's it. There's no part two, chapter two, or second book. And all we can do is just let it go."

My eyes start to get moist. He takes me into his arms. The warmth it offers is reassuring.

"Your ship is still anchored in the past. Let go, Hanna. There are other horizons to explore."

I nod. After a minute, I look up at him.

"Thank you. This has been a very good first date."

"Do you want to go home now?"

"No, that's not what I meant. I'm thanking you for shaking me loose."

"The past is something we've become familiar with. But it's not safe to stay there."

"Letting go is difficult for me."

"It is for almost every one of us. Don't think that it's any way easier for us men. We just handle our emotions differently than you ladies."

I smile at him.

"You're more beautiful when you smile."

I tip on my toes and give him a smack on the lips.

"Thank you."

"You're welcome. And you're welcome here."

He presses my hand on his chest. His gesture is melting my defenses like jelly. How can one heart ignore the promptings of another, especially when it comes with a pair of beautiful blue eyes?

**

Soft knocks on my door interrupt my thinking.

"Babe?"

"Come in, Ash."

"You just got here?"

"About an hour ago."

"So how was it?"

Her excitement has not waned yet.

"I think it went very well. He's a really sweet guy and seemingly matured. I like him."

"Where did you go?"

"We had lunch at a Lebanese restaurant and spent the afternoon at JBR."

"What is it, babe? I can see something on your face. Is he single?"

"He said so, yes. Maybe I can confirm that from his parents, if I get to meet them when they come."

"His parents are coming to meet you?"

"They're coming to visit him. He asked me to help him arrange his apartment to get it ready for them. I doubt I'd get to meet them, though."

"Why? If you two really hit it off, I don't see why he will not introduce you."

"That seems too soon and too fast for me, babe. Perhaps I'll pass."

"What is it? There's something on your mind, woman."

"I'm just getting blown away by how fast things are happening. The conversation we had this afternoon, I've never had that with anyone, not even with Zaki when we first met."

"You and Zaki met in a different circumstance, and all these years you've only ever been around him. I can understand why you find the newness of things a bit perplexing. But it will soon pass."

Will my feelings for him soon pass too?

"What is it, babe? You seem troubled."

"Zaki's love defined me as a woman. Who am I now without it?"

Tears start to drench my face, coming out hot and fast.

"Oh, babe."

Ashley cradles me in her arms, and I cry out the confusion and fear that chains my heart inside.

A good ten minutes later, I have a runny nose and swelling eyes, and a heart no less lighter.

"I didn't know that it still hurts you this much. All these months, I thought somehow you're getting better. I asked you before I went on vacation if it was alright for me to leave you. You said nothing."

"Your life should not stop just because mine felt like it did. It's not fair for you or Lana or anyone to be affected by my pain."

"It's not about that, babe. I could have just stayed here with you."

"You're here with me. You've been here with me. That's more than enough. Just please be patient with me and keep me tuned in to the present. Keep me here. The memories are still too strong, pulling me back to yesterday. And I feel so weak to resist thinking about it all."

I feel so bare having to admit my losing struggle against the past. Ashley's hand rubbing my back, its warmth and intensity, is like charging the dying battery of my heart.

"Moving on doesn't need to be on the clock. You have the right to take it at your own pace. But please, babe, do not overindulge."

I simply nod.

"What did you tell Saad?"

"I'm open to seeing him, but I need a bit more time to be ready for another relationship."

"And he's okay with that?"

"He said so. I intend to see through this and start over. I'm physically fit, but it feels like there's so much extra baggage around me."

"The excess weight inside your heart isn't something your hula hoop can help shed off, babe."

"You're right. Maybe it's about time that I store the past in the attic of my memory, so I can start a new story with Saad."

"Sounds like the Hanna I know. Just take it easy. You'll get your rhythm back."

"Thank you, babe, for being here for me."

"You're welcome. Now get some rest. Healing is a tedious process."

Her kiss on my forehead is a promise that I'll always have another heart ready to listen and support.

**

"Hello, Saad. I'm sorry I missed your call earlier. I was inside the boss's office."

"It's okay. Are you free tonight? Do you mind giving me a hand to bring my new TV home?"

"Sure. What time do you need me?"

"I need you every hour, Hanna."

He's very good with words. His comebacks are difficult for me to equal.

"My time is not cheap, mister."

"Whatever it takes, I'm ready."

But am I?

"You always know what to say, don't you? I'd be done by 6:00 P.M."

"Are you okay for me to pick you up directly from work?"

"Sure."

"See you then, Hanna."

Whatever it takes. Does he mean it?

My best friend Molly has always warned me not to overthink. The heart that's been through pain is expectedly skeptic.

I'm occupied with tasks when a call comes into the main trunk line. It registers the caller as being from France. My breathing suddenly quickens. I pick it up on the third ring.

"Hello."

I forgot to answer in my usual greeting. The sound of the ring feels like a jagged knife inching its way fast to my heart.

"Hi, Hanna! How have you been?"

My ears are very familiar with the voice on the other line. Never in a millennium will I forget it.

"Zaki."

There's so much I want to say, but not one word will come through right now.

"Hanna. It's been a while. Is everything okay with you? How's everyone there?"

Is everything okay with me?

"Hanna?"

"Hi! I'm sorry. There's just this email… I'm good, I think. It's always busy around here. What about you?"

"The usual, busy as well."

Have you thought of me at all?

"What made you call?"

"I need to speak with Roshie. I tried her extension, but she's not answering."

"She's outside for some visa work for a new colleague joining in two weeks. Is there something I can help you with?"

Or can we talk about us instead?

"I see. I'll just call her back. I'll speak to you again soon, too."

When? Why not now?

"Hanna?"

"Y-yes, sure, Zaki."

I know he knows why I'm disoriented. A simple phone call pulls me back to him in an instant. All these months of separation have done very little to distance me from his memory.

"It has been difficult for me too. But I undermined the impact that my simple call would cause you today. I'm sorry, Hanna."

"I miss hearing your voice, Zaki. It's a welcome surprise to hear it again now."

What I wouldn't give to keep hearing it.

"That's really nice of you to say, Hanna. It's good to hear yours too. I will have to drop out now, though, as I have a meeting in ten minutes."

"I understand. Till next time then."

"Till then, Hanna. Take care."

As in life, minutes after he hangs up, I'm still clutching the receiver, listening to the busy tone, unable to let go.

Why is it so hard?

**

"So how was it today at your office?"

"Busy. Yours?"

"Same, though I feel more tired today. I serviced six companies."

"Why didn't you opt for the TV to be delivered instead?"

"The model I wanted wasn't available at the time of my first visit to the store. Then they called me days after and told me that it would be there today, so I asked for one to be reserved for me. We're going now so I can pay, too."

"How big is it?"

"55 inches."

"I'm sure that you're more than capable of carrying that on your own," I say so teasingly.

"Of course, yes, with these muscles. But I'll make every excuse I can think of to be with you."

Then he winks at me.

I mouth silently the word "flirt" back to him.

The TV is not as heavy, though it's a challenge to carry it alone. Upon reaching his apartment, I'm surprise to see Ikea boxes filed on one side.

"Your new furniture had arrived too."

"Do you think you can help me with those as well?"

"Of course."

I want to tire myself so I can sleep right away once I'm home.

The less I think about it, the better. Conscious effort is the only way to move forward, to heal.

I'm inspecting each of the Ikea boxes to determine which one I should start on when he opens the conversation again.

"Where are you?"

I look at him in confusion.

"You seem to have drifted off in your own thoughts."

"I'm sorry. It's nothing. Should we go for this one first? So we at least have something to sit on after everything."

He just shrugs his shoulders. I reach for the scissors and start unboxing the dining table, then the chairs. He's positioning the TV on the stand.

"Did something happen at work today?"

"Nothing out of the ordinary. What made you ask?"

"You're a bit off tonight."

"In what way?"

"I'm not sure. You seem distant."

"I'm right here."

"Physically, yes. We could have done this tomorrow or on the weekend if you had told me earlier that you're not up for this."

"I am up for this. Just like you, I'm a bit more tired today than usual."

Because of his call.

I feel a kick inside at the thought. Ten strides forward, and with a single phone call lasting not even five minutes, I'm back to zero in my progress chart. Saad's not buying it.

"It's a daily struggle for me. I don't know how to move on."

"Do you *want* to move on?"

"I must."

"But do you *want* to move on?"

I feel the weight of his words through his tone.

"Because if you *want* to move on, not even life or fate can stop you."

"I don't know how to take the first step."

"You have taken more steps than you actually realized."

"Put that into context for me."

"You've agreed to go out with me. Or I don't count at all?"

What does he mean by that?

His words immobilize me.

"Do you want me to bring you home now?"

"You want me to leave?"

"Right now, you don't look like you want to be here."

"I don't usually go to a guy's place, especially one I just met."

Silence. It's true, but unnecessary to say right now. I walk towards the door.

"Whenever you're ready."

The drive back to my place is expectedly awkward, but one I prefer since I really don't want to talk right now. There's a lot I want to say, but not to him.

"I'm sorry for tonight. I didn't mean to upset you. I'm really trying here. But I cannot walk as fast as life expects me to. Please understand."

I'm starting to feel emotional.

"I do. I'm sorry if you feel pressured by anything that I said. It's not my intention …"

"I know. I appreciate your concern. I really like spending time with you, Saad. But a heart as badly hurt as mine can only limp right now."

"I know what you mean. But continuously carrying the past this way will not make it any lighter. You're only becoming accustomed to the weight."

Home run. No point in my responding. The rest of the time till my place, we're in relative silence.

"Will I still see you?"

"Of course. Why would you think otherwise?"

He lifts both shoulders in a nonchalant shrug.

"See you on Saturday."

I kiss his right cheek gently and step out of his car. I walk straight inside my building without looking back. I feel ashamed.

**

With my boss out of the office, I look forward to a light and easy Friday. I make a mental note of my tasks today while preparing myself to go to work.

Attendance, the vacation table of the team, and the visitors next week from Europe.

I have just enough to keep my mind occupied. A wandering mind is dangerous, and I'm one who's prolific at daydreaming.

Sometime after lunch, as I'm reviewing the vacation table of our team, Erdem comes to my desk.

"Hanna, do you have a paper weight?"

"What is that?"

"Something to hold down the papers and other documents on my desk. I want to open the door behind me, just a bit to let in some air. But I have a lot on my desk that can be blown away."

"Will this do?"

I hold out the smallest of the pyramids amongst my display. He checks its weight.

"Are there more?"

I hand him all three.

"Careful with those. They're from …"

"I know who they're from."

He winks and walks back to his office. Five minutes later, I'm still deconstructing and reconstructing what he said in my mind.

Is it love or fear that's holding me down? Am I just using Zaki's memories as a "paperweight" to keep me grounded because I'm afraid to be blown away by the changes that our separation has brought?

It's both embarrassing and refreshing for me to dawn on this realization. How should I act upon this changed outlook now? I'm afraid to tip the balance in this connection with Saad. He has been the perfect gentleman so far. I don't want to hurt him in any way, just because I'm still hurting myself.

"It's the weekend, girl. Any plans?"

Joan's question surprises me, so I check the time on my computer. 6:10 PM.

"I'd be with Saad for sure."

"That's nice! Things seem to be developing well between the two of you."

"He's a very thoughtful and sweet guy. Funny as well. I like being with him."

"Fun is good for a broken heart."

I feel a pang of guilt hearing her say that. I don't know why.

Do I genuinely enjoy his company, or is it only because he makes me feel less lonely?

**

"Why do you have to overanalyze everything?"

Molly's beginning to be exasperated with me.

"This is how I have always been, Molly. I cannot not think things through."

"I'm not saying that you shouldn't, but be less of yourself. Allow things to blossom organically. Let life lead you on how to live again."

She slum dunks that one into the basket of my consciousness.

"What are you afraid of?"

"Pain."

"Then adapt a hermit life. Leave the common world and go into the mountains. You'll be safe there, but utterly unhappy."

That's a three-point shot made from half court. I need to take the bench.

Hours after our video call, Molly's words are still playing in my ears, like a song on repeat. Saad's call pauses it.

"Hello, you!"

"Someone's cheerful. That means you'll go out with me today."

"What makes you think that I won't?"

"Our row last Thursday night got me thinking that maybe you will stop seeing me. Hanna, if my mere presence pressures you, please know that you can walk away anytime. I will not take it against you."

He hits a major artery in my heart with that one, so to speak.

"I do want to see you again. I really like being with you. I just get confused at times. And I don't like it when I lose the reins on my own thoughts."

"Let's talk some more later. Would it be okay if I pick you up at 4:00 PM?"

"Sure. See you then."

**

"It's hard to catch you lately."

It's a slight jab, but Lourdes' words over lunch land on my lower jaw, almost disabling me from speaking.

"It's been busy at the office a lot lately."

"And on the weekends, you keep yourself busy with a guy! Tell me the details."

"He's a smart blue-eyed cutie."

"Where is he from?"

"Originally from Armenia. He was born in Syria and then grew up in Lebanon."

"Seems like one with a story. Is he good?"

"Yeah, he's a good guy. I like him a lot."

"I meant in bed."

"I cannot even open my heart completely to him. What more my legs."

"They're two parts independent from each other. Besides, who's to stop you?"

"It's not who. It's what. I'm not ready."

"When do you think you'll be?"

Is there an approaching train that I have to be ready right now?

"Babe, we're in Dubai. Men here don't have the time to fall in love. But they certainly can spare you hours for sex."

That's Lourdes – unbiased, uncensored, but real.

The arrival of our orders saves me from needing to respond. It's one thing to banter with Saad. Lourdes knows Dubai way better. I cannot compete with her wit in this regard.

"So you haven't had sex yet. I'm telling you, if he will not get it from you, soon enough he'll move on to the next available one, wherever he can find her."

It's like a wine cork gets stuck in my esophagus, hearing her say that.

"Just saying, babe. I don't mean to spoil your fun."

"You're not. I understand what you mean."

Though I certainly can't do as you said.

"How long has it been now?"

"Just a little over three months."

"Wow! No sex since… That's something. How long do you intend to keep this going?"

Would his affection expire in another month if I prolong our nonsexual foreplay?

"I just can't do the usual. Besides, wouldn't sex lose its romantic appeal if done without any feelings?"

"Babe, they don't know that here. This is a different kind of jungle. Here, a horse would do a rhino if that's the only option for him at the moment."

If one has never understood Calculus back in school and is studying it again now – on their own – they'll be whacked in the brain. That's how it is conversing with Lourdes sometimes. But her truth has foundation, not just some unruly opinions formed from random experiences. I sometimes struggle to compose my thoughts around her – like today.

"We might get there eventually."

"Don't tell me you're still on to Zaki?"

Just the mention of his name still has an impact. I look away.

"You got it real bad, babe."

"Stronger than the Spanish Flu."

"You have to move on at some point, if you haven't yet. Be fair to yourself and give yourself the chance to be happy again."

That knocks me out flat.

My journal records my defeat.

A boxer can recover after each match.

Some hearts can't do the same, and as fast.

I'm still in the ring, but just fighting my own emotions.

**

"I'm immigrating to Canada."

I'm neither deaf nor mute, and I can speak and understand English very well. However, right now I feel totally incapacitated. The shock pounds my consciousness so hard as to render me speechless.

"Hanna?"

"I'm listening."

For it's all I can do at this very moment.

"I'm moving to Canada."

"That I heard."

"I just received a word that my application has moved up in the processing stage."

I may be sitting across from him, but my ears are right by his mouth, in a manner of speaking, waiting for specific words while my heart readies for further assault.

"I might be able to move there before this year ends."

Ten grenades explode inside me simultaneously.

"Hanna?"

"I'm sorry, Saad. I have been listening, and I think this is great news. Really, I'm very happy for you."

I reach out for his hand. He squeezes mine, and I return the gesture.

"I'm just a little shock."

"Just a little?"

His lips may be teasing me, but his eyes convey laser-focused seriousness. I smile shyly.

"I guess a little bit more."

I playfully dig my nails on his palm. When I raise my eyes to his face, his eyes are on mine, burning with an intensity I cannot fathom. I feel a surge of heat flush my cheeks. I instantly feel self-conscious. I retreat my hands to my lap while looking down. I'm confused by my own actions.

"You really like me. I'm sure of that now."

"What's not to like about you?"

My dad once said that a real gentleman is like a gardener. He knows how to handle a rose because he understands its thorns. Saad is the same.

"So, you'll still see me?"

"Yes. I don't see why not."

I may not know if my feelings will develop more, and how much pain that might bring afterwards, but I'm certain that I still want to see him while he's here in Dubai.

"Then I'll make sure you'll only have good memories to masturbate on once I'm gone."

That draws a hearty laugh from me. In an instant, the tension inside me starts to diffuse.

No doubt he knows his way around women – how many there have been, I do not want to know. I just want to revel in his attention right now. The initial shock of knowing his imminent departure is wearing off, but it is being replaced with another feeling, something I'm well familiar with by now. Sadness.

The future of Syria is hanging in the air. I will not stand in the way of Saad securing a citizenship in a country where he will not only be safe, but the promise of a strong and abundant future also awaits.

**

"He's not the one, girl. Perhaps he was just loaned to you by fate in order to help ease your separation from Zaki."

Who needs therapy when one has a friend like Lana?

"I hate this kind of game."

I lie down on her sofa.

"It's not a game. This is life."

It's not? It does feel like it. A game of chess where I'm losing with each move that I cannot make.

"What happened to those guys who sent you messages on Tinder?"

Lana's question arrests my concentration quickly enough.

"Don't tell me you deleted the app?"

"No. I forgot about it, though."

She stretches her hand out to me, and her eyes are demanding my phone. I hand it to her without qualms.

"There are so many messages now waiting for your response. They might unmatch you if you keep them waiting longer."

"I couldn't care less."

"Girl, your happiness is at stake here. You need to be proactive about it. How will life be able to serve you what you want if you're not even going to check the menu in front of you? Tinder has international cuisines. I'm sure there's something in it that will suit your taste."

"Maybe after Saad leaves."

"Why wait? You two are just dating."

"Is it because he's leaving that our time together does not qualify as a relationship? We do the usual things that couples do. And I doubt there are many out there who share the depth we have in ours, even in the short time we have been together."

"Did he tell you that he loves you?"

"Does every relationship start with love immediately?"

"Fair enough. But it's been months! He should be in love with you by now."

Am I in love with him?

"I still think that you shouldn't hold out on yourself for him this way. Since he's leaving, he should allow you to date other people so you can establish a more secure relationship for yourself."

"I could barely keep up with this one. I think seeing more men right now isn't a good idea."

"Says someone who hasn't even tried."

I head for the kitchen with our used plates and glasses before Lana can nail me to my seat.

My friends share the same argument. I don't take it against them. But *moving on* are two words that, when put together, paralyze me. I lost Zaki without even being given the chance to fight for him. How do you accept a defeat forced upon you by fate?

Fate's Contingency Plan

The vibration of my phone on the bedside table startles me. I'm on the Preface of Robert Lacey's Inside the Kingdom.

Another match. Incredible.

I thumb open my phone. There's a message from an Alfred. I don't remember seeing that name amongst the previous matches.

Alfred: Hi. I'm Alfred. In here just looking for a friend.

Quite an odd place to look for a friend. Let me see your photos. Not bad at all. And you're a vet.

Me: Hi, Alfred. I'm Hanna. Nice to meet you.

His quick response surprises me. It's almost midnight.

Alfred: Hello dear. Glad to meet you too, but I'm hoping that to be in person as well, one day. Not to be too forward, though. Just that I'm an old fashion fella, quite matured as well to be in here and doing this.

And yet, here you are.

Me: I agree. I'm very new to this as well. In fact, you're the very first one I ever responded to.

Alfred: Oh wow! I'm flattered. I'm sure there are plenty clamoring for your attention.

Me: They all seem to want only one thing.

Alfred: Oh? Well, you look very attractive in your photos. Are they really you?

The photos! Holy dang!

I immediately go to them and deleted all except for two which I believe are decent enough even though a good portion of my cleavage is showing.

Me: Yes, it's me. My best friend created this account for me. She took all the liberty to choose what she used here. Thank you for reminding me. I deleted them.

Alfred: Why? They're all very nice.

Me: Thank you. But I don't think they're appropriate.

Alfred: I agree with you to a point. Can I ask you something?

Me: Sure. I'm all ears.

Alfred: Is it okay with you if we exchange numbers? I want to rather speak with you on the phone than here, if meeting in person is too soon for you.

He's a bit forward yet reserved enough for my taste. I don't see the harm in sharing personal information this early. After all, I can block him should he turn out to be a jerk. I put the book on the bedside table in anticipation of his call. In just three minutes, my phone lights up.

"Hello, Hanna."

"Hi, Alfred."

"Nice to be speaking with you. And thank you for sharing your number."

"I honestly don't see any problem with it. Unless you start hounding me after this one."

He chuckles.

"Do you have a dog?"

"No. What made you ask?"

"You said 'hound.' I thought perhaps because you have a pet. It's not a word I usually hear people use as a verb, unless they are dog lovers and familiar with the different breeds."

"You have a quick pick up."

"Two things, Hanna. I'm old and I'm a vet."

"Oh, yes. I saw that on your profile. Is there a particular animal you specialized in, or are you a GP in a way?"

"Horse. I look after the collection of a prominent local."

"That must be nice."

"It comes with perks, definitely, and challenges."

There's a hint of sadness in that last word.

"What about you? What do you do?"

"I'm an internal affairs person in an international company. It, too, comes with challenges."

"Where are you from? I can't place your accent."

"Philippines."

"Ah, beautiful country. My family and I have had the chance to visit once, when my children were still a bit young."

"How many do you have?"

"Two – a boy, 16, and a girl, 14. Are you married, Hanna? I'm sorry if you find me a bit forward. I'm curious, of course."

"No worries. I'm still single. I'm seeing someone, yes. Just started some time back."

"I see. Where is he from?"

"Around here."

"Is it okay with him for you to be talking to another guy? I have come to know the temper of the men in this region when it comes to their women."

"Don't worry about him. He's a cool one. Level-headed. What about you? Your wife is alright with you being on an online dating app?"

"Ah… that's a story all on its own."

Here we go.

"I think one good thing about speaking with a stranger is the liberty it offers one to be just themselves."

I cannot refute that.

"Looks like you have something in your chest, Alfred. And it seems heavy too."

"Very. Can I tell you about it?"

"I'm all ears."

"I caught her in bed with another man. In our own home."

Holy fox. How audacious!

"Did it happen recently?"

It's a challenge for me to remain collected at this moment.

"Quite recent, yes. Four months ago."

No wonder he's looking for a friend.

"Do your children know?"

"No. They just know that we are having problems. We are not yet divorced. But we have been in separate bedrooms since."

"Have you spoken to anyone, your friends, about this?"

"Does a horse count? No. I couldn't, and I don't know how, either. I'm very ashamed. But I informed my parents."

"What did they say?"

"They're here. They're staying with us for a month now. My mom was especially upset. She's not speaking with my wife. Or soon-to-be ex-wife, I should say."

"I can't blame her. Your mom, I mean. I would be upset too. Well, I am, and I am a complete stranger to you. Cheating is something that I still struggle to come to terms with."

"It's devastating."

"It must be. I can't imagine it any way less than that. How are you holding up? Have you two spoken about it?"

"We have, yes. But I don't think I can forgive her. I told her that. It's just too much, too painful. Of all places, it was right on our own bed!"

If it's possible to hear someone's heart shatter again after it has been crushed, I think I just heard his break into a million more pieces now.

"I'm so sorry to hear this, Alfred. I'm sorry for your heart."

I'd love to embrace him right now if he's here. Silence. I don't prod. Let him take his time.

"I'm sorry to have dumped this on you like this, Hanna."

"Apology is not necessary. I understand. Thank you for opening up to me. Somehow, I'm glad I could listen."

"You gave me that impression right from the first minute. You have a really nice voice, by the way. I think you're a nice person, Hanna."

"Thank you, Alfred. I can say the same about you. I normally ignore when my phone buzzes and it's from Tinder. But today, I just thought, 'Why not?' You look non-threatening."

He gives a gentle laugh at that.

"I'm a vet, not a hoodlum. And I'm a father. I really want to look and be respectable for my children. I love those two. They are my world. They'd be devastated as well should they find out. My son has been asking. At his age, he knows something terrible had happened for us to sleep in separate bedrooms. But I don't know how I can tell them. They're very close to their mom, my son especially. I don't want their relationship to corrode. I worry about the damage it would have on their psyche."

Even I, a complete nobody in their lives, cannot swallow this story. I cannot begin to think how they, at their age, can fully comprehend the seriousness of their mother's betrayal. I'm lost for words.

"I'm sorry again, Hanna, if I make you uncomfortable about all this. It's not a proper subject, especially when we just met. Or connected, I should say."

"Again, it's alright. It's heavy to take it all in. I feel like I'm beginning to have a headache myself."

We both laugh at that.

"I feel like I already know you. And this is just one of those calls we exchange just because."

"I'm really pleased to hear that. And it's mutual. I feel I can trust you as well."

"Do you have a story yourself?"

"Don't we all?"

"I suppose so. Well, whenever you feel like it, I'm here. I could be your friend. And I wish we could be that. Can we, Hanna?"

"Aren't we already?"

To hear him laugh wets my eyes. I wonder how long ago his last laugh was, or if he has laugh again since it happened.

"Thank you, Hanna. Really. I was not expecting this. But I feel somehow lighter. Thank you for swiping right for me on Tinder."

And that draws a hearty one from me.

"I'll tell my best friend you're giving your thanks."

"Oh, yes! Perhaps we three can meet one day for coffee."

"That sounds very good to me. Let's plan that sooner."

"We must. So, till then, Hanna."

"Till then, Alfred."

I give out a big sigh when the line cuts.

Wow. That sure was something.

**

After a 30-minute phone call to my mom and older brother, I resume reading Inside The Kingdom. The first chapters are very engrossing. Love, indeed, comes in many forms, is felt in many ways, and sometimes expressed in outlandish fashions. While I understand, and to some degree share, the fervor of some highly religious people, I do not, however, condone the use of violence in the expression of one's devotion. The disturbances brought about by Juhayman Al-Otaybi and his group created a temporary civil unrest, and desecrated what's considered a holy place for the Muslims, all because of their flaming love for their religion.

This may not be in any way related to what happened to me and Zaki, and yet somehow, it's making me think right now what kind of problems we might have brought upon our lives and those we love had we taken the bold decision to go against our families' wishes. Like Juhayman, I, too, felt then that we should rebel against what I thought a very constricting beliefs of Zaki's family for him to marry only a Muslim woman. I know, even now, that had I persisted in persuading him, we would have been married. But we would be alone in that marriage, with no outside sustenance from our families.

Too much love can kill you in the end.

I close the book. That's what I love about reading. I can stop and bookmark the page whenever I feel like it. When something in it shocks me, appalls me, scares me, or in any way makes me uncomfortable, I can close it, halting the effect, maybe temporarily, but still affording me control. And to a Scorpio, that means a great deal. Surprises frustrate me, especially the kind that shifts my balance. I'm a planning fanatic. Saad's *not* on my calendar. Fate put him on it. And just as we change calendars each new year, chances are he will not be on mine come 2019.

That troubles me. I do not want to experience new things just to be alive. I am alive. I may not be living like the others here, actively swiping left and right for their happiness, but I am living my life the best way I know I should, given what happened. But to my friends, it seems that's not enough. A woman is not enough on her own. She must have a man or someone.

"Babe?"

Ashley pulls me out of my mind.

"Hi, Ash."

"You seem to be in deep thought. Anything the matter?"

"Nothing really serious, babe. Though I'd like to ask you something."

"Shoot."

"Saad might leave before the year ends. He applied to immigrate to Canada. If you're me, would you continue seeing him despite knowing that it's not going to end up favourably for you?"

"Oh, babe. I don't know. That seems like a dilemma."

"It is, indeed."

"So what are you going to do?"

"I've grown fond of him all these months. I love being with him. He emits a very positive energy all the time. He makes me laugh. He's very caring and utterly sweet. He's smart, and those beautiful blue eyes win me over every time. I don't feel so broken anymore when I'm with him. But his imminent departure is casting a shadow over my heart, and it seems to be growing every day, if you know what I mean."

She nods, but her face displays her confused mind, too.

"Lana said I should start seeing other guys. Since he cannot give me a proper relationship, then there's no point dragging this on."

"But it's evident that you don't agree to that."

"It's not a bad idea, but yes, I don't agree to it. Something inside me does not agree with it."

"Your heart was hoping that he could be *the next one.*"

"Was it wrong for me to want that?"

"Of course not. Only that time isn't on your side on this one."

Ah, time. What a perplexing enigma. Our entire lives are ruled by it. The time of our birth and the time of our death. We must perpetually take it into consideration whenever we make decisions.

"We hear people saying, 'At the right time.' But when is it really? And why can't we determine that ourselves?"

"I don't know, babe. It screws up my head, too, now and again. One thing, though, perhaps meeting Saad is just like a trial run to show you who's out there and who you can possibly meet."

And there's fate, another tease. We are given minds to think for ourselves, but we are never absolutely free, for there are forces far greater than us that subjugate us under their influence.

"Perhaps you can do as Lana suggested, but put a twist to it. Continue to see Saad, but on the side, entertain your matches on Tinder. There's no harm in that. And I don't think you can call that cheating, given your setup. Just try to mingle, and then take it to the next level when you're ready to make that step forward."

"I'll think about that. Thanks, babe."

"Sure thing. What is that you're reading now?"

I flip the book to show her the title.

"Why are you reading that?"

"A colleague gave it to me. He said he picked it up at the airport while waiting for his flight. It seems interesting. I've been curious about Saudi Arabia for some time now."

"Why?"

I shrug my shoulders.

"I guess it's just human nature. We are always curious about things or matters we know very little about."

"Or should I say *Hanna's nature*?"

I respond with a chuckle.

Ah, yes, my curious nature. My innate hunger for knowledge and desire to know everything – and control everything.

"Anyway, where is he? Aren't you guys going out today?"

"We were together yesterday. I think I'd spend this day alone."

"Alright, babe. I'll go get ready. I'll be heading out."

Something in what Ashley said stayed with me long after she left my side on the sofa. The possibility of meeting another guy similar to Saad is like a promise that gives me an ounce of hope moving forward.

**

The constant vibration of my phone on the table shoots me back to wakefulness.

Tinder. My, my, my.

Brett the Brit: I don't understand why you swiped right for me and then not respond after we matched.

Me: Life. I'm living it outside of this app.

Brett the Brit: Fair enough. But why be here if you much prefer to be out there?

Me: It's not like that. I'm just occupied a lot lately. And I'm very new here. I really don't know what to expect or how to be.

Brett the Brit: I see. So am I. I just arrived in Dubai less than six months ago, and a friend suggested this. I thought I'd give it a try and see what it is about.

Me: And how has it been for you?

Brett the Brit: Well, so far, I've met two, and both were unsuccessful. My friend warned me about gold diggers and working girls, and I strongly felt like those two were either which.

Me: And yet here you are still despite the initial failures.

Brett the Brit: Yeah, sounds silly, I know. But I'm still hopeful to meet someone decent. I'm actually excited matching with you, I'll tell you that.

Me: And why is that so?

Brett the Brit: Well, you look really attractive in your photos – supposing it's really you. And you have a well written bio. You mentioned "friendship." I like that. Nothing too forward or too needy or very pretentious about it.

Me: Thank you. Nice to hear that.

Brett the Brit: Where are you from, if I may ask?

Me: Philippines.

Brett the Brit: Nice. How would you like to exchange numbers perhaps and continue this on WhatsApp?

Me: I prefer talking on the phone. I'm lazy in typing.

Brett the Brit: I think that's alright too. So, may I have your number?

Two minutes, and my phone's vibrating to an unlisted caller.

"This is Hanna."

"Hi, Hanna. I'm Brett. We were chatting on Tinder just now."

"Hi, Brett."

"So."

"So. After two failed tries, here you are working up a third."

"Oh, no! I hope not. Actually, I have a feeling that I'm not going to fail this time around."

"Oh, how so?"

"Gut feeling."

"That's not something accepted in the court of law. You know that."

"True. But still, I feel you are not like them."

"And if I happen to be so too?"

"Then I'd delete my account and forget about Tinder completely."

"Well, why are you there to begin with?"

"Why are you?"

"My best friend created the account for me while I was sleeping."

"Ah! Sneaky one, that friend of yours."

"In a manner of speaking, yes."

"But I'm glad she did that. Otherwise, we will not be talking right now. I want to ask you something, if you don't mind."

"Go ahead. I'm all ears."

"Is that really you in the photo?"

"Yes. Why?"

"Nothing, just want to be certain. My friend also told me about some girls using fake photos."

"I see. Well, be assured that it's me, and what's written on my account is true. I'm single, never been married, and have no kids."

"Very nice. Now I know that what I thought about you is correct. I was hesitating to swipe right. Now I'm glad I did."

"Nice of you to say that. Can I ask you something too?"

"Of course. Anything, my dear."

"Why are you on Tinder? What are you looking for? What are you expecting to happen?"

"Well, why is everyone in it? Companionship, I guess – well, at least I know that's what I'm looking for. What about you? Are you really just looking for friends?"

"It can start from that. I really don't know what to expect from it. Now that you asked, however, I think I need to sort that out."

"I know it's not proper to ask a woman her age. But I'm really curious."

"I'm turning 35 in two months."

"We are in the same age bracket. I just turned 36. And I just got divorced."

"Is that why you moved here?"

"Well, it's partly the reason, yes. Also, the work offer I got is something I cannot pass up."

"Do you have children?"

"No, and somehow, I'm glad about that. It made the separation easier."

"How are you now?"

"I'm alright, really. We wanted different things, and we couldn't see a way to compromise. So we thought it best to go our own separate ways."

"How long were you married?"

"Four years. We have been dating since college. We decided to get married after she had a miscarriage. But life, as they say, happened, and we just sort of drifted apart."

"Ironic. Just as when you're already married."

"Yes, but life's like that, as they say. What about you? Why haven't you settled down?"

And there's that proverbial question asked of every woman when they passes the age of 30.

"Well, to borrow your words, life's like that for some."

"Smart girl. But I think I shouldn't be surprised. Many a smart woman is single or married very late in life."

"I might be on that list, alright."

"The world is not perfect, my dear. And neither is anyone of us."

"I know that for a fact. And I'm not looking for perfection."

"Then who are you looking for?"

"Good question."

Who am I looking for, indeed?

"Well, to borrow your words once more, gut feeling. I'd go with what my instincts will tell me."

"And what have your instincts told you about me so far?"

"It's very early to tell."

"Have you met anyone from Tinder?"

"I've spoken to one on the phone, but we haven't met."

"I see. Are you up to it?"

"I'm not sure, to be frank. You're just the second guy I responded to there."

"I see. Have you thought of how you're going to carry this out then?"

"Again, to be frank, no. I'm still nursing a badly broken heart. My friends think Tinder is a good start on the road to recovery. I'm not against the idea. I just really don't know yet how to move forward from here."

"How long ago was it?"

"Well, he left four months ago. He was transferred to our headquarters in France."

"You had to separate only because of that?"

"No. We're of differing religions, too. Our families did not agree to our relationship."

"Religion is a complicated matter. But why did you get into a relationship with him if you knew he was from a different faith?"

"I never thought it would matter."

"Well, it shouldn't, but it does to some. How long were you together?"

"There was no relationship *per se*. It was mid-2015 when I realized that I was falling for him. And it was a sweet surprised to find out that it was mutual. It was last year when we declared our plans to marry, but our families made their thoughts known to us."

"Romeo and Juliet. Only yours was made complicated by religious ideologies. But tell you what, I think it is better this way. Don't quote me for it, but love and religion shouldn't mix, just like water and oil."

"I cannot disagree with you on that."

"I'm a Christian, by the way."

And we both laugh at that. How he makes light of my earlier predicament takes away an ounce of its sting, so to speak.

Ashley's right. This could work to my favor.

"So, Hanna, given the current *state* of your heart and mine, what do you think about sharing tea one afternoon soon?"

"I don't see why not."

"Good. When you feel like it, when you think you're ready, or even just when you're bored, try to remember me."

"Brett the Brit."

"Hanna the Filipina."

"Thanks, Brett. I appreciate the call. It's quite a refreshing one to have."

"Yeah, same here. Alright, Hanna, bye for now. Tea on me soon."

"You bet. Bye, Brett."

If all the men I'm going to meet are like that – matured and seemingly genuinely nice – then I think Tinder is really worth a shot. I can carry on having light conversations like that. It's a good way to start things – friendly and non-threatening, emotionally speaking. I don't think I'm afraid of change or starting over. I think I'm more concerned with the aftermath of any actions I take moving forward. The heart can cope with any situation sometimes better than the mind. But it needs its own time. I don't want to rush myself just to get out of this sad situation and end up getting hurt again. Besides, there's nothing wrong with playing it safe next time around.

**

"Hello, you!"

"Hi there, princess! What have you been up to?"

"Nothing special. Just been thinking a lot."

"Do you also think of me?"

"Of course."

"Care to share?"

"Well, the thought of you leaving has been on my mind a lot lately. Do you know when you might have to go already?"

"You're asking because you're eager for me to leave, or you'd rather that I delay it?"

"I'd rather that you don't go at all. But I understand that it's not for me to interfere with your decisions or that of life itself."

"That's really sweet to hear from you, Hanna. If there's another option, I wouldn't hesitate to take that if it meant that I could stay here with you."

Zaki had left. Now Saad is leaving. Who had I unconsciously offended in the past, so I'm being served with these karmic experiences now?

"Hanna?"

"I'm still here."

I'm still here after Zaki left. I'd still be here after you do, too.

"Your silence worries me."

"I'm sorry, Saad. I guess I'm just a bit more tired today."

"I see. Well, we can just talk tomorrow then."

"No, it's alright. Is something up? You heard from the immigration again?"

"Yeah."

A heavy metal door slams loudly in my head, the effect of which cascades to my heart. I close my eyes. Though I know that whether I keep them close or open them again, the reality is the same.

"I'm flying out on November 30. I will go see my parents in Syria first, then I'll take a flight to Canada from Beirut, perhaps, or back here in Dubai."

Beautiful destinations, but the initial departure flight is from my heart's airport. The control tower cannot really stop any planes from flying out, for everything must run according to schedule. And time isn't something my heart has any control of. What a sick joke this all is.

"Hanna?"

"Sounds like you're all sorted out."

He's silent, perhaps unsure of how to respond. I cannot think of anything else to say, either.

"Well, there are still two months before then. Are you still up to spending some of those days with me?"

"Sure. Why not?"

"Really? You know that you will not offend me by saying no."

Our spending together during his remaining time here will not change anything. However, I can delay facing my reality until he leaves. Whether that will serve me any good or not, it is something I'm willing to do.

"I'm sure about it, Saad."

"I'm happy to hear that, Hanna."

"I'm glad you are."

**

The vibration of my phone startles me in the middle of composing an email. I hesitate to answer. It's Sunday, and I am deep into work.

"Molly, I can't really video chat now. I'm in the office."

"Why are you always taking the martyr's route?"

"I'm sorry, the what?"

"What is the point of you choosing to keep seeing this guy, knowing too well how it's going to end?"

Now I realized that I shouldn't have sent that message last night on Messenger.

"Well, for the time being, I don't really have any other interesting options."

"Is that really it, or is it because you're hoping for a miracle here?"

"Ouch, Molly!"

"Am I right?"

"No, not at all. It's just that I still want to see him. Why must there be a reason all the time why we do things?"

"Knowing you, Hanna, you don't do anything at random. You're an overthinker."

"Well, yes, I am. But what if in this particular instance, I have no other reason except that I just really want to be with him more?"

"Okay, have it your way. But just so you know, in those two months, if you open yourself again to someone else, you would have built something substantial by then. Just saying."

Point taken, but not enough to merit a change of mindset from my end. Saad has been the perfect gentleman since day one. If anything, I'm doing this out of respect for him. Besides, if there's a buffet that I can feast on later, why can't I enjoy my à la carte of choice for now?

"What's in it for me? That's my guiding mantra when making decisions, especially if it involves people. What benefit will I get out of choosing this option over the other? I think that's the reason why your friends question your decision. Perhaps from their end, they cannot see its benefit to you."

"I just really want to be with him still."

"From what I have observed about you for years now, you're one who's not shy from making hard decisions or choosing the unconventional options. You're constantly pushing the boundaries of your own limits. And I think that's a good thing because you're always able to see beyond or above what many of us commonly miss. I really admire that fearlessness in you. I think you have a good grasp of this matter. So don't let the voices of others, though they may be your friends, confuse you."

Kaycee's refreshing take on my situation counteracts the effects of my conversation with Molly earlier. Not that there's anything bad about it. But it's nice to have another friend – who can also cook delicious Adobo – pull the string on the other end as a way to balance the spectrum and help stabilize me. My lunch today has been more filling than usual.

**

"You can have these chairs after I leave. Just don't let another guy sit on mine."

It may have been just a few months, but I'm fairly certain that it would be difficult to top someone like Saad.

Ashley is right. I wanted him to be *the next one.* Apart from his attractive physical attributes, his matured character is another reason why I'm very fond of him. I'm always drawn to old souls perhaps because I am one myself.

It has always been easy being around him. I don't have to hold my tongue. I don't have to restrain my feelings. I don't have to wear a mask. I don't have to behave in a certain way because I know that he likes me, understands me, and accepts me for all that I am. I'm a Scorpio. We may be some of the most attractive people in the zodiac, yet we are one of the hardest to love. But Saad has always made me feel like I'm someone special. He has a way of opening me up without using force. He puts my heart at ease without any pressure. Any woman who would meet a man like him would want him to be *the one.*

"We're all unique in our own ways. And you, my dear, you're a star all on your own."

It's one of the most earnest compliments I've given anyone. He lays out his hand in my direction, and I place mine on it.

"I hope that you will not forget me fast enough."

"I hardly forget, Saad."

"I think I can believe that."

He turns to me with a pained look on his face.

"I'm sure that after I leave, you will still think of him. But I hope that the memories we shared will make you think of me more, time and time again."

I feel a tiny prick in my heart. A tear readily escapes from my right eye. He tenderly wipes it away with his thumb.

"Is this for me?"

I nod.

"And for me too. For a love that could not be. You're like the wind for me, Saad. You were just meant to pass me by."

"Ah! You can also have the electric fan I have in the apartment. Whenever you turn it on, think of the air as me caressing your body."

I playfully dig my nails on his palm.

"What else are you going to leave behind for me?"

He pulls my hand closer to his heart.

"No. No, you cannot leave that to me."

"Why? Is it because you're holding someone else's heart still?"

"No. But you cannot leave your heart to me when we both know someone else deserves it more."

"Your mind flew ahead to Canada before me."

"I'm all for romance and love, and what have you. But I'm also a realist."

"LDR?"

"Let's not chain each other in a promise that life may not allow us to keep."

"So you don't want us to even try?"

"How many attempts do we need to take just to make life understand us?"

Silence. The tide is rising. It's now coming to our feet. Saad is startled. He must have been in deep thought not to realize.

"Relax. It's not enough to drown you."

"I'm not afraid of deep waters even though I don't swim that far out all the time."

I understand his underlying message. I opt not to say anything back, though. There are times when silence is better than words. This afternoon is one of those times.

******

One quiet weekday, in the early afternoon, as I'm readying to get up to head to the pantry for lunch, my phone starts buzzing on my desk.

"Alfred. It's been a while. How are you?"

"Hanna. I'm good. Everything is good. What about yourself?"

"Just as beautiful."

"Now that's something I'm really interested to see for myself. Not that I don't believe you."

"Well, you wouldn't have to wait very long. We can schedule the meet-up in less than two months."

"Two months? That's still in the future. What's up?"

"Remember, I mentioned to you on our first phone call that I was seeing someone? He's immigrating to another country by the end of November."

"Oh, is that so? And until then, you cannot go out for coffee even with a male friend?"

"We connected on an online dating app."

"And I went full-on drama on you from the get-go."

"Hey, don't say that. It wasn't drama at all. That's real life. And I appreciate you opening up to me. How are you, by the way? How are things in relation to that?"

"Well, I have commenced the legal proceedings of our divorce. I cannot forgive her for what she did, and so I don't see the point in staying married."

"I can understand, and I think you're doing the right thing. But what about your kids? Do they know already?"

"Not yet. My parents and I have been talking about the best way to do that."

"I don't know what to say, Alfred. I just hope that things will work out well for you and the children. And needless to say, but I'm here. I'm always willing to listen."

"Thanks for that, Hanna. Yes, I think for now that's what I need the most. Someone to talk to and give me an unbiased opinion about my situation. I still cannot see the way forward, but mind you, I'm really excited to get divorced. It's like I'm looking forward to my liberation. I know it's a bit harsh to say that, but that's really how I feel."

"It's a normal feeling to have. Alfred, you're talking to a friend. I don't need many words to understand, particularly about your situation. Feel free to express yourself in any way you feel comfortable. I'm here to just listen. So don't hold back."

"I have to say that you're one of the silver linings in these dark times. I think I can wait until it is okay for us to meet in person."

"Thank you, Alfred. I appreciate your understanding. I just don't want to be disrespectful to him. He's a gentleman, and he's been so good to me. I'm actually sad that he's going away. But I wouldn't stand in the way of him having a more secure and safe future."

"By the way, I did not get to know where he's from."

"He's from Syria."

"I agree with you. I think it's a really good thing for him to move to Canada."

"Indeed."

"Well, all the best for him – and for *you.* I hope you will not be very sad after."

"I hope so, too."

"Don't worry, Hanna. I'll be here whenever you need a friend."

"I know. Thanks, Alfred."

"Alright, till next time. I just called to check on you."

"That's sweet of you. Thank you. Glad to hear from you again. Call me anytime."

"You bet I will. Take care, Hanna."

"Take care, Alfred."

They will all have to wait until Saad leaves. I will give him all the respect he's due. After all, he rebooted my heart from its dead state. Will I shut down again after he leaves? Who's to know? Right now, I don't want to concern myself about that. I just want to maximize our remaining time together. I don't know why or how I came about this thought, but I think Saad and I will never see each other again. We're like those people who have to meet in this lifetime because there's something we can learn from each other. But we are not meant to stay together longer because fate does not see it fit. And just like with Zaki, I'm not one to force my way against the natural order of things. If something has to go, it will go, or life will take it away, because it has to be somewhere else.

The will of the wind.

For a sign that goes through so much transformation in its lifetime, we Scorpios also have so much difficulty when it comes to change. But I think, irrespective of zodiac signs, change is one of the most challenging endeavors for us all, especially when it involves the heart.

I've spent half my life
looking for the reason things must change
and half my life trying to make them stay the same

So goes the lines of one of my favorite songs. I think it's not pointless to mull over things and situations that happen in our lives sometimes. It helps put everything in perspective. Saad's unexpected arrival and sudden departure, however, still perplexes me.

Nothing is random in this life – at least that's what I believe. Our choices have shaped this world into what it is now. Series of actions deliver certain results – some of which alter our lives completely. And the timing of it all, when something should happen, that is a complete ball game altogether for me.

Perhaps he has to come into my life just to show me that it's time for me to open myself again to the world. Otherwise, I might miss the chance of meeting another great guy like him.

Something's gotta give.

He merely has to open the door for me. But he's not meant to be in there with me, wherever the door might lead. If that is the case, then I shouldn't disregard his effort by allowing my current confusion to immobilize me.

Maybe it's time for me to explore more of this world of opportunities that lays before me. Maybe it's time for me to see and experience more of Dubai and the people who are here.

And as if to reaffirm such a thought, my phone buzzes with another match from Tinder.

Inertia. I was not fond of Physics at school. Understanding it, though, sure does help.

**

"You didn't get to experience that with me. Now they're taking it away."

The movers, after dismantling his bed, are now taking it out of his apartment. It's heading to the home of a Russian woman who just arrived in Dubai.

"I got to experience you, though. So I think I still got the better end of the bargain."

"No, princess, it's not quite the same."

"Really? How so? They say a man is his bed."

"Oh, but think of the fun that we could have had on that bed!"

"Didn't we have fun off of it?"

"There really is no way around it with you, huh?"

"I'm set in my ways, Saad. I don't mind having sex within my personal relationship. However, I don't want to have it purely out of carnal desires."

"Fair enough. But I'd always be jealous of the man who'd get to do that with you."

"And I of the woman whom you're going to love."

**

"This Brett guy is really good-looking. Square jaw, chiseled cheekbones. He looked like an army guy. When are you going to meet?"

"How did you know that we haven't met?"

"You'd have told me."

"After Saad leaves, I promised to meet Alfred. Maybe around that time, I'll see Brett too."

"When is Saad leaving again?"

Less than a year ago, she asked me the same question, only it was Zaki who was leaving then. Back-to-back losses. I hope that this will not become a trend in my life.

"Lana, if you're going to keep swiping right, please don't just consider their looks. Please read their bio as well."

"That's for you to do after you match with someone. And if you don't agree with my choices, you can always unmatch."

Is this how it's going to be for me moving forward, matching and unmatching with men?

"By the way, do you have reservations about nationalities?"

"How can I have any when I don't even know what or who's out there?"

"With your mind and outspoken personality, I think you're better suited to a European. However, if possible, choose one who has not been married before, or if he's divorced, at least someone who has no kids. Nothing against them, though, just that I don't want to compete with my man's attention and devotion."

"Okay, noted."

"What about age? Do you have any preference?"

I shrug my shoulders. All these are alien concepts to me at the moment.

"Do you remember Malik? He's ten years older than me. I was reluctant at first, but he was so sweet and persistent that I relented. Then, just weeks into dating, his manipulative tendencies started to show. There came a point where he wanted to see what I'd be wearing even before we went out!"

"Wow. I had no idea he's way older than you. I think ten years is a stretch. It's a full generational gap, Lana."

"I know. I just thought I'd give it a try. He's a very smart guy. I like smart guys. I mean, who doesn't? But his age began to run our budding relationship. I had to cut it off."

"You were seeing another Egyptian guy some time back. What was his name?"

"Which one? I met several already. But I think you're referring to Mohammad. You met him. He's another story. But I think every Mohammad's story is the same."

"What do you mean?"

"While he was in the shower one time, I opened his wallet and saw the Emirates IDs of his family."

"You went through a guy's wallet?"

"I have this nagging feeling. It wouldn't go away. You know me. He's very evasive, but my gut's telling me something else. So when the opportunity presented itself, I went for it."

"Did you confront him about it?"

"Not right away, and not in a manner that you might expect. But one time when we were out, and I chose a fancy restaurant in a nice hotel, mind you! I asked him where he thought this was going. And I asked straightforwardly if he was married. Of course, he tried to stir – again – the conversation in another direction. But I told him that it's a deal breaker if he was."

"And he admitted that he was?"

"Yes, so that was that. After he dropped me home, I blocked him completely."

"But where's his family?"

"The wife and kids are in Egypt. They'd come during school breaks and holidays. Thinking about it now, we met in September, just the start of the school year."

"You have been to his place. There were no signs, pictures and toys, and what have you?"

"None whatsoever."

I'm lost for words. Lourdes may be right. Dubai does seem like a more dangerous jungle than the natural ones.

"This is just me saying. I think it is okay to go out with Arab men, Egyptians, and whatnot, but don't dabble into serious dating with them. Chances are, they're married or have been arranged to be married. Add the Pakistanis in that list too."

That tugs at my heart. Have they found someone for Zaki?

"Another thing. If they ask for photos on WhatsApp before meeting, block immediately."

"Why?"

"What do you think they'll need more photos of you? You have it on Tinder already. If they say that they just want to be sure it's you, tell them you're open to meeting up."

"Okay, noted."

"If they ask you if it's okay to meet at their place for the first date, flat out decline. Maybe not all women are worth the effort to go out for, but you certainly are. And those types are only after one thing: sex. Some would hint that very early on, and even in your conversations. So be wary and discerning."

"Ah, you swiped right on some of them."

"Really?"

"Yes. Their messages are still there. I haven't responded to any of them."

"Well, why didn't you unmatch? If you find them vulgar or indecent, I don't see why you'd even spare a minute."

"Frankly, I just forgot. And now that you reminded me… You know what, why don't you delete them now? Or what if I respond but in a lighter, *cleaner* way?"

"That might work, but after the first attempt, just unmatch. I think when a guy really wants sex, he will get back to that point right away. Otherwise, he'll just happily move along to someone else who might be more liberating or open than you are. There are many fish in the ocean. A seal does not have the patience to chase after one that swims away."

"You have a point. And since you have been on the app far longer, I think I'm more inclined to believe you than my own perceptions."

"There's still a lot more to talk about, but I can't think of anything in particular to focus on right now. Just keep in mind that whenever you feel uncertain about any of the guys you'll connect with, before you meet them, talk to me. You just got a new match. Check him out."

My phone vibrates again with an incoming message as Lana hands it back to me.

"Maybe later. Right now, I just want to rest. What you shared with me was more than a mouthful. I'm still trying to wrap my head around it, especially about Mohammad."

"Okay, up to you. I'm going for my parlor appointment now. Do you want to tag along?"

"No, some other time perhaps. I'm scheduled to change my beddings and put them into the wash."

As I'm fitting in a new sheet on my bed, I wonder how many times Mohammad has to change his. He must be one very meticulous and organized guy in order to hide away traces of his alternate life. It's good thinking on Lana's part to check on his wallet. But then again, that's typical of her.

When something ruffles her tides inside, she will not stop until she finds the cause of it. I can't say that I can do the same. So I think I'll take the discerning route instead.

**

My birthday will be in two weeks. Last year, I celebrated it with Zaki and our colleagues. This year, I'm not keen to observe it in the same fashion.

I'm turning 35 years old, but I feel a lot older than that. I think pain has a way of ageing you, though not physically. But inside, I feel like I have had enough more than one should have in their lifetime.

The sound of the biometric machine opening the door halts my melodramatic train of thought.

"Hanna! Just the one I need to see."

"How are you, Jaro? What's the update on your wedding?"

"That's exactly the reason why I've been looking for you since morning. Our parents have already decided on a date. It will be on the 11th of this month. I'd love for you to come, Hanna."

"Oh! That's quite soon. How are you going to prepare for everything with that little time?"

"Well, our parents have taken care of everything. It was just the date that had to be decided upon. And today, both sides agreed to have it on November 11. So it's 11/11."

102

"I see. Let me check with the boss and Roshie. If my workload permits it, I don't see any reason why I cannot attend. I'll come back to you tomorrow for an update."

"Great! I'll tell the others too. Anyone who wants to go is welcome. And I'll cover the hotel for anyone who comes."

"That's just perfect, Jaro! Now I'm more eager to go."

He leaves my desk beaming ear to ear, while I'm filled with excitement at the possibility of visiting India for the first time.

"How long will you be there?"

"Just for a week. One of my colleagues is getting married."

"Are you going alone?"

"No. Another female colleague will go too. But she will leave the day after the wedding. I'm thinking of roaming around for a few more days before coming back."

"You want to roam around in India by yourself?"

Saad's reaction is a bit exaggerated. I'm not sure how to respond.

"I don't think it's a safe idea, Hanna."

"Travelling is therapeutic for me."

"I can understand that, but travelling alone in a country like India?"

"Have you been to India? Do you know the situation on the ground?"

"No. But do you?"

"Then I'll hire a driver just like what I did in Egypt. I'll take all the necessary precautions. I will not stay out late at night and will go only to tourist spots where security is surely enforced."

"Why do I have a feeling that I will not be able to dissuade you from going?"

"Because you won't be able to. It's as simple as that."

"Okay, but promise me that you will keep in touch with me all throughout the day while you're out. And you will inform me once you're back at your hotel. I also want to know what hotel you'll be staying at."

"Sure, I can do that."

I think apart from security concerns, time is another reason why Saad does not want me to go. With him leaving sooner, a week away in India will impinge on our remaining time together. I feel a little guilty over my decision, that I must admit. But I know that I have to ignore the promptings of my heart right now and just go with what seems right in my mind. Maybe the clarity I need will come to me in one of the chaotic streets of India. Sometimes, the most unlikely of places offer the best lessons in life. I'm not expecting to stumble upon my own little miracle in there. But I'm certain that going will do me good. It will take me away from him, but it might bring me closer to myself.

**

The familiar noise and chaos in the airport do not confuse me. There's a certain vibe in the air that doubles my excitement in a way.

"Where are you?" Kaycee asks.

"Just here, roaming around the place. How long was I out?"

"About ten minutes, I guess. What are you thinking about?"

"What *they're* thinking about."

"Why would you concern yourself with the troubles of other people?"

"To forget about my own troubles."

"Oh. Are you and Saad not okay?"

"We are. But he's leaving soon. By the end of this month, actually."

"Oh, why didn't you just stay and spend these days with him instead?"

"Will it change anything?"

"Perhaps not, but at least you're together."

"That's the point. I'm afraid I'm not fond of that idea anymore. I feel cheated again by life. Last year, it was Zaki. Now it's Saad. What is this? Why is this happening?"

"You're Nancy Drew. You're the one who loves riddles and puzzles. I'm sure you'll figure this out on your own at some point."

"Why do I have to figure everything out on my own? Why can't life be just plain and simple for once?"

"You're not plain and simple, Hanna. You may think that you are because you got yourself figured out. But if you ask for plain and simple, you'll be doing yourself a disservice."

Being left behind is not a disservice to me?

**

The venue looks like a Bollywood movie set. It's grand and elegant. Gold and red colors dominate the entire place. There are fresh flowers of different varieties neatly arranged on the walkway leading to the main function hall and on the stage. It's hard for me to estimate the number of seats. From the looks of it, though, it seems more than five hundred. Kaycee and I are the only foreigners attending this celebration today. We choose to sit closer to the stage and by the aisle so Jaro can easily see us.

Nearly half an hour later, guests are still pouring in, filling the empty seats around us. As my eyes busily roam around, enthralled by the sheer number of people, the music that suddenly plays from the stage startles me. Turning my gaze, I see two male musicians humming while beating their drums in a ritualistic tempo. Then, not long after, they step down the stage and follow the lead, holding a trumpet. A small procession of women holding candles on an elaborately ornate plate follows them. They walk towards the direction of the entrance.

Momentarily, Jaro's entourage comes into view. In front of him and his family are three pairs of women beautifully dressed in white and gold, dancing as they walk forward. Jaro smiles and waves when he spots us from the crowd. Once he and his family are settled on the stage, his bride's entourage marches into the entry hall. The bride is preceded by a group of men wearing only white loincloths, their chests covered with white shawls. They're chanting as they walk. They are followed by the same group of women from the earlier procession. Just behind them is the bride with her father, walking under a canopy of flowers. The wedding ceremony commences when she and her family take their places on the stage alongside Jaro's family.

My eyes are glued to the stage. An Indian wedding is very ritualistic and pregnant with symbolism, heavily influenced by their culture and Hindu traditions. What I'm witnessing right now is in no way comparable to any of the weddings I've been to before. It's like watching a movie. What an enriching experience this is. I'm glad I came despite Saad and my earlier indecision.

When the formal ceremony is done, Jaro waves at us to come up onto the stage for photos. Then we feast on traditional Indian cuisine. The official reception will be two nights from now. Kaycee has excused herself from that and will be flying back to Dubai tomorrow afternoon.

"So what will be your itinerary for the next two days?"

"I will fly to Jaipur and tour the city. Then come back in the afternoon prior to the reception."

"All reservations for that are arranged, I suppose?"

"Yes. I booked the hotel. Well, it's more like an inn, really. A very old house turned into a mini hotel. It's in the city, close to a few tourist spots. I also arranged for a driver. I'm all set."

"That's good. All the best on your solo wandering then."

"And a safe flight for you. I'll see you in the office next week."

**

After a brief morning of pleasantries with Kaycee, I head to the reception and check out. We're very close to the airport. In less than twenty minutes, I'm queuing to check in for my flight to Jaipur. There are fewer people given the time.

After just an hour, my flight's called in for boarding. The short distance will not allow me to nap. But that's alright. I'm fully awake because of excitement. Two days may not be sufficient to see Jaipur, but I'll make the most of my time while I'm there.

Upon reaching the inn, I head upstairs to my room to drop my backpack and come down right away to rejoin my driver. His suggestion is to visit the City Palace first. I happily obliged. I find myself roaming inside its complex in almost no time.

I think the City Palace is aptly named because the courtyards and museum within it seem to make up a small city. This is the first time I have seen Mughal architecture and design. I'm blown away by how detailed and elaborate the decorations on the façade and in the interiors of each building are. The doors and balconies are intricately painted with peacocks and flowers. Colors are boldly used throughout the premises, but they all come beautifully together, with pink being the predominant hue. The place is an extravagant show of craftsmanship. It has a royal appeal even to this day, I wonder what more then. This place is a museum of its own kind, with each building an artifact. Two hours can fly by in a heartbeat when you're in a place like this.

A short distance from there is the Hawa Mahal, another pink-painted structure used by women in the olden times to peek at men on the streets without them being seen. It has the same sophisticated design as those buildings in the City Palace. There's no way to stop for a photograph, so I content myself with a snapshot while inside my service vehicle.

We're heading to Amber Palace now. It will be lunchtime soon. I have not had breakfast. I'm still full of excitement, though. I know, however, that it's not wise to continue without having at least a snack. As per Google – and my crude estimation – Amber Palace is bigger than the City Palace because of the adjacent Jaigarh Fort. Better have a stopover for a quick bite.

My driver suggests a short visit to an elephant sanctuary where I can feed the animals with fruits, and I can have my lunch there as well. I readily accepted. I have always been fond of elephants.

All of creation is a wonder, but I find elephants exceptionally amazing. They have complex emotions, almost similar to ours. They openly express sorrow and never forget. I, too, can never forget. However, I cannot wear my heart on my sleeve. It's not in fashion, and it will never be in trend.

This is my first time seeing elephants, and an hour is not sufficient. But that's all I have for now. If I had known, I would have spent an entire day here.

Amber Palace and the connecting Jaigarh Fort fare well with my expectations. The palace has retained its old grandeur. The ceilings, walls, and windows are truly works of art. The courtyards and gardens are well-maintained and echo the sophistication of Mughal art. However, I learned that the style used here was called Rajput architecture. They have a few similarities, but the distinction is there if one would really look closely enough.

The Jaigarh Fort is an imposing structure, on the other hand. From above, one can see the snaking walls that extend all around the perimeter of the palace. It's similar to the Great Wall of China.

I check the time. I'm breezing through the day without realizing it. It's close to four in the afternoon. I thought it best to head back to the inn. My feet are starting to complain as well.

On the way back, we make a quick stopover for photographs in front of Jal Mahal. It's a five-storey palace in the middle of a lake. When the lake's high, four of its floors are submerged in water. I want to know the story behind its construction, but my driver speaks little English. I'll settle with Google later then.

Once back in my room, I look at the photos in my phone. Jaipur is a living museum. These structures are not just proof of the genius of a particular time or person. These are a testament to man's desire for immortality; to always be remembered, be revered.

**

I love museums. They are the repositories of history. Going about in the Albert Hall Museum transports me back to the glory days of Jaipur. The collections are impressive and speak highly of the arts and crafts of the time. The magnificently elaborate depictions of their many gods on brass and other metals, stones, and woods, and the bold use of colors on their painted ceramics, draw from me a deep sense of respect for their skill and extraordinary talent. Indian art is truly one of a kind.

The Egyptian collections housed in the basement are a sweet surprise. I was not expecting to see a mummy here. I'm once more hit with a strong longing to see Zaki. But the past is the past. If very old things are placed in museums for safekeeping, I must learn to file the past in a folder that belongs to its time. These great objects once served their purposes, but are stored here now because they no longer offer benefits to the world of today. The past, our memories, must have its own place too. And it's not in the present. I left the museum feeling a little sad, having been reminded of Zaki. But a renewed sense of purpose is beginning to sprout inside my heart.

Back in the inn, while having snacks at the rooftop restaurant, a middle-aged female staff member approaches and offers to do a personal tarot reading for me. I'm taken aback. I'm familiar with the art. However, knowing what can happen tomorrow activates my paranoia. With my confused state of mind, it's the last thing I want.

"Don't worry. It's free."

"I'm not actually concern about that. It's more of …"

"Your aura is heavy. There's a lot on your mind. Maybe I can help clear some of your worries."

Now what do I make of that?

"You don't have to believe everything or follow my advice. But knowing might help you. Do you want me to proceed?"

She has already piqued my curiosity. What's the harm in listening to her?

"Sure."

She shuffles the cards so fast that some are flying off her hands. She laid them down flat on the table. All five cards show swords in them. The images are vivid and evoke certain emotions in me. She studies the cards, then looks at me.

"You have a very inquisitive mind. You question life's mysteries, that you experience headaches sometimes. You need to be careful about your thought processing. Not all the things that our minds can conceive are true. Do not let your own thoughts deceive you and create self-limiting beliefs that can hamper your own growth or hurt you. Find your center again."

Bullseye. She shuts my logic down with that. She draws in more cards from those on her left hand.

"Give your mind a rest. I think that's part of the reason why you are here."

I think she knows that my silence is an affirmation. She continues.

"No one can get ahead of life, of nature, or of the universe. Let them take their course on their own time. You create your own unhappiness by trying to control everything. Are you a Scorpio by any chance?"

My cheeks grow red with shock. I simply nod.

"There's nothing wrong with being intelligent. But if it's the only force you'll allow to influence you, then you'll be creating an imbalance in your life. We have emotions because we are humans. Allow yourself to live. Get outside of your head."

Wow.

I look down at the cards in quiet introspection of this stranger's words. Then she picks them and shuffles them a few times before speaking again.

"I hope in any way that that was helpful."

"Yes, yes, it's very helpful. Thank you. You're very good. You're on point."

"I'm very pleased to hear you say that. I hope the coming days and weeks will be better for you."

She leaves the table without another word. There's nothing I can say more as well.

**

The reception is a relatively smaller gathering compared to the wedding, but in no way less grand. It's a full-packed night of entertainment. There's not a minute of silence. The band keeps playing music, both from Indian and Western artists. The dance presentations of different cultures, including that of the Egyptians, are the highlight of the evening for me. And it brings with it an important realization.

Life will continue to put me in situations where I'll be reminded of the past, not to test my patience, but to help me learn to accept that it's over. Saad is right. My ship is still anchored to yesterday's post. It's about time to set sail again. And the tarot reader is correct. I think too much ahead. My fear has no foundation in reality, and yet I'm allowing it to direct my actions at present. This has been a very good trip, though short. I'm coming home with the gift of enlightenment.

**

I miss him. My short vacation in India has created a thirst in me which I'm now trying to quench with his kiss.

"I've wanted that all this time."

I feel the full impact of the emotions that come with those words.

"I know. But I was not prepared for you. I have not come to terms with my loss then."

"And have you now?"

"This short time away has been good for my mind. I think when you step away from a situation, you then get a better understanding of it."

"I'm glad. But it's a little too late for me, though."

"The heart cannot be rushed, Saad."

"I know. Just saying."

Just saying what? He knew he didn't have the luxury of time for a proper relationship. So, what he is trying to just say now?

Voicing my thoughts will only sour our remaining days together. I do not want to be a bad memory for him.

**

Saad: The TV set will be collected in an hour, and the couch tonight. My friend has also agreed to take my car. So tomorrow we are going to start the paperwork to transfer the ownership to him.

Receiving this WhatsApp message from Saad stops me from what I'm doing. I accepted some time back the reality of his leaving. But it's only now that it's starting to really sink in. My heart is once more awash with the unmistakable feeling of sadness. I don't think it's something I'll ever get used to, no matter how many times the emotion visits my heart.

Me: That's good. You're able to dispose the majority of your things.

Saad: There are some things here that I thought of giving to you.

Me: That's very thoughtful of you. Thank you.

Saad: If you're free later or tomorrow, I can bring them over.

Me: Today and tomorrow would be good.

Saad: So, should I come today? What time would you like me to be there?

Me: Feel free to come by after office hours. Will you be able to visit me again tomorrow?

Saad: I actually intend to see you every day until the last day.

Until the last day. It packs a punch. I respond with a smiley even though in reality I feel the exact opposite.

**

"Ashley, are you home?"

"In here, babe."

I walk in on her folding her fresh laundry.

"What's up?"

"Is it okay with you if Saad comes by? He's going to drop a few things."

"Of course. Why not?"

"Thank you, babe. He's giving away stuff in his apartment, and he said he has a few for me."

"That's really nice of him."

I let out a deep sigh as I collapse on her bed.

"You'll be alright, babe. You got through something worse than this."

"Yeah. But it hurts just the same."

"But you've one resilient heart. You'll pull through."

When you have no other option but to survive, yes, one's heart pulls through.

Saad shows up outside our apartment with a variety of items from his place: two beach chairs, a beach umbrella, a small cooler, his stand fan, a floor lamp, and a pillow tucked under one arm – physical proofs of his imminent departure. I'm momentarily taken aback, unable to decide which one I'll put my hands on first. So I kiss him full on the lips instead.

"Now I was not expecting that."

"Neither did I, nor all of these."

He hands me the pillow first.

"This is the main one that I used. To help you sleep better and hopefully make you dream of me. The lamp, because you said it's cute. The fan for your steady supply of cold air."

He winks flirtatiously.

"And these you can use with Ashley when you go to the beach. I'd rather she be the one sitting on my chair than another guy's ass."

"Wow! This is very thoughtful of you, Saad."

"I don't want you to forget me that easily."

"As if I'd be able to. Can you stay a little bit? I prepared something for you."

"Oh, wow! That's nice to hear. Will it be cabaret style?"

"You want your dinner served in that way?"

"Wouldn't mind it at all!"

"I'm sure Canada will not disappoint you in that regard. But I don't think anyone there will serve you this. My own spaghetti recipe."

"Looks delicious and smells good too."

"I hope you'll like it. There's still half of the cheesecake I made over the weekend. Would you like to try it as well?"

"Wow! Do you usually do this to men when they come here?"

"For the record, you're the first guy I've invited to come into our apartment."

"Very nice. I feel special."

"You should, because you are. And you will always hold a special place in my heart, Saad."

He pulls me to an embrace and goes straight for my lips. I kiss him back ardently. When our lips part, his nose nuzzles mine.

"Are you still not willing to try LDR?"

"Let's keep in touch, sure. But let's not put undue pressure on our hearts to make it work through the distance. What my heart went through was massive. And I don't want to start anything again with a confused mind. Besides, you're starting a new life in a new place. That alone is a huge undertaking. I don't want to rob you of the time and energy to have a good start there."

"Your wisdom never fails to amaze me."

"Drop your charms and eat my spaghetti. I want to know how you find the taste."

"I don't mind having this and you every day."

"Won't you get bored being served the same thing every day?"

"With the same food, yes, for sure. But you, I highly doubt it."

"Do you really find me that attractive, or are you just saying all these because you're still hoping to bed me?"

"I've given up on my sexual dream over you right after the first month. But it doesn't mean that I don't jerk off thinking of you."

My cheeks readily flush at his admission. I cannot stifle a giggle.

"I love your personality and your mind, Hanna. Sex is easy to find here. And if a guy has money, as some women come with price tags, he can have what he wants, however he wants it."

"Have you tried it?"

"I'll never pay for sex."

"I'm curious to know one thing."

"I've not been out with anyone else since meeting you."

"How did you guess that?"

"You seem the kind who would have thought of that. And if I can be very frank, I have thought of that. But the thought of having another girl in my arms and looking at her face, but nothing seeing yours… it stops me every time."

That's one of the sweetest things a man has ever said to me. Tears are threatening to escape my eyes. He reaches for my hand.

"I wish you could just stay."

"I wish that too. I'm not expecting for my application to get approved that fast. Otherwise, I wouldn't have invested in my apartment and got a car. Or pursued you."

"But I think the sooner is better for you."

"I feel better here with you, Hanna. But as they say, we play the cards we're dealt with. We can hope to win, but never to expect it."

"Life is sometimes more unfair to those people in love. But I never would have wished to have never met you, regardless of how things turned out for us."

"Same goes for me, Hanna."

"By the way, I never got to ask you what made you approach me that night."

"Funny you asked that. I don't know. I saw you sit down and flopped back, staring at the sky. I thought you were drunk."

"And yet that possibility did not deter you from coming forward. Or you saw it as an opportunity, thinking that my guard would be down because of alcohol?"

"A drank girl is an easy win, yes. But the possibility of me cleaning after your mess once you reach my apartment almost made me run for the hills!"

"Yet you approached."

"I thought you were cute."

"And you thought you could bring this cute girl home."

"I'm actually glad that it didn't happen, because that made me look at you differently. And the more that I got to know you, the more my respect for you grew. And along with it my affection."

"You're just the sweetest, Saad."

"Am I not the most good-looking as well?"

"I have no one to compare you with."

"What about him?"

"You two cannot be compared to each other. He's an Arab. You look more like a European. You are very fair, with dirty blonde hair, and those blue eyes... I can still remember very well that night when I first looked at them."

"Now that you said that, what were you thinking then?"

"Nothing, really. But I felt excited, ecstatic, along with other emotions. Fear too."

"Fear? Why?"

"I don't know. I've talked to my friends about you. They've all encouraged me to press on and see where things go."

"And this is how things went."

"And this is how things went."

"Any regrets?"

"None whatsoever. What about you?"

"Just that I cannot stay longer."

"Karma's a bitch, but time is like a boss who fucks us all when he wants to."

"Just try not to forget me too fast."

"Why do you keep saying that? You know it's not possible for me."

"My friend saw you on Tinder. He showed me your profile. He's interested in you. He swiped right for you. Why did you never wear that dress when we went out?"

I feel like all the blood in my body goes up to my face.

"I can explain that."

"No need. It's okay with me. But when did you create your profile there?"

"I didn't. My best friend did while I was asleep on her couch one weekend. When exactly, I can't recall."

"Are you chatting with anyone there?"

"I spoke to two guys over the phone. Friendly conversations. I haven't met either one in person."

"I see."

He looks surprised. He remains as composed, but I can see the hurt beginning to manifest in those beautiful blue eyes.

"I just wanted to see what it's about. Those two came off as very friendly. I didn't see any harm in having conversations with them, so I shared my phone number."

"Will you meet them after I leave?"

"Yes."

"I see. How soon?"

"I don't know. But if it would appease you in any way, both of them knew about you."

"Where are they from?"

"One is from the UK, while the other is Swiss. Both are divorced, or the Swiss will be too. He found his wife on the bed with another man in their own home."

"Disgusting. You need to be very careful with the men here, Hanna. Not everyone will treat you the way I do."

I simply nod.

"Are you angry with me?"

"No. I'm just surprised. I wasn't expecting you to be there."

"My friends think that it's time for me to move on. My best friend said that it's a good platform to connect with men and establish rapport prior to meeting them in person. I thought that was a safe approach for me. Again, if it might make you feel better even in the tiniest bit, I have not swiped right to anyone as of yet. I haven't really explored it. I just kept reading the messages and never responded. Until Alfred and Brett."

"Does either of them look better than me?"

I crack out so loud enough to draw Ashley out of her room. I reintroduce them to each other.

"So, I heard you're moving to Canada."

"Apparently so."

"I wish you all the best. Although you're going to make someone here sad."

I raise my hand, then shrug my shoulders.

"But she won't be sad for a long time. She will be meeting a lot of men after I leave."

"Oh, come on, Saad."

"Does he mean the Tinder thing?"

"Yeah. His friend saw me there."

"Oh. I overheard you and Lana here talking about it very recently. Last week, was it?"

"Yeah, sometime then. She was giving me pointers."

"What pointers?"

"She's teaching me how to use the app and who to avoid, and all that. She told me stories of her Tinder dates."

"Well, just be very careful, habibti."

I nod earnestly.

"Do you mind going with her on her dates?"

Now it's Ashley cracking up to him. He does know how to handle any situation. He can sense perhaps that I'm not comfortable with the subject anymore.

**

The last day has come. No matter how many times I tell myself to pull it together, I just cannot concentrate. My overwhelming sadness is like lava flowing out of the volcano inside my heart. The sediments from last year's "eruption" have not cooled yet, and here are fresh layers to top it up. I'm not hoping to get out of this unscathed, but I'm hoping to get out of this.

'Don't go ahead of time, of life, or of the universe.'

I wonder what the tarot reader means by that. How can I get ahead of anything when I'm being left behind?

The Men Buffet

Alfred readily accepts my invitation for lunch. After all, this is a long time coming.

If likened to a car, he is an older model of Mercedes-Benz. He may not have the modern appeal of the latest releases, but he definitely has the old-school charm typical of the well-bred and educated kind. He's not bad for a 55-year-old man.

"Pink suits you."

"Thanks. But I have to say that sadness is not a good shade of eye makeup for you."

"He was a really good guy. He was a loss for me."

"As I'm sure you are to him, too. But life's like that. It always fucks up a good story."

"What about you? How have you been?"

"I'm divorced. It was easy enough. But sitting down with my children and talking about divorce is not something any parent can easily muster in their lifetime."

"How did they take it?"

"It was particularly hard for my son. He knows that there's something that I'm not telling them. But my parents and I agreed that, when the time is right and they're both a bit older, we'll tell them the real reason. For now, we just explained to them that their mom and I have grown apart. For tensions not to escalate further, it's better to separate."

"What about her? What did she say about all this?"

"What else can she say that would matter? She's going back to Switzerland. My parents will be staying with us for some time longer. I also hired a professional to look after my children while I work."

"How do you intend to move forward from this?"

"There's work and my children. This coming school break, they'll spend the Christmas holidays with their mother in Switzerland. And I'm thinking of taking that time to go somewhere and shed the old skin, so to speak."

"Ah, yes. Christmas is upon us."

"Do you have any plans?"

"None. I actually almost forgot about it."

"By the way, any interesting prospects from Tinder?"

"Ah, that. Well, it seems that my best friend took the liberty of swiping right for almost everyone who is here. My phone has been buzzing all the time. I'm matching with so many guys, and I'm swamped with messages."

"Well, I think that's good, isn't it? You will have options. How many have you met so far?"

"You're the very first one, Alfred. I waited until he left, out of respect. And now, frankly, I don't know how to go about it."

"Maybe you can take the same route as we did. Talk to them on the phone first, get a feel of things. And if you think that it's okay to see them, you feel safe, then you decide and take the shot."

"Yeah, sure, I'd do that."

I will not allow life to further coerce me. I'm taking the wheel on the drive forward. So, upon reaching home, I go through the messages from the past weeks, and I start unmatching except for three: the pilot, the Pakistani doctor, and the pastry chef. They seem decent with strong professions. All claims to be single still, but I'll see about that. After sending responses to each of them, I got one back right away from the doctor.

Pakistani Doc: Would you like to have dinner at my place tonight?

I can hear Lana's voice in my head protesting against this preposterous invitation.

Me: I don't go to a stranger's place on the first meeting.

Pakistani Doc: Fair enough. Where would you like to meet?

Me: There are plenty of cafés or restaurants around. Also, I prefer to speak to you over the phone first before we meet. You know, just to get to know each other a little bit.

Pakistani Doc: Okay. Please share your mobile number.

No calls till the day closes. A new week starts, and more pressing matters push Tinder to the side of my mind. The pilot, however, brings it back to my consciousness with a message.

B777 Pilot: I was on a long-haul flight and a short trip in the region after that. I'm sorry for my delayed response. Well, you took your time too. We matched more than a week ago, but I only got your message two days back. Anyhow, if you're free this week, perhaps we can meet for dinner.

Me: Aye, aye captain!

B777 Pilot: Where do you live? I'm in Marina.

Me: We're practically neighbours! I'm just in JLT.

B777 Pilot: Nice! So when do you think would be a suitable time for us to have dinner?

Me: I'm free tomorrow. If you are too, then let's set the time.

B777 Pilot: You work in an office, I suppose?

Me: You guessed that right, captain.

B777 Pilot: So it means you'll finish around 5 or 6. Would 8 p.m. be okay?

Me: Yes, that's fine with me. There's one thing though before we meet.

B777 Pilot: Go ahead. What is it?

Me: I prefer to speak on the phone before meeting in person. You know, to establish rapport and find a common ground. So it won't be awkward when we meet.

B777 Pilot: Sure. Call me whenever you're free.

I want to pull the time so it's lunch already. I want to hear his voice. Work does not make me wait longer, though. It rushes the day for me, in a manner of speaking.

He seems like a smart guy, with a healthy sense of humor. He's a good conversationalist. He knows what's happening in the world, not only because he's a pilot, but also because he's genuinely interested in its affairs.

**

The joint venture meeting with our partner from Saudi Arabia extends beyond our working hours, affording me less time to prepare for my dinner date. While in the shower, I'm already thinking of what I'll wear. It's winter, though it's not as cold. As soon as I leave the tub, I hurriedly open my closet and scan what's in it.

Right, this should be okay.

White t-shirt with a deep neckline, paired with an A-line red chiffon skirt and a denim jacket over it. Feminine and sexy, but not too put-together. And I'm glad I thought of wearing my heeled espadrilles. He would have dwarfed me. He's so tall.

Mid-dinner, the jukebox in my head starts playing the song *Every Breath You Take*. I look at him. He's curious why I'm grinning.

"You look like the younger version of Sting from the band The Police."

"Funny you say that. My mom thinks so, too."

"Can you sing too?"

"Oh, I do that all the time in the cockpit. Sometimes, if I'm really up to it, I sing during the entire flight, to the detriment of my co-pilot."

I laugh at his comical admission.

"Are you close to your mom?"

"Yes. Why do you ask?"

"Just out of curiosity."

According to Lana, a guy who's close to his mother is either a mama's boy or a gentleman. It's too soon to make anything out of this conversation. I'm open to seeing him again whenever he's down here on the ground.

Upon reaching my building, I chance upon Ashley by the elevators.

"Babe! I'm surprised to see you out this late."

"I was just on a date."

"With someone from Tinder?"

"Yup. He's a German pilot."

"Wow! That's nice. Is he single?"

"He said so. I'm inclined to believe him somehow. Isn't it difficult to maintain a relationship when you're always in the skies?"

"I suppose so. But you know men. It's easy for them to lie. Not that I'm saying he is. You're getting what I'm saying, yeah?"

"Absolutely, babe."

"Will you see him again?"

"Yeah, I don't see why not. I like talking to him. He's funny, and he has some good stories to share. But I don't know when the next date will be."

"Wait a minute. Is he based here?"

"Yes. He's an Emirates pilot."

"Very nice! I'm happy that you've found a way to entertain yourself."

"Yeah. Good night, Ash!"

"Night, babe."

Diversion. That is what this is about. It's a trick to stop me from living in the past. As if it's a disease that could contaminate me should I linger a minute longer.

**

Thursday night, and I'm on my wits' end. What a tiring week. I think I'll just have a night in and get back to my reading. The books I ordered from Amazon have been delivered. I run the bath and go through the parcels. *Evil Under The Sun* by *Agatha Christie*. It seems like a good read. Perhaps I'll start with this one. My phone vibrates on the bedside table, interrupting me from reading the blurb. It's a message from a recent match.

Pastry Chef: Back-to-back weddings. Whew! I'm flat already this week. I'm so looking forward to the weekend, chillin' by the beach. Would you like to join me?

Me: Oh, tell me about it! I'm about to soak myself in the tub to soothe my stresses away. Which beach will you be going to?

Pastry Chef: I live in Marina. I usually go to JBR. Where do you live, by the way?

Me: JLT. I go to JBR myself, mostly on weekends too.

Pastry Chef: Perfect! So it's a date then.

Me: There's just one thing, though. Can we first talk on the phone tonight?

Pastry Chef: Sure. As soon as I get home, I'll call you.

He's South African. He's got quite a personality. His arrogance is slapping me through the phone. I'm not sure about this one. I'll sleep it off. If tomorrow I still have reluctance over him, then I'll bail out.

**

The sun's blinding light fills my entire room. I glance at the wall clock.

Holy fox!

I hastily grab my phone, but it's not where I usually keep it. I'm paralyzed momentarily, thinking where I put it last. Then it starts to vibrate. I listen in carefully, trying to determine where the sound is coming from. It's on my study table. Three missed calls from Jackson. I press the call back button, and he picks up in one ring.

"Good morning! I'm so sorry I overslept. Are you still at the beach?"

"Just about to leave. I'll pack and go as soon as I finish my beer."

"Isn't it a little too early for that? And since when has JBR allowed for anyone to drink openly?"

"I woke up at 4:00 AM. I already had breakfast. I actually prepared a sandwich for you. As for the beer, it's in my canister."

How brazen. Somehow, I'm not surprised. He seems like the kind who'd do something like that.

"I'm sorry again for failing to wake up early. Would you like to have lunch with me instead?"

"Frankly, I'm annoyed right now. I'll pass."

"I can understand. Though I hope it's not enough to ruin your entire weekend. I'll see you around next time."

I hang up without waiting for his response.

He repeats his rhetoric in his WhatsApp messages. A queen will not go down to the level of the fools, especially just upon waking up.

I flop back down to bed, intending to resume my sleep. I feel a hard item underneath my duvet. It's the book I'm reading. *Evil Under The Sun*. How apt. I open the book to see where I'm at in it when my phone vibrates again.

Oh, come on!

I sit up, bracing myself for another assaulting message from Jackson. I'm pleasantly surprised to see that it's from Ralf. It's a picture inside a cockpit with the accompanying message "ATM."

Me: Where are you?

Ralf: We just landed in KSA. Dammam.

Me: I see. You look good.

Ralf: Thanks!

Me: Will we see each other this weekend?

Ralf: I have a flight to Munich late in the evening tonight. I'd be back on Wednesday. So perhaps by then.

It's a hard chance with this one. Might not be for my best interest to invest more in him. But there are plenty of options to go around, so it shouldn't be an issue. And this weekend is a good time to start looking at those.

I don't want to be too serious in my approach. But I must be careful in order to avoid the pitfalls that Lana has warned me about.

"Don't be too trusting. That way, you'll become vulnerable. Remember, a bear may be cute, but it's still a predator. Don't make yourself an easy prey. Don't go out there wearing Iron Man's suit, either. There are difficult men out there, challenging even, but nothing that your intelligence can't handle."

Right you are, Lana.

After a few swipes to the right, I'm ready for my daily hula hoop spin. In 15 minutes, my phone's vibrating constantly with matches and messages.

Let it roast a little bit.

Once my timer hits 30 minutes, I drop the hula hoop and grab my phone with the excitement that I've never felt before.

Hello, boys!

**

I look at the outfit that I put together. Red mini dress with cap sleeves, red ballerina flats, cream double-breasted coat that's just a little longer than my dress, and a gold clutch just big enough to carry my essentials: lip gloss, cards, key, and phone.

We're meeting at one of the restaurants just blocks behind my building. It's an easy route home for me, just in case. He's a Chemistry teacher from Spain. He's neat, reserved, and almost nerdy, sans the glasses. His English is very good. His accent can make one wet. Yes, ridiculous as it may seem, but that's how sexy he sounds when he speaks. I wonder how his female students are during class, if they're actually listening.

"If you don't mind me asking, where are you from?"

"Isn't it obvious?"

"In your bio, you put Asian, but I can't really place you. Your accent… I'm confused, really, but in an intriguing way."

"I was born and raised in the Philippines. By blood, I'm of Spanish-Chinese descent. As for my accent, I don't know what people can hear, really. This is the way I talk."

"Oh, so can you speak Spanish then?"

"I can pick up simple and small words. We didn't use it at home. We grew up with English as the main language. But believe it or not, when I get really upset, I swear in perfect Spanish."

"Si. Si. Let's try not to upset each other then."

His laugh is even sexier. And those thick curly hair…

Stop it, Hanna!

"Are there topics that are off the table for you?"

He seems the communicative type. I like that.

"Well, I don't think it's proper to discuss intimate details about one's life, given that this is just the first meeting. I'm okay with almost anything, but I still have my sensitivities."

"So the subject of sex is not welcome, I presume?"

"For now, I think it is best we forego it."

I cannot allow myself to be tempted beyond my threshold, especially by a hot teacher like him.

"I see. Are you religious by any means?"

"What made you ask? Is it because I do not want to discuss sex?"

"Yes. And just out of curiosity, really."

"No. I'm not religious. Though if it can be helped, I do not want to talk about religion as well. It's very subjective and can be a divisive topic."

"Agree. So why don't you propose a subject for us to talk about? As for me, I'm open to anything."

"Why are you on Tinder? What are you hoping to find or get from it?"

"To be frank, nowadays all I'm getting from it is sex. Not that I'm complaining. But after a while, you question whether that's all there is to it."

"Since you said you're open to anything, I'd like to pounce further on this."

"Okay. Shoot away."

"Those that you have had casual encounters with, are they different women each time? Do you meet anyone of them again?"

"There's one I really like, so I see her now and again. But she's married, so it will just be purely sex between us. The others, no, I prefer not to see them again. I will never pay for sex."

"What do you mean?"

"They were asking for money the morning after."

That's a hard one for me to swallow. I'm blinking non-stop. An oddity that I find annoying.

"You look shock. I hope you're not getting upset by this."

"No. No, far from that. I'm more curious. I mean, they're asking for money? What do you mean by that? I'm aware of wandering married people, but women asking for money from their dates… That's completely new to me."

I remember Saad mentioning this in passing in one of our conversations. Men giving gifts is one thing. Women asking for money from someone they just had a one-night stand with… What's that?

"How long have you been here?"

"Four and a half years. Why?"

"The other guys that you've met, they never mention this to you at all?"

"I've met only two so far, and one of them is going through a divorce. I connected with another guy from the UK. He did say something about this, but I didn't pay much thought to it because I did not know the circumstances surrounding the situation."

"Well, I was just as shocked as you when I first experienced it. So I started talking to some of my close colleagues. Apparently, it is normal here."

A lump forms in my throat. How can such a reality be an accepted norm?

"I'm sorry to have brought it up. It looks like I stirred your mind."

Stirred my mind? My whole being is shocked at the moment. Sure, I can understand what prostitution is. I did a paper about it in college. But this is something else.

I take a sip of my cold Coca-Cola. I think the sugar helps in regaining my composure.

"Don't worry about me. I'll still be able to sleep tonight."

"I'm relieved to know that. I was worried for a moment that you might not go out with me again because of it."

"You want to see me again?"

"Yes, for sure. Why? The feeling is not mutual?"

"I'm just pulling your leg. Of course, I like talking to you. I like smart men."

"If you don't mind me asking, and it's not about sex, when was your last relationship?"

"The first one in this country ended last year. I dated another one this year. It could not mature, though. He had left for Canada already."

"Are you looking for someone to be in a relationship with, or are you just meeting people for now?"

"I don't know, to be frank. But I do want to see what's out here for me."

"So that's why you're on Tinder. You're looking for prospects."

"Yes. And if it's not going to reach a level that I can deem satisfactory enough to turn into a relationship, I'm open to friendship."

"I don't think guys would want to just be friends with you."

"Well, that's beyond me to do anything about, isn't it?"

"I like you. I think you're really smart and mature enough. I would really like to keep seeing you. If you're open to that."

"I don't see why not."

Upon returning to our apartment, my phone is vibrating to an unlisted number.

"Hello?"

"Hello! Hanna?"

"Yes, it is I."

"Hi! I'm Echo. We connected on Tinder."

Echo. Echo. I repeat his name over and over in my mind, but no information bounces back to me.

"Are you using the same name on Tinder?"

"No. On Tinder, it's the Pakistani Doctor. Remember, you said you want us to speak on the phone before we meet?"

"Ah. I was expecting your call much sooner."

"I'm sorry about that. I got tied up with some family matters. You know, Friday is family day for us."

What about Saturday? A whole week has gone by!

"Hello? Are you still there?"

"Yes. I'm still here. I'm just surprised by your call. I'm not expecting to hear from you anymore."

"It seems like I've upset you."

I roll my eyes in slight irritation.

"I just came back home. Can we talk at another time?"

After hearing one affirmative word, I cut the call.

Save your bullshit for someone else.

I have other plans for my time. On my study table is my list of *Men to Meet.*

Ah, Brett!

I press the dial for his number.

"Hanna! What a pleasant surprise."

"Hi, Brett! How have you been?"

"All's good. What about yourself?"

"Just as beautiful. Thank you. I'm wondering if the tea offer still stands?"

"Of course! Of course, it does. When would you like to have it?"

"When are you free?"

"Tomorrow would be lovely. What do you say about that?"

"Sure, tomorrow suits me fine. See you then!"

Now, who's next on my list?

I don't like the rest of them. I open Tinder and start scouting. Lana has cautioned me about the Egyptians. But they are some of the most good-looking lot. Some of them have insanely tantalizing eyes with lashes that can shame many a woman's. I don't think it would hurt to go out with a few. I'm curious to hear their stories myself. I make a few swipes to the right. And now it's a waiting game. The other books on my study table remind me of the one I'm reading currently.

Let me get back to Poirot then.

As I'm about to get comfortable on my bed to resume reading, I remember my tea date tomorrow. It's mildly hot mid-morning.

Sleeveless might be a good choice.

My long white floral chiffon dress catches my attention from amongst those on the rack hanging in front of me. The neckline's attractively low, though. I place a purple cardigan over it.

Right. This one then.

**

Square jaw, aqua blue eyes, and thick, dirty blonde locks. He looks like a typical model, only he'd be shorter than most. We're almost the same height, with me on my heeled espadrilles. I stand at 165 cm.

"Hanna, Hanna, Hanna. Finally! I thought we'd never meet."

"Well, here we are."

"You look younger than in the photo, and definitely prettier."

"Thank you. That's nice of you to say. Your eyes are bluer in person. Very arresting."

"But expect none such from me. Today is for tea and good company."

Apart from his strong British accent, Brett is a mild guy of modest opinions and seemingly even temperament. He is my ideal character for a man. But he gives me the impression that he's more interested in exploring my body than this chance we have to get to know each other better. No worries. As my dad used to say, "The ocean has fish aplenty!"

**

The pharaohs are out of their tombs, and I'm meeting three of them this week. Zaki and two other colleagues are the only Egyptians I know so far. I'm not sure what to expect in meeting others.

"My work is here, and they're in Cairo. Through the years, our marriage degraded. I thought it best to divorce her than carry out relations here while I was still married to her."

Mohamed has been an engineer working on government projects for ten years now, and has been in and out of relationships with women from my country in the last five.

"Why only with Filipinas?"

"It's cheaper to maintain a relationship with women from your country, and you're all very caring and sweet. I really like that about a woman."

"Why are you not in a relationship now?"

"My first priority will always be my daughters. After some time, my past girlfriends became very demanding with money. I lost interest, so I broke off the relationships."

Ahmed's story is different. He's been living with a Filipina for years, only to discover her infidelities on her laptop one night while he was using it.

"I carried the weight of the pain from that experience into my marriage and made it collapse after some time. I realized I had not completely healed from it."

"How are you now?"

"I'm okay. I'm living each day as it comes. It's been two years since my divorce, but I have not been able to start a new relation with anyone. Well, not a proper one, I mean."

"And what exactly are you hoping to find on Tinder?"

"Good question. Frankly, I don't have an answer for that. I just want to bring fun into my life again, in whatever form or way it would come."

Karim is on the same boat. His family is in Egypt, and his loneliness being by himself here makes him long for female companionship.

"Why don't you just bring your family here?"

"It's more economical if they're there. My wife's not working, and I have two boys who are both in high school. Once a year, they come for a visit, or I go there."

And it's more convenient for your cock for them to be away.

"You may think that I'm the only one who benefits from this arrangement. But the women walk away with at least AED 500 from me each time."

"What do you mean by that?"

"Some women would like gifts, Pandora, a gold bracelet or necklace. But the majority want money, so I give them that."

Wow. I'm dumbfounded. This is another version of what the Spanish teacher shared with me.

"I can see that you're not comfortable with our discussion."

"Don't worry about me. It's just that some realities are hard for me to take in. I want to know, have you ever fallen in love with any of them?"

"It has not happened yet. And I don't know if there's anyone out here who's worth falling in love with."

I am, but I don't want love from someone like you.

The truth is burning my ass. I cut the evening short. I'd rather be watching videos on YouTube of ingrown toenail extractions than sit longer with this guy.

**

I've always loved the French fries from McDonald's. With my period days away, it helps ease my cravings. However, this place leaves a sour taste in my mouth tonight – of all nights! - for the guy who sounds every bit a man in the phone turns out to be a college student. 15 years my junior!

"Age is just a number. Who's to know?"

And of course, he lacks the tact and maturity of an older man.

"Shouldn't you be dating people your age?"

"I'm not interested in them. And I don't think they have anything to offer."

"And what do you think I can offer you?"

"Look, I've been out with two older women already. They're around your age. We had good times. So why don't you give me a chance?"

"How about I buy you a ticket back to Moldova? Are your parents aware that you're here, cavorting with older women?"

"Look, it wasn't just about sex, if that's what you're thinking."

"Really? You're young, yet you have the body and some charm of an older man. What do you think an older woman could possibly want from you?"

"You're too strict. Loosen up a bit."

That's my cue. I grab my large fries and walk away without looking back.

Instead of heading straight home, I go to the nearest Starbucks to let the steam off. Less than an hour during my stay, a wrestler-looking guy approaches my table. I look straight into his eyes without saying a word. He holds my gaze for a few seconds.

"Do you mind if I sit with you?"

"What's wrong with the other chairs?"

"Probably nothing, but it looks like you need some company."

"What made you think that?"

"I think you're emotionally eating right now."

I'm still pissed, and the last thing I need is a conversation like this.

"Leave."

"Excuse me?"

"I don't like repeating myself."

I don't need a rifle to scare anyone off. My eyes alone can make people shit their pants.

He leaves without further qualms. Good for him. At the current state of my mood, I'm prepared to take this situation further, any which way it will go.

Sometime after, I thought it best to get going, and so I walked in the direction of the beach. I'm transfixed at the red ball of fire setting on the horizon. There are still a few people frolicking in the water and others lounging on the sands.

"Mesmerizing, isn't it?"

"Captivatingly so."

I look at him and give a curt nod.

"What happened back there in Starbucks?"

I instantly become alarm, thinking that others have overheard my vulgarity.

"I was seated behind you. I was ready to intervene, but I thought you got a good grip of the situation."

"Really?"

"Yeah. You're ballsy."

"He was more so. The audacity! Ugh!"

"I overheard everything."

"Don't ever do that."

"Tell women that they're emotional eaters? It's not even lame. It's downright appalling even for me as a man. I'm Ken, by the way."

"Hanna."

"Where are you from? You sound different for an Asian."

"Philippines. I always get that. Frankly, I don't know how I sound like."

"I was thinking perhaps Malaysia or Singapore. Never would have guessed the Philippines."

"Close enough. They're our neighbours. What about you?"

"From the way I talk, you can't tell?"

"American. I just don't want to be embarrassed in case I'm wrong. But the way you enunciate your words is a giveaway. Which state?"

"North Carolina."

"What are you doing here?"

"Work. I'm a financial consultant. What about you?"

"Internal affairs, global company. Have you been here long?"

"Couple of years. You?"

"Four and a half."

"Married?"

"Would I be in Starbucks alone if I am?"

"Just checking. I'm single too. And I don't know about you, but I find this a strange place to be single."

"I don't follow you."

"I mean, there are tons of single people here—"

"Or so they say."

"Or so they say! Exactly! Today I was on a date with someone I connected with on Tinder. On her bio, she wrote that she's a single mom. But she told me earlier that she's actually still married, only separated from her husband. It's a deal breaker for me."

"I met someone earlier, too. On Tinder, he put his age as 35, but he was just 20!"

"That's a big gap. You didn't notice anything in his photos?"

"He had beard in them, which helped in his lie. He had a very masculine voice on the phone. He talked like a matured guy. He's clean-shaven when he showed up earlier, so his real age became evident. I grilled him and he admitted. I walked away."

"And you ended up in Starbucks."

"Yes, only to be hounded by the Hulk."

"High five on our failed dates."

"You kind of saved the day for me, though."

"I have to say the same about you."

"Let's have a drink? I can easily get us into three of the hotels in this area, with free drinks perhaps."

"That sounds really good to me."

I can tell Ken is a very smart guy. He can hold a conversation really well. I like him. I fail to notice the time until Ashley calls.

"Wow! It's almost 11 PM."

"Yeah. I had a really good time with you today."

"Same."

"Can I drop you home?"

"Oh, you must because you kept me out late!"

"Did I now? You were talking a lot yourself!"

When I really enjoy someone's company, I am particularly chatty, and I have the same effect on the guy. The 20-minute drive to my place seems like five.

"So, tomorrow, same place, same time after our dates."

"Deal."

After a simple peck on the cheeks, I step out of his car.

**

Another day, another date. And now I understand why he's insistent on picking me up, and it's not for my convenience. He's driving a Ferrari. We're at breakneck speed on Sheikh Zayed Road. He's trying to show off. I'm not impressed.

After ordering, he takes the stage, so to speak, and dominates the conversation. I'm nodding now and again, and when the food arrives, I happily eat my heart away with the Turkish delicacies in front of me.

"Well, don't just listen. Converse with me!"

Who said I'm listening?

"You sound so absorbed in your storytelling. I thought it best not to interrupt."

"Oh, I just love history! I can go on and on!"

Oh, I don't doubt that at all.

"What about you? What's your take on the subject?"

"I love history as well. My favorite is that of the ancient Egyptians."

"Ah, do you know we have an ancient site in Turkey that predates the pyramids for thousands of years?"

"Gobekli Tepe. Yes, I know."

"Oh, I'm so impressed that you know! The previous dates I had, pff! Empty tanks. They only move when pushed. Tsk! Tsk! Tsk! So sad."

So sad for them, too, to have to endure someone like you.

"Have you been to Turkey?"

"No, not yet. But it's definitely on my bucket list."

"I'd love to take you. I'll show you around. I'd be your personal tour guide. When would you like to go?"

His enthusiasm drains me. I think I need another bottle of water – or make that wine, please!

"I don't know. I haven't made any plans about it. But I surely would love to go one day."

"If money is the problem, just let me know, and I'll take care of everything for you."

"You're willing to do that for a complete stranger?"

"We're not strangers anymore, my dear. Right now, we are already acquaintances. Soon enough, who knows, we might become lovers."

I choke at his words. I'm so tempted to excuse myself and call Ken and ask him to bail me out. But he might also be out with his date now.

"Why? What is it? You don't like me? I can take very good care of you. I'm very generous with my women."

"It's pleasing to hear that. But let's not jump the gun here. I'm not ready for anything. I just really want to meet new people for now."

"You mean you still want to play around?"

"I'm not playing around. Meeting people is not the same as playing around. I'm checking my options, trying to see who's out here and all."

"And you think I'm not a good option?"

"I didn't say that."

I want to say more, but I think I will only complicate it. Time to leave.

"If you're done, I'd like to go."

"We have not had desserts yet. What about coffee? Have you tried Turkish coffee?"

"I don't drink coffee. I really want to go now."

He mimics my action when I stand. I offer my hand and bid him goodbye.

"I can drive you back."

"No need. I'm meeting a friend. Thank you, though."

I turn my back and walk forward without stopping. The sight of the approaching train offers relief to my irritated mind. Something about this date hits a sensitive nerve inside me.

**

"You have a strong sense of self. You're one of those women who built themselves from the ground up. You know every brick and stone that made up your kingdom because you built it yourself. A man like that who flashes his wealth right on the first day appalls you because you feel like you're being bought. But you can never be bought."

"No human being should be."

"There are women with price tags dangling from their ears, Hanna. He might have encountered some of them. Forgive the guy. Many of us are still clueless about women right up to adulthood."

"What about common sense, Ken?"

"As they say, common sense is not common."

I roll my eyes and take a big gulp of my drink.

"Also, maybe he really liked you, so he thought that showing off that way would make you like him back."

"Every sensible woman knows that's crap."

"And every crappy guy doesn't have a sense of that. Cheers!"

"I thought you were supposed to be out today as well. What happened?"

"She wanted to try a restaurant at a hotel. I told her I'm okay with it so long as we split the bill. She unmatched me instantly. Of course, I would not make her pay. It was just a test. I wanted to see how she would react."

"I hope she matches my last date. I think they're perfect for each other."

We clink our beer bottles to cheer on the thought.

"Who's next on your list?"

"There's a Lebanese guy who asked to meet up. I haven't agreed to any date yet."

"Why? What's holding you back?"

"I feel taxed from these encounters. I'd like to rest a bit."

"How many have you met so far?"

"Nine in less than two weeks."

"Wow!"

"I know. I have one or two matches every day. But many failed at step three."

"Step three?"

"Yeah, the phone conversation. I insist on speaking with them on the phone before the meetup. You know, just to get a feel of them. I like a good conversationalist. If they cannot engage my mind, I'd rather stay at home and watch videos on YouTube of people's ingrown toenails being removed."

"What?"

"It may sound gross, but I really enjoy those videos."

"You're joking, right?"

"No, Ken, I'm not. I also like watching pimples being popped and—"

"Okay! I got it!"

He raises one hand to my face.

"Do you want another round? You look like you need it. It's on me."

I make a quick order to a passing crew.

"So, anyone faring well amongst those you met so far?"

"There's the pilot. I like his stories and the photos he took from the cockpit. But he's constantly flying."

"I know what you mean. I connected with an Emirates flight attendant two months ago. Her schedules are insane."

"So it would be to our best interest to stick with the ground people."

**

As I'm fishing for my key from my purse, I can smell something delicious from outside our apartment door.

Ashley is home.

"Oh, my god! Look who is here! Babe, you've been in and out of this house. What have you been up to?"

I'm laughing as I embrace her.

"The boys from Tinder got me busy, babe. What's this? It smells so good."

"You can try. It's just chicken, but it's so spicy. So consider yourself warned."

She's not joking about it being spicy. My throat's burning!

"How can you eat this?"

"So, tell me who you have met so far? And how many?"

"Less than ten so far, and the pilot is still in the lead, followed closely by the Spanish teacher. The others I can forget about, except Alfred."

"They were that bad?"

"Let's just say that they weren't how I expected them. Not that I know what to expect beforehand, really. And you want to know something else? They talk as much as we do!"

"Yeah? And what did you guys talk about on those dates?"

"Some of them opened up about sensitive details of their lives with people they've met online and those they've had relationships with. I don't mean sex, okay? Other life stuff. And there's one thing that keeps coming up in those conversations. Money. Apparently, there are women who are asking for money from their dates the morning after. Some expect gifts."

"What?"

"That was my initial reaction, too. But then I thought that perhaps there's more to it than what I'm actually realizing now."

"What do you mean?"

"It's like a transactional relationship where both parties benefit from each other."

"Wow! I don't know what to say, babe. I have to admit that I'm shocked by this."

"Yeah, me too. But I think I'm just scraping the tip of the iceberg."

"Oh my god! I cannot imagine what's underneath the ice!"

"Neither do I."

**

"I was ready to forget you, if only I could find someone with your brains with whom I could discuss world affairs. Where have you been bitch?"

"You told me to date. So I am. I'm meeting guys from Tinder."

"Aha! And how has it been for you?"

"Entertaining is one of the ways I can describe it."

"Any good lay so far?"

"Lourdes, I said I'm meeting men, not *mating* with them."

"My darling friend, in this place, those words are synonymous."

"Well, not in my vocabulary."

"No one is hot enough for you amongst those you've met?"

"I'm not looking for someone to have sex with."

"Then what are you looking for?"

What, indeed, am I looking for?

"Don't look for people that life has already taken away from you. Don't litter your present with spoils from yesterday."

"I heard you loud and clear. I'm just taking my time. That's all."

Lourdes looks at me with willful regard.

"You'll be fine."

"You don't look convinced."

"But I trust my gut."

"Okay. What's up with you? Anything that I should know about or any new man?"

"Which date would you like me to start?"

I give her my usual classic dumbfounded look.

"Come on, Hanna. You know me. I don't like the restrictions of a relationship."

"But doesn't the lack of structure make you feel lost?"

"I'm not a college student anymore. I have twins in their high school, just to remind you."

I'm old enough to have a kid of my own, but I cannot live the "anything goes" kind of life. I cannot imagine living without pen and paper to jot down my everyday routine. I need to follow a course.

"I've had my chance at love. Not my cup of tea. I don't think we're all cut out for it."

Am I cut out for it?

At 35 years old, I have had no relationship solid enough for me to boast about to my friends.

"What are you thinking about?"

"If I can live the same life you have."

"You're a romantic, babe. You believe in love and all its theatrics. My lifestyle will not fit you."

But does love fit me?

I have the tendency to fall silent during conversations. My friends sometimes have to pull me out of it.

"Those you've met, where were they from?"

"Arabs and Europeans."

"How do you find the Arabs?'

"I've met Egyptians mostly."

"It would be a challenge to find one who's not married or has been or will be."

Have they found someone for Zaki to marry?

"You're thinking of him."

"He's an old story that still aches."

"If men are the cause, men are also the cure. For everything else, use your credit card."

"I don't have one."

"Then use theirs. That's what some women are doing. They can't get the love that they want from men, so they get everything else that their money can afford."

"I heard about that."

"And you'll hear and learn more. So try to keep an open mind. The struggle for love is different for every woman."

In my journal, I write what I cannot ask openly to Lourdes or to anyone.

**

I'm hesitating to answer, but the thought of calling him back is less than appealing.

"Hello."

"Hello! Hanna?"

"Yes."

"This is Jackson."

"I can see your name on the screen of my phone."

"Oh, I thought maybe you had deleted my number."

"Why would I do that?"

"I don't know. So, how have you been?"

"I'm okay. What made you call?"

"Just checking, you know, if you're still up to meeting me."

Now the idea of blocking him suddenly becomes interesting.

"Hello? Are you still there?"

"Yeah. I'm in the middle of something. I'm at work. Can we talk at another time?"

"It's a simple yes or no, Hanna. But I think I got my answer."

The sound of the dial tone pleases me more than his voice.

**

After the customary Christmas call home, I grab a new *Agatha Christie* book from the shelf and position myself comfortably on the bed. A few minutes into the first chapter, I can hear Ashley at my door.

"Hi, babe. Any plans for Christmas?"

I raise the book in my hand. She comes closer to my bed.

"No way! It's Christmas! You cannot be reading a crime novel."

"Why not? This is actually the best time for me to catch up on my reading. I have no plans, babe."

"Maybe we can have dinner later then."

"Sure. I'd love that."

"I'm surprised that you don't have a date tonight, of all nights."

"I don't like the idea of spending this day with a complete stranger."

"What about your friends?"

"We agreed to meet before the new year. There's always so much hype during this time. We want to avoid it."

"True. But why didn't you go home this year?"

"I was thinking about that last night. My mind is out of proper focus this year, same as the year before."

"I understand. While there's no shortage of men for you, the opposite can be said about me."

"No progress on the matrimonial site?"

"None, babe. Zero."

"Are we really just too picky, or is there a shortage of quality good men?"

"Or is love no longer in fashion in this modern world?"

Ashley's words are like ghosts, haunting me until dinner. The world is here in Dubai, and yet here we are talking about men when we should be with them.

**

As the new year rolls in, there is an outpouring of greetings and messages from my matches. I line them up starting in the first week. Hosni, a Lebanese, kicks start 2019 for me.

Suppose I'm to describe him in one word: sex. His looks, his smell, his voice, his action – he is *it*. Our whole

165

conversation is about sex, but in a fun way I never thought possible.

"One time, there's this girl I was doing from behind — and I can be rough at times, be warned! I pressed her head against the pillow. The next time she was up, there were two black lines left on it! Her eyebrows rubbed off on it! Oh, she was pissed!"

It's not just the story that I find funny, but also the way he's retelling it.

"Another girl lost one of her false eyelashes during sex. We couldn't find it even after half an hour of looking. I gave her 100 Dirhams to buy new ones. She got upset because she's going home without them. But the worst was when I pulled a girl's hair while we're on doggy. And it came off! She screamed so loud! I pulled out instantly and believe it or not, I've never seen my dick grew limp that fast."

"Ouch! You pulled her extensions."

"Yes, I did, and she was raging mad at me. Oh boy!"

"Well, I think it's needless to say that you didn't meet again after that."

"We did one more time, but we didn't have sex again. She asked me to pay her for the damage I supposedly inflicted on her hair."

"Oh. And did you?"

"Yeah, and then I opened the door and sent her on her way."

"Do you mind if I ask how much?"

"I had one thousand Dirhams cash in my wallet at the time. I gave it to her."

"Was she from your country?"

"Yes."

"And the others?"

"Mixed. From all countries."

"Did you see anyone of them after?"

"Others, yes. But the majority, no. Those that I see again, they must have enjoyed the sex, so they're coming back."

"I want to ask you something, and it's quite personal. I understand if you don't want to answer."

"I'm an open book. Go ahead. Ask!"

"Do some of them ask for money?"

"Few have asked, yes. The ones I regularly see. They messaged me asking for help. Why do you ask?"

"Nothing. Just out of curiosity, really."

I'm surprised by his bulge when he stands to go to the men's room. I'm no saint myself, for I'm wet between my legs right now. Since I don't wear panties, except when I have my period, there's nothing to contain it.

Hosni has a strong sex appeal. When he comes back, he sits leaning forward to me and eyeing my legs with lust. It arouses me.

"Do you like sex, Hanna?"

"Who doesn't?"

"But do you?"

"Why are you asking me that?"

"I'm curious."

"Have you ever been rejected?"

"No."

He slouches on his chair to show me his asset outlined on his loose trousers. I copy his actions. I spread my legs and have my two hands cover my naked sex. Then I abruptly stand.

"I'm wet. I need to dry myself in the ladies' room."

I'm surprised to find him outside the door with a sexually charged look on his face. His tanned, muscular arms press me against his equally muscular chest. His eyes tell me what his lips aren't saying.

"I don't want to be one of your dolls, Hosni."

"Dolls?"

"I deserve to be more than just another warm body beside you."

"Why do you have to be so smart?"

"You'd rather that I be the opposite?"

"Just a wee bit less, yes, so your legs are not tightly held together."

"I'm password protected, Hosni."

He releases me as I motion to walk back to our table.

"What do you want, Hanna?"

"Love. And I know I'm asking from the wrong person."

"Why do you want love? It's a complicated world already. Why else do you want it?"

"Because I can earn my own keep. But to love myself is not enough."

"I'm a complicated man, Hanna. I don't want to hurt you."

"Neither do I want that. Will you drop me home, or I'll get a taxi?"

"Any taxi driver will give you a free ride with that dress. But I will not give him that luxury."

Immediately upon reaching home, I release the pent-up tensions in my body using my fingers.

Damn you, Hosni.

**

A WhatsApp call jolts me up to wakefulness. I can't call back without connecting to a VPN. Instead, I send a quick message back to Jake confirming the dinner.

Upon being seated, I regretted accepting the invite not long after.

He's an American military pilot. He's currently on vacation and wants to meet women who can make this trip *extra memorable* for him. His cockiness puts me off, and his overzealous patriotism stretches my patience. Who goes on a date and talks about one's country's national security concerns? Even if someone points a gun at me, I will not see him again.

In the taxi on the way home, I get a message from a recent connection for a brunch date tomorrow. I readily confirmed.

**

What would make any normal Saturday morning special? Waking up to your sexy date's voice on the phone.

Jean-Luc calls to confirm the location of the restaurant. I engage him a bit. He's a Belgian businessman who flies in and out of the UAE to meet with his partners. Another hard option.

"I thought that it would just be the two of us."

His words confused me. I give him a quizzical look.

"I can see someone else in your eyes."

"What do you mean?"

"I'm a highly perceptive man, Hanna. There's a memory walking with you."

I feel a tug in my heart hearing him say that.

"I don't want to make you feel uncomfortable. But your emotions are overflowing."

My eyes are growing heavy with tears that I thought had dried up. He takes both my hands in his.

"Writing is therapeutic. Why don't you write about it? It seems to me that you have quite a story to tell."

"I don't even know what I feel exactly. How can I write about it?"

"Concentrate. Apply yourself to the task, and I'm sure you'll be able to write a compelling story, something the world might need to hear."

**

"He's right. You're very good with words. Why don't you try? If it scares you to have it published for the world to read, then just write for yourself."

"But where do I start, Kaycee?"

"In your heart, Hanna. It's time to empty it of Zaki's memories, so you'll have space for a new beginning."

How is it possible to empty one's heart of another's memory?

I cannot force myself to eat anymore, although I know it's my heart that's full.

"How are those Tinder dates going?"

"Oh, Roshie. I wish you hadn't asked. There's nothing much of substance that has come out of it so far."

"Girl, you just started. Stay on it. Who knows?"

171

"Yes, I agree with Joan. How many have you met so far?"

Roshie, though the only one married, is always the giddiest amongst us when it comes to talks about men.

"12, 13, maybe. I'm meeting three this week."

"Where are they from?"

To egg the conversation further, expect Joan to ask the right questions.

"They're all Egyptians."

"They're one of the smoothest talkers around, so you'll be very careful. My flatmate got her heart badly broken by one."

Joan's tone comes with both caution and worry.

"Why? What happened?"

My voice goes a pitch higher than usual. I'm beyond eager to know, of course.

"After three years of dating, she found out that he's married. And take this, he has kids!"

We react in unison. Roshie's making a flicking sound with her tongue in dismay.

"How did she find out?"

Kaycee will not let the story stall too long. She'll pounce with questions to keep it going.

"She's been insisting that they go to Egypt. He kept giving excuses. She got fed up and badgered him until he cracked."

"I think it has a lot to do with their culture. Many of them are promised to someone since birth, usually one their families know."

Kaycee's words hammer a big nail straight to my heart.

Who is Zaki promised to?

It takes me some time to realize that the three of them are looking at me.

"I'm sorry. How long was I out?"

"No judgment, Hanna. We know what you're going through. But again, don't overindulge yourself. Memories stay alive if we keep thinking of them."

Another point for Kaycee for that. But how does one's heart start the process of moving on when it doesn't have enough strength yet to do so?

**

I'm sitting in front of a different guy – the third Egyptian this week – whose story is the same as those before him. Seems like there's only one life pattern for Egyptian men.

"Is there no way to resist these arrangements?"

"How? When something has been decided for you since birth? For some, it happens even before they are born."

"What happens if you decline their choice?"

"They'll just simply look for another."

"What a torture for one's heart."

"And sanity! Because you'll never know what you're going to get."

"But how come you're single?"

"I am now, but I had been married twice."

"Oh? Any children?"

"I was careful about that. I know it's going to tie me down, if ever. With my first wife, it was easy. She didn't like me either. We stayed married for six months, then divorced. We made that agreement on our first night.

"The following year, I met another girl. She's a family friend of one of my relatives. This time, I was excited about marrying again. But she was only after money. I didn't drag it longer when I realized it wasn't what I hoped for."

"That's some story."

"Such is the life that some of us have. How about you? Ever been married?"

"No."

"What are you looking for?"

I'm not expecting that. The question captures my tongue. I'm relieve when he takes the spotlight back to himself.

"I've carried out relations with women from your country. I tried with Europeans as well, those from the eastern side."

"What came of it?"

"Why do you think I'm sporting a bald head now? I've lost my hair with their drama!"

It's no laughing matter, I understand, but I fail to contain myself. Mostafa is a smart, comic guy. He loves to talk too. I just allow him. Hearing their stories makes me forget mine.

**

What's with men and boobs? This French toast in front of me can barely take his eyes off my cleavage. His responses are laden with sexual innuendos.

"I'll have a Wet Pussy. You may want to try their famous Dick Sucker. I heard it's really good."

"I'm more on the classic, traditional side. I'll have a Heineken, please."

"Oh, so you're a plain old vanilla Jane."

"Is this how you're going to talk all night?"

"Why? Am I getting you aroused?"

"I'm afraid it's the opposite. You're making me uncomfortable."

"Oh?"

"I'll just go to the ladies' room."

"You said you're not wet yet."

"I want to poop."

I love the look on his face. I walk away laughing inside. I turn my back and quickly take the exit when he faces the bar again.

**

I'm zooming through the month. It's January 31st, and I'm looking at my calendar. 25 dates in 31 days, the majority were Egyptians; 15 to be exact. Different faces, but very similar stories.

I am starting to wonder if their marriages are problematic by default – given how many of them came about – or the huge variety of options that they are now offered at this place is causing it to collapse.

There's always a choice, one may argue. But how can the right choice stand against the alluring alternatives that are parading in front of them? One goes to JBR, and some of those options are almost completely naked. Another visits any bar, and there are boobs and asses of varying sizes and colors on display.

"This place is like a banquet. When you're offered something that you're not normally served at home, what do you do? You feast."

It's an unsettling thought to think, but one that makes a lot of sense.

"You're looking for love. Leave the truth on the wayside."

Lourdes and her hardline belief system can unhinge a weak character.

"I don't want to be just an option out of many."

"The whole world is here. We're all options until somebody makes us their choice."

Who needs a self-help book when you have a friend like her?

**

Options are good. It can help deepen or widen our perspectives. But this guy in front of me is one option I'll never consider, even if he's the last one there is. I cannot stand arrogance. I can't even feign indifference to it. Halfway into dinner, I abruptly stand under the pretense of needing to go to the ladies' room. There's another door on the opposite side of the Cheesecake Factory in JBR. I walk straight out through it.

The doorbell draws Ashley out of her room.

"Babe, I didn't know you were home. I ordered only for myself."

"It's okay. I was just out with friends. I thought you had a date?"

"I did. I left him at the table. I'm still hungry, so…"

"Oh? What happened?"

"Pompous ass."

"Where's he from?"

"Lebanon."

"Wasn't the other guy you met, and you said you really like, also a Lebanese?"

"Yeah, but the one I met tonight was no way near the caliber of Hosni."

"Why don't you just see Hosni again then?"

"If your mind can't trust someone, why would you let your heart be close to that person? With Hosni, I'll just be the number one, not the only one."

"Wow. Some guys never stop playing right through to adulthood."

"He got married twice – or as he said, got *fooled* twice. He thinks he's smarter now by not getting into relationships anymore. He loves women, but might never settle for just one again."

"Hard pass, babe."

"Definitely."

**

February. It will be Valentine's Day soon. I'm a no flowers and chocolates type of woman, but about this time each year, my sadness is more emphasized. I'm in a place where there is no shortage of men, but there seems to be a deficit of love.

"While you're looking for love, why not have some fun on the side?"

"That's not a bad idea."

"You're 35. Enjoy yourself! Now is the best time."

I raise my glass as a form of acknowledgement to Lana's suggestion. Even bars are full during this time. Many people are out to enjoy themselves. I'm enjoying myself. I've not met this many men in such a short time before. It's like reading books. Not all of them and their stories are as interesting as the others, but they all have a lesson to impart. And I'm a sucker for information. I can't explain it well enough now, but I know someday I'll find a pair of patient ears willing to listen to all the madness that I've hoarded in my head. He will come with a mind that holds judgment until he hears the period in my sentence. And his genuinely good heart will match the rhythm of mine.

"Girl, this is not a place for you to think. Forget about Prince Charming for now."

"I'm just wondering if he's stuck in someone else's pussy."

"In that case, you'll have to settle for another dick."

Maybe in their past lives, Lana and Lourdes were sisters. They sure talk the same way.

**

"Good morning, stranger."

"Good morning, Miss Starbucks. Any plans for Valentine's Day?"

"I'm saving that for you. I prefer to sit down with a soul I'm acquainted with than a seemingly aimless character wandering about with an erect penis."

"Looks like you have great stories to share with me. Can't wait to hear them."

"Same place as usual?"

"Yeah. Why not? If all the restaurants in JBR are full by then, we can just take out our food and sit by the shore."

"I think I like that better."

"Alright. Then we're settled. See you."

True to expectation, there are no available tables anywhere. JBR pulls people to it regardless of the occasion.

"Why are you wearing a dress? You knew there'd be a greater chance that we'd be sitting on the sands."

"I'm a lady. What am I supposed to wear?"

"Pants, maybe, for greater comfort."

"I'm more comfortable in a dress. Thank you."

"Suit yourself, princess."

Upon deciding on the spot, I pull out the shawl in my small backpack.

"You're prepared, soldier."

"I'm a warrior. I prefer the sword to the gun."

"Bullets kill faster."

"I'm a fighter, not a killer."

"How are they different from each other? In the end, someone dies either way."

"Not necessarily. For not all fighter kills. Besides, anyone can shoot. It's just pulling the trigger. To learn to handle a sword takes discipline and patience."

"You must be a warrior princess in your past life."

"Queen. I'm a queen who matured in her throne alone."

"Ah, speaking of that, how are those dates? What's your tally now?"

"35."

"Does that include me?"

"If I'd count you, then 36."

"How are you able to keep track?"

"They're in my calendar, Ken."

"Of course. An old soul with OCD."

"I like everything organized."

"But love can be messy."

"Perhaps with the right person it's not."

"Define that. Who would you consider right for you?"

Should be easy enough to answer, yet I can't. That's one advantage of the bullet over a sword. It can paralyze the target immediately.

"Hey, I'm not trying to put you on a hot seat."

"My friends and colleagues ask me the same question. You're not firing at a fresh target, Ken."

"Yet here you are, eluding us all with an answer."

"Not all questions have to be answered when they're asked."

"And as usual, your intellect bends us backwards."

"I meant no offense."

"None taken. But unless you fill me in with all that happened to you while I was away, we're not even."

Someone like Ken is my definition of who's right for me. But I must feel that attraction towards him, that distinctive desire that pulls you to the other person.

It's so easy to talk to him. I don't have to filter my mouth or slow down my brain. We're on the same wavelength in more than one front.

"I've met interesting fellas, but none I'd consider starting anything with, not even thinking of seeing them again for a second date."

"Where were they from?"

"Majority were Arabs, Egyptians mostly. Some from Europe."

"No Americans?"

"One. He's a military pilot. He was here only on vacations."

"And?"

"I don't mean to be rude, but I don't care about your national security issues."

"You talked about that during the date?"

"Awesome, right? I was so thrilled that in less than two hours I ejected myself."

"I've never talked about my time in uniform with any of my dates, either there or here."

"You served?"

'Yes, milady. Two tours, one in Afghanistan and the other in Iraq. It's not an easy life."

"But that's not why you quit."

"Some people are built for war. Believe it or not, that's a fact I've seen myself. But I'm not one of them. What you develop with those you're with is as deep as marriage. You're bonded for life and death."

"You lost someone, haven't you?"

"As they say, war is a necessary evil that comes with a price."

"How long ago was it?"

"Nearly four years."

"That's why you're here."

"I've always been good at Math. I have a degree in Economics before joining the army. I took a short course upon returning home to refresh my memory."

"Or alter your focus."

"We cannot let dead memories bury us alive, Hanna."

Ken's words echo in my consciousness for days. What am I really doing with my time? Fun is not all that my heart needs. I want substance. I don't like anything fleeting. I want something that's constant. I want stability. I want something solid that I can hold with my hands. I want to build something with someone.

Where are you, love?

I just started my late lunch, and here comes Roshie rushing me out of the pantry.

"Zaki is on your line one. He said it's important."

He's bringing the entire European team to the Middle East for their yearly meetup. I just crawled out from the ground, and now it looks like it's ready to swallow me up again. I speed dial the number of someone who I know will keep me unburied.

"Hi, little sissy! How are you?"

My enthusiasm sounds fake. I'm hoping she will not notice.

"All good, big sis. What about you? It's been a while."

Hearing Gregely's voice is like having tea during the rain.

"I know. That's why I'm calling. I have a week to spare. Can I come and stay there with you?"

"You're always welcome here. It may not be much, but this is home. So come home."

After making all the arrangements for Zaki and his team, I filed for an emergency leave. Upon reaching home, I pack my trolley with clothes for a week-long stay and some books. Come Thursday night, I wheel it out of the apartment.

I'm just reaching the Abu Dhabi Falcon Hospital when my phone buzzes with Ashley's call.

"Hi, babe."

"Babe, where are you? I just saw your note."

"I'm just taking some time off with a friend here in Abu Dhabi. I'd be back next weekend."

"Okay. This is so sudden. Is everything alright?"

"Yeah, babe, nothing to worry about. I just thought I could use some days off."

"Alright, babe. Enjoy yourself there!"

No hint of suspicion in her voice. Good. I don't like making my friends worry.

"You just arrived, and they already want you back?"

"She's my flatmate and close friend."

"You can rest now, then we'll talk tomorrow. But if you're up to it, I'm all ears."

Gregely and I go way back to our college days. She's one of my most trusted friends. She knows me a good deal.

My lips are not ready to talk, but my eyes are. I burst into tears. Bottled emotions are highly combustible. And after what feels like infinity, my ducts are finally dry.

"Can you walk? You need some fresh air."

Abu Dhabi Falcon Hospital is a huge facility. It's especially quiet at night, so you can clear your head as you walk within its perimeter. And tonight, there's a full moon, so it makes it perfect. We walk in silence for a few minutes, and then Gregely speaks.

"Big Sis, what I'm about to tell you will hurt you a little bit more. My intention is not to add to your pain, but instead to offer clarity.

"When we are in love, we focus on the good stuff. We ignore the little details that are critical in completing the picture of the entire narrative.

"I believe that he truly loved you, and he could have been a very good husband if given the chance. I also believed that he knew right from the beginning that such a chance didn't exist."

Her words root me at my spot, as if an assault rifle is pointed at my heart, disabling me from moving or speaking because of shock.

"He led you on, made you believe a possibility that's obscured by questions that even he had no answers for. He sold you a fairytale that, in the end, turned out to be a nightmare. He probably thought he could pull this through. But then he realized that family and faith will always be greater than love."

I feel like our surrounding grows dim because of the darkness that's beginning to develop inside me.

"You're in the same world but living very different realities. Your conversion could have dissolved that great divide. But we don't take on another religion because of our love for one man. That's called compromise. It has to be a willing act of faith for it to matter."

Gregely is not even five feet, and yet her wisdom dwarfs me right now.

"Bring him down from the pedestal you put him on. Only then will you be able to see how other men fare against him. There's been better choices all along, sissy. Don't deny yourself that chance now to explore your options."

I'm still lost for words, though my internal compass seems to be getting back in alignment with my true north.

"I don't know why you had to meet. Fate is a cruel joker. But now that you realized the joke wasn't funny, start looking for your real happiness.

"He's out there. He's looking for you, too. He doesn't know who or what he should be looking for. But he needs the kind of love that you can offer. He's out there. Go find him."

"They say love is more elusive when you search for it."

"I'd rather search for the unknown than endure longer what fate has made known."

That carries so much weight. There's a tone of finality in her admonitions, too.

Ash, Gregely's Ragdoll cat, and the *Agatha Christie* books keep me company while she works during the day. *The Sleeping Murder* particularly impresses me. Why can't we leave old memories alone? This thought haunts me throughout the rest of my stay.

**

Before allowing me to get into the taxi, Gregely sends me off with a strong message.

"Let the past sleep. Stop waking it up each time you're lonely."

That and many other thoughts knock me down during the two-hour bus journey back to Dubai.

**

I'm bouncing from one friend's arms to the next. Ken's is equally warm as that of Gregely. I cling to him closer when he makes an attempt to pull away.

"What's wrong?"

"What if you were not in Starbucks that day? Or that you didn't approach me at the beach?"

He's quiet for a moment, contemplating my words.

"But I was there. And I'm here."

188

I want to say something, but my eyes beat my lips. I slide inside the passenger seat.

"I hardly cry before the world."

"Would you like to come to my place?"

I nod as I dry my cheeks. His studio apartment mirrors my room: clean and organized. I feel at ease right away. I down a big gulp from what he hands me.

"That's not water, Hanna."

"This is better than water. In fact, I think when someone is crying, she should not be offered water but alcohol. The effect is better."

"I got you covered, just in case."

Standing on the opposite end of the kitchen island, he opens a cupboard just above the sink.

I raise my glass to him and empty its contents.

"So what happened in Abu Dhabi?"

He refills my glass as he takes the spot beside me on the sofa.

I share with him the conversation I had with Gregely. He listens with the patience of a doctor and the loyalty of a friend.

"You never looked at him in that way before. So you never perceived that side of the situation."

"It does make a lot of sense, but it's so painful to think of it."

“Then try not to think of it. The past is no longer real, Hanna.”

“But neither is there anything real in my present.”

“Because you don’t want anything or anyone to matter. No one will be able to measure up to him, not even to his memory, because right from the beginning, he had an unfair advantage above all men.”

“I feel stupid right now.”

“Why?”

“You all learned the story from me. I lived it. And yet I failed to see that angle.”

“Don’t be too hard on yourself. We all can lose footing from time to time when we are emotionally attached to someone.”

“It’s more than just an emotional attachment between us. I’ve always felt it stronger than that.”

“I believe you. Otherwise, you wouldn’t be this affected still. But Hanna, that time is over.”

I nod in quiet acknowledgement. I don’t need to be constantly told that it’s over. His absence in my life confirms it, and the pain inside me solidifies that fact. But the heart has its own time. And it doesn’t follow the human calendar.

**

“It’s Holy Week!”

Ken's tone is loaded with guilt feelings, but falls short of hitting me.

"So? Is there a law that prohibits us from dating during this time?"

"Perhaps none, but isn't this a time for quiet introspection and solemn prayers?"

"Yeah, for those who practice their religion. I don't."

"And why is that?"

"Are you practicing yours?"

"I've always been pragmatic about it."

"Then consider me the same."

"But you fell in love with a Muslim guy."

"I fell in love with a man who happened to be a Muslim."

"Would you consider falling again with another one?"

"I'm not actually ruling that out."

"Even with the guarantee that you might suffer the same plight?"

That corners me. Am I really willing to go through the same devastation? Suppose there's another Zaki. Is it worth the pain to experience the same kind of love?

"Where are you, Hanna?"

"I'm sorry. How long was I out?"

"Are you ever anywhere since, or have you been out with him somewhere in your thoughts?"

Now I feel boxed. Where have I been since Zaki left? Who have I been? Ken shifts in his seat. I always make people uncomfortable with my silence.

"How many Egyptians have you met so far?"

"I don't know at the top of my head. Why?"

"I hope you're not meeting Egyptian men because you're looking for someone like him. I hope it's just happenstance that you're matching with them."

I think praying to an unknown god is easier right now than to sit across from Ken and confront realities that I'm not prepared to see.

"Hanna, I'm a friend. It may not seem like that sometimes, but all I'm doing really is to help you."

"I know, Ken, and I understand. I just need time and the right kind of distraction, I guess."

"Or you can channel your focus outside of the story you shared with him."

I can't even remember what I was like before Zaki. Some love is so strong that it can give you a different identity. I'm not saying that I'm a different woman, but definitely something has changed in me.

**

"You've met over 30 Egyptians, but you've not been out with them again for a second date. Are you sure you're not looking for him in every one of us?"

I feel embarrassed hearing Amr say that. Guilty too, though I'm not sure why. My silence alarms him.

"I'm sorry. I don't mean to offend you, Hanna."

"You didn't offend me at all, Amr. Don't worry. But in my defense, I'm not looking for him. In fact, if I can be frank and candid about it, I really don't know who or what I'm looking for."

"I think that's a more serious dilemma than my former thought."

"I won't overly concern myself about it, if I were you. I'm just really using my time to see what's out there for me. Options that I have ignored before."

Amr does not seem convinced. I don't blame him. There are many a day like today when I can't convince myself, either.

"How's the hotel doing nowadays? Are you full?"

"We are, actually. Even our two sister hotels are fully booked these days. There are a lot of tourists from Europe and Asia."

"Well, that's very good then, considering all the competition around. And you must be busy yourself, so I should leave you now. I need to go back to the office, too."

"Let's do this again soon. I want to hear something better by next time."

I opt not to say anything back. I don't like making promises that I can't keep. After a quick peck on both cheeks, I hail the first available taxi on the stand.

Amr is one of my closest guy friends. He's our account manager in one of our partner hotels. Through the years, he and his team have helped me with all my booking reservations for my colleagues from Europe. Ours is an easy friendship right from the start. I remember Zaki being jealous of him at one point. *Zaki.* How do you leave a chapter in your life where you feel most alive?

**

Rani: I'm flying back to Dubai this Friday morning. I want you to be ready by then. I really like it when my girl is made up and polished. I will reimburse whatever you'll spend in the salon.

I roll my eyes in slight irritation upon reading the message. Lourdes sees my reaction and probes me.

"There's this Lebanese guy I matched with on Tinder. He wants me to go to the parlor before we meet."

"What the fuck? Are you serious?"

I show her the message.

"May I look around?"

"Be my guest."

"He's quite a good-looking guy. Though I think he's not actually single."

"Aren't almost all of them?"

"Have you met a good lot of them?"

"Lebanese or men in general?"

"Lebanese, in general."

"No. Why?"

"Tell me what you think of them once you do."

"Why don't you tell me *now* what you think? Looks like what you know is something that I should know too."

"I don't want to sound judgmental. For all we know, I might be the only one who thinks this way."

"But nonetheless, tell me. I want to know."

"I find them very vain."

"Could it be that they just want to look good all the time?"

"I can understand that. But to go through so many modifications? I mean, they don't need it. Majority of them are a good-looking lot."

"Well, the mirror is the best liar, and many of us fall victim to it."

"You've been here a while. Your eyebrows still look the same. You have not adapted the usual look that's on trend."

"My eyebrows are naturally thick. And I'm comfortable with the way I look."

"It makes a lot of difference when you have confidence supported by intelligence and inner fortitude."

"Thank you, babe. That's nice of you to say."

My phone vibrates inside my purse. I fish it out to check the notification.

"I just had another match. Take a look at him."

"He's asking when you'll be free for dinner."

"Respond. Tell him tomorrow is cool with me."

"He's asking for your mobile number now."

I recite my number aloud to her.

"He's European. He looks really hot. When you meet tomorrow and you don't fancy him, don't forget that I am here. A new message just came in for you from another guy, Colin."

"What does it say?"

"He's asking when you're going to meet."

I pause, going through my calendar entries in my mind.

"Tell him Friday lunch should be good."

"But you're meeting the Lebanese guy then."

"I'd try to meet Rani at dinner time instead."

"But he's saying that he wants to see you for lunch on Friday. You'd have to schedule an early parlor appointment then, if ever."

Her tone is both teasing and mocking me.

"You think I'd oblige him? Even if he pays me triple the amount, I won't."

"But you will still meet him?"

"Yeah. Why not? Just to satisfy my eyes. I think it would be like most dates I had: bordering to nonsense."

"Then why do you still keep meeting them?"

"The food! Who would say no to free meals?"

"Where do you usually go?"

"Nothing too fancy. The Cheesecake Factory and the likes. Other times, just in a café. Tim Hortons, Starbucks. One time, I met someone in McDonald's."

"Why not go somewhere nicer, like a hotel?"

"I'm not entitled to their money, babe. Besides, it's just the first date."

"And they might expect something more from you if you go somewhere more expensive."

"Exactly. However, I know not all men think that way. But better be on the safe side."

"Has anyone been sexually suggestive or forward to you?"

"Almost all of them. That's why I lose interest right on the first date. I know that at some point, sex will come into the picture. But I wish they'd be smoother in injecting it into our conversations. Some seem after just to score, so they have something to brag to their friends during a boys' night out."

"That's highly plausible."

"I just got another match. Terrific."

"How many have you met so far?"

"Close to 40, I think. This one's a French guy. Check and tell me what you think."

"Chiseled. But he looks like a dad."

"Yeah? What does his bio say?"

"He's a dentist. And yes, he has a son. Divorced. He's asking how you are, where you're from, and what you do."

"You know the answers to all those. Be me for now."

"When can you meet?"

"My Saturday is still free."

"Why not this Thursday night?"

"I promised my flatmate that I'd go with her to Barasti again."

"He's asking what time on Saturday."

"If he's free for lunch, then better. That way I wouldn't have to cook or order my food."

"There. All set now."

**

Our last-minute administrative meeting with our boss delays my departure for home. I'd have to go straight from here for my 7:00 PM dinner with Emil. At 6:30 PM, I'm rushing to leave the office only to be stranded on the ground floor lobby because there are no taxis. After ten minutes, I'm beginning to be frantic. Emil is sensitive to time. But a minute after someone gets off at my building, I hop into the taxi he has just vacated.

Five minutes before 7:00 PM, I'm running past the people in JBR on three-inch heels to get to P.F. Chang. When I hear him call out my name, without looking at his face, I collapse in his arms.

"Are you okay, my dear?"

"Yes! I was rushing to get here. We had a last-minute meeting in the office. Took me time to get a cab. Plus, it's always tight coming here during this time. I was afraid I won't be able to make it."

"Well, you could have sent me a message, and we could have moved it a bit later."

"We agreed to meet at a certain time. I'm a woman of my word."

"I'm pleased to hear that. And I appreciate you making all the efforts to come on time."

Once we are seated, I close my eyes and steady my breathing. I'm startled when he reaches for my clasped hands on the table.

"I'm sorry, Hanna. I didn't mean to—"

"It's alright. No issues at all. It's just that I wasn't expecting it."

"Yes, it was stupid of me. I should have waited, at least, until you opened your eyes again. I just really want to put you at ease."

"Don't worry. I'm good."

Emil is 32 years old and a German aviation engineer with Emirates. He just moved to the country. I like his easy and open approach to life. He has a seemingly relaxed personality. He's the only one so far who has not asked me where I'm from and why I sound the way I do when I talk.

"Do you like to get married someday?"

It should be easy enough to respond to that. But I don't have a ready answer for it.

"To be frank, I don't know. What about you?"

"I'm okay either way. If the girl isn't into it, no pressure from my side. I don't believe a piece of paper can keep two people together anyway."

"Same here, though I know my family would want me to settle one day."

"Well, why aren't you yet?"

"It's not as simple as taking a shower. Getting married is not merely being soaked with water. It's taking the plunge down to it."

"That's a nice analogy. I agree with you."

I want to make a witty respond to that, but I'm unable to when I get a glimpse of the staff carrying a tray of orders precariously on her hands. And before I can finish processing my thoughts, our orders come pouring down on Emil. He yelps when the hot soup makes contact with his body. I'm rooted to my seat opposite him, unable to think what to do first. Emil is speaking fast in German. The commotion stops other diners. When he stands, the ramen, sliced chicken pieces, and everything else come off his pants. The manager tries to assist, but Emil is too annoyed now to accept any help. He asks for my hand, and we hurriedly leave the restaurant.

"I need to change out of this and get a proper shower."

"Most certainly, yes. Of course."

"Can we just go home now?"

"Yes, absolutely. It's perfectly fine with me."

We're already out of the underground parking of JBR, but he has not asked me yet where I live. I'm a little too awkward to open the conversation. Once we're out on Sheikh Zayed Road, it becomes apparent to me that going home means his. I should have said something sooner. But we just came out of a highly annoying situation. If I ask him to bring me to my place, he might think that I'm ditching him. I don't want to aggravate his mood.

Seeing the Metro station within walking distance from his building gives me relief. I don't know why.

Upon reaching his place, he walks straight into the bedroom, leaving the door open. A moment later, I can hear his clothes dropping to the floor. I'm reading Ashley's message when Emil walks out, completely naked. I keep my eyes on his, though I can see the hardwood below his waist. No word comes out of my mouth.

"Would you like to join me in the shower?"

The gong in my head gives a loud bang. A moment more, and I manage to force my tongue to work.

"Why don't you go ahead and ready the shower? I don't like it cold, but not too hot, either."

"Yes, ma'am."

And he gives me a playful salute and a wink.

I sigh in relief and silently mouth "Wow" as he retreats into the bedroom.

"I'm getting in!"

My heart's beating madly in my chest hearing him say so.

"Okay! I'll join you in a moment."

I hurriedly remove my shoes and rush to the main door. His apartment is fronting the door to the fire exit stairs. I make no second thoughts and speed down to it. Before reentering the apartment floor below his, I put my shoes back on and took the elevator going down from there.

I'm sorry, Emil. I'll pay for dinner next time, but I cannot be the substitute for a failed one tonight.

Walking towards the main entrance door, I'm relieved to see an empty taxi waiting. The driver has just veered into Shekh Zayed Road when my phone starts to vibrate inside my purse. Emil is calling. My heart is still excitedly beating. I'm afraid I'll stammer if I answer him now. Twenty minutes later, I'm at the entrance of my own building. I press the call back button for Emil. He picks up in one ring.

"I'm sorry for walking out on you. For a moment, I thought I was ready to accept your invitation."

"You could have just stayed, and we ordered dinner."

"When I don't know how to handle a situation, I prefer to extract myself from it. Your door was my main view from where I was seated."

"You must have thought of me as a pervert."

"Not at all, and I was not displeased with what I saw. It's just that it's not what I was expecting tonight."

"My bad. I'm sorry. Really. Thinking about it, I realized perhaps I shouldn't have done that."

"It's happened. If you're still open to meeting me again, so am I."

"Yeah. Let's keep in touch then."

Of course, I know what it means. Strangers don't keep in touch.

Well, might as well not.

**

Saturday night, while in bed, I think of my most recent dates. Colin certainly is a boorish class on his own. He's only a high school graduate and has no significant work experience back in the UK, and yet he thinks he's underpaid for receiving AED 8,000 as a hotel staff member. Majority of the people from my country who are working here in the

UAE have bachelor's degrees and solid work backgrounds. They're paid just half of that.

Rani would have appalled Lourdes in the first minute. Lana would have shot him in cold blood if only that were allowed. What case can we slap the liars with? He wants his women to be made up and polished, and yet he's the one who needs a lot of help on that front. His pictures on Tinder might have been five years old – or older. He's short and stocky, with a bulging stomach.

The French, Giullaume, is the opposite. He's tall and fit. Yet I'm having a hard time believing that he's only 45 years old. He looks a lot older than that to me, but with the libido of a younger guy.

"If I can invite you to my home, there's something special I'd like to show you."

Any woman may be thrilled to be invited to a man's home. But I feel ominous about it.

"It's not customary for me to go to a man's place, especially on the first date."

"I see. Maybe I can just show it to you in the car."

I oblige. I can easily get out, if ever. Once inside the car, he takes my left hand and places it on his crotch.

"Do you want to see what's underneath?"

"I know human anatomy well enough."

"Maybe. But do you know what we can do with our anatomy to enhance our pleasures?"

"I'm not sure I'm interested in knowing."

I try to pull my hand away, but he keeps it firmly in place.

"Trust me. You would be most pleased, my dear."

He rubs my hand hard against his cock from outside his pants. Then I feel it. Tiny, seemingly circular objects moving inside his cock.

In glorified horror, I ask him, "What have you done?"

"The ladies have enjoyed it."

"Doesn't it come with some serious health risks?"

"No. Otherwise, I wouldn't have gone through it. You don't look pleased."

"I think I'd prefer a traditional penis."

I pull my hand away.

"Well, if we're done here, I'd like to go."

I open the door and am about to go out when he stops me.

"I can drop you home."

"Thanks. But I can do that on my own."

A new week starts tomorrow. What's in store for me?

**

Blue: Fancy meeting you, kabayan.

Me: Same here.

Blue: I was doubtful at first because of your chinita (Chinese) eyes.

I have often been mistaken to be from different Asian countries other than the Philippines. Some even thought I was from either Kazakhstan or Uzbekistan. One time, a staff from McDonald's thought I'm from Tibet.

Me: You don't look like a Filipino yourself.

Blue: I know. We took so much more after our dad. When we visited the Philippines for the first time to see my mom's relatives, no one could believe we were her children.

Me: What brought you all the way out here?

Blue: I just want to see what's here. There's a big fuzz about Dubai back in the States. So I thought I'd come and see what's this place is about.

Me: Are you here just on vacation then?

Blue: Well, that was the initial plan. But I got a job, so I'll stay for a while. What about you? What brought you here?

Me: Change. When I get too familiar with a lot of things in one place, I get bored.

Blue: I see. How long have you been here?

Me: Five years.

Blue: Have you met anyone interesting on Tinder so far?

Me: Oh, all of them are, in their own little ways.

Blue: Okay. That sounds like something. What do you say about us meeting?

Me: Sure. I like that.

Blue is the eldest of three siblings. He has two younger sisters named Red and Purple. I don't want to know how that came about. With Filipino moms, sometimes it's hard to tell.

I love talking to people, and I especially like it when a man can carry on conversations really well. Blue is an intelligent guy. He makes it known to me right from the first minute. It would have been a shame for a good-looking guy like him to be an empty head. However, he's a little too puffed up. I can't hold him against his opinions. But I don't like the way he expresses them. I can say some unpleasant things about my own people and the Philippines in general, though I will not dare utter a word outside of a solid friendship I share with a few whom I've known for a long time. But as they say, you can take Americans out of America, but you cannot take America out of Americans. Another hard pass option.

******

It is just the second day of the week, but I feel like it is Thursday already. Walking back to my apartment building, I thought of soaking myself in a tub of warm, soapy water once home. Minutes after arriving, my phone starts buzzing on my bedside table. Two new matches on Tinder. I run the bath while I go through the messages. They're Arabs. Their accounts are bare, but they're heating up my phone with messages.

Smooth Criminal: Hi

I'm particular with the written word. The lack of punctuation marks in his sentences turns me off. But he seems like a nice fella, so I'll let it slide. Perhaps he's just lazy, as some men are.

The other guy is wearing a kandura in his photos. I can't be certain if he's a local. I've never met one, and other nationalities wear the same.

Smooth Criminal is a police officer in Abu Dhabi, and he lives in Dubai. He's a Jordan national. His eyes are a beautiful lime green pair with eyelashes that women pay thousands for to have. He's funny and polite. I would like to see him again if only he didn't smoke.

Zayed is 33 years old and is working in the government. He's been divorced. He's quick to admit his guilt for the destruction of his marriage.

"Marriage is a man's business and not of a guy who's just on his way to becoming one."

"Or a woman's, in my case."

"Have you been married before?"

"No."

"On Tinder, you put your age to be 35."

"That's correct."

"Your family is okay with you staying unmarried till now?"

"Seems so, yes."

"That's not a typical situation in your country, as I've learned."

"They're quite open-minded. But there are some non-negotiable conditions, should I decide to marry someone."

"Oh yeah?"

"Religion is one. I fell for an Egyptian not long back. It was a big deal to my brothers. They objected strongly to our marriage plans."

"You said they're open-minded."

"I said *quite*. His mother couldn't accept me as well."

"So there's no chance of me marrying you at all? Not even with 50 camels?"

We both laugh at that.

"Seriously, though, I understand your brothers. Religion as a subject alone is sensitive and confusing to talk about. What's more, having it actually play a part in one's life?"

"I agree 100%."

"But you swiped right for me. I'm sure in the photos you could tell that I am an Arab."

"Religion or what, nothing can stop me from swiping right for good-looking men."

Then I wink at him.

"Oh… you think I'm good looking? That's flattering. Thank you."

"Why did you swipe right for me?"

"I think you're pretty, too. And decent, if I may add."

"How can you determine that based on the photos?"

"Instincts. I've been around, Hanna. After some time, I know who's a pro and not."

"Have you…"

"No. I'll never sleep with one."

"That's not what I wanted to ask."

"Yes, I have met some, even helped two of them to get proper jobs."

"That's very nice of you."

"We all have to live. At the end of the day, that's a human being who has needs."

"Would you ever consider one?"

"Intelligence in a woman is very important to me, Hanna. A real intelligent woman would not willingly prostitute herself when she knows she has a worthier prospect."

"Fate can be cruel even to the most well-meaning of us. Some are denied the worthier chance."

"That's the most fitting way to describe how I feel about meeting you today. I'm denied the worthier chance because of the religion I was born into."

I'm not expecting that. His words tug at my heart. Chance is a gift that many of us may not be given in this lifetime. And if ever we are, it's just for a fleeting moment, just enough to touch our hearts and make us hopeful.

Once we're in the basement parking and realizing that we are alone, I pull him to me for a kiss. He responds with equal ardor. After a minute or two, I push him away to catch my breath.

"I thought you can't be with a Muslim."

"But it doesn't mean I can't kiss one."

And I gently smooch his lips once more.

"Can you please bring me home now? I have an early start tomorrow."

**

Another evening, another guy. Armi is from Armenia and works at Etisalat as an engineer. He's tall, dark, and handsome – sexy too! He has an angular face and chiseled body. Typical model look. But he lacks tact and makes no effort to hide his true intentions for being on Tinder. He's surprised that I turned down his invitation to go to his place.

"Don't tell me you're expecting to find love on Tinder."

"Why is that wrong to your opinion?"

His laugh is mocking me. His fake apology offends me more. When he realizes that I'm not amused, he tries to explain himself.

"It's Tinder! Why would anyone think that love can be found there? It's an app for people to hook up."

"The app is a tool that connects people. Could it be that your understanding of it is incorrect?"

"Whatever. I just think that you should not keep your hopes high on this one."

"On this one meaning yourself? I've no illusions of any kind. Thanks for dinner."

I stand abruptly and walk away without another glance back.

Brute!

**

"You've met over 40 guys from Tinder? Are you doing an experiment or something?"

"No, I'm not. Is it really unusual?"

"I find it so, yes. But I meant no offense."

"None taken. Though I have to say that your reaction was surprising."

"I am super surprised. I've never met anyone who had met that many people before from the app. That means you're very active on it and matching with people every day."

"Actually, I am, yes. I have at least two matches a day."

"Wow. And where are those guys from?"

"Everywhere. But you're the first Indian I've swiped right for. I thought perhaps you'd be a good match for my friend."

"She's an Indian?"

"Yes, from Kerala."

"We're from two different worlds."

"Oh, is that so?"

"One country but many worlds within it. I'm not in favour of these distinctions amongst us, but they've been there long before I was born. And there's absolutely no way to change anything now. Not even love can do anything about it."

"Is it beliefs, politics, or money?"

"All of the above. And love has no power over any of it."

"Such has what became of our world, huh?"

"Amen."

"It's sad, isn't it?"

"Very. Good thing we're over a billion. There are options for me still."

"Why did you swipe right for me?"

"Doesn't mean because I can't marry you that I can't date you."

"But why bother when you know how it will end?"

"There are many ways in which our mindset differs from women. We're good at compartmentalizing."

"Simply put, you can do without emotions."

"And that too."

As much as I like honest and open conversation like this, there's also something unsettling about it, especially with a man.

"If not for your friend, would you have swiped right for me?"

"Yes."

"Why?"

"Curiosity."

"But you will not consider me for anything else?"

"Frankly, no, especially with what you have in mind."

"Your *kabayans* and I have had some good times together."

"I'm not a girl just for good times, Raj."

"Too bad. Imagine the fun that we can have."

If it's ice cream he's offering, even a curry-flavored one, I might try it.

**

Guido is a Lebanese and an executive of a mobile phone brand. Quite an odd name for someone from this region. I thought perhaps one of his parents might have been from another country with Latin American origins.

"Your penis's name is Guido?"

Hardly anything shocks me now, but this shakes me good.

"Why do you seem so surprised? Doesn't your kitty have a name too?"

I endeavor to wake up very early every Friday, despite it being a weekend, because I want to do my laps in the water while there are very few people. JBR is a hot weekend destination. It starts to get crowded around 9:00 AM. I have breakfast at Chowking after swimming. I while my time here people-watching as I let the food settle in my stomach. Today, I want to kick myself for inviting this guy over.

"So what's your name?"

"Anas."

"Why didn't you tell me that when I asked you over the phone?"

"You're the only one who saw through the façade. No one I've met on Tinder had questioned me about my name. And because of that, I consider you special."

Men and their lame lies. In a time and age where it's not hard to get laid, what's this charade for? If he can't be upfront with just his name, what can I expect from this one then?

"I mentioned your name several times during our almost hour-long conversation, and for once you never—"

"I love the sound of it from your lips. I had an erection—"

"Stop it!"

I'm a woman of strength, and I know too well when to employ it.

"I need you to leave my table so I can continue with my breakfast."

"Ugh! I can't believe this. Over a name?"

"You gave me the name of your genitalia."

"I told you the truth!"

"You told me the truth because you thought it could lead to an outcome you're expecting. You probably think I'd giggle or find it cute, and be eventually interested in meeting your Guido. Even on the phone, your overreaching libido was unmissable."

If my silence can make men uncomfortable, my words can fry their testicles.

"Can we start over again?"

"I lost my interest in you."

It may just be a name, but why tell me that it's that of his penis? He could have kept that from me and told me that he just fancied the name Guido. Like what Saad has done when we first met.

Despite my annoyance, I finished my breakfast and order for their famous *halo-halo* for dessert. As I'm enjoying it while looking at the passersby, my phone vibrates to Ken's call.

"Hey, stranger."

"Hey, you, other stranger. Where are you?"

"JBR."

"Let me guess. Chowking?"

"Just had my breakfast. Can you come now?"

"Sure. Give me 20 max."

I like a guy who keeps his word, especially in relation to time. After 18 minutes, Ken's striding fast in my direction in deep purple shorts and a white polo shirt.

"Wow! Purple."

"Do I look funny in it?"

"Not at all. In fact, I think very few men can give justice to that colour. You're on that short list."

"Thanks. So how was he?"

"Oh boy, where should I begin? Or how?"

"So it's another one of those unpleasant meet-ups."

"Do you have a name for your penis?"

"What?"

The tone of his voice and the expression on his face somehow validate my own displeasure.

"His name on Tinder was Guido. When we were talking on the phone, I asked him if it was his name because I thought it was unusual for someone from this region. He said yes. Guess what? It's his penis's name."

"Who gives a name to their genitalia?"

"Apparently, he does."

"Did you ask him why?"

"Ken, why would I give a fuck about that?"

"Sorry. I just want to understand the logic behind it."

"Unbelievable, right?"

I start laughing uncontrollably. Ken joins in, though I think he's mostly being carried away by my laughter.

"The most peculiar ones sure know how to find you."

"I'm beginning to wonder myself about my luck."

"Hanna, don't overthink this. I think it's perfectly normal. And nowadays, normal has evolved widely. People are more experimental and expressive."

Of course, he's right. Many people are now exercising their freedom in unprecedented ways. I think more than the expression itself, what unsettles me are the consequences of it, because inadvertently, whether I like it or not, all these changes in our world affect me. And if I'm caught unaware of this, it can potentially shift the balance in my life. As a Scorpio, such sudden changes are disturbing.

**

I'm surprised to see pictures of him with a woman in them. I'm sure they're not there before.

Me: Hey.
Me: You added new photos here.

Chris: Yeah. She's my wife.
Chris: We're in an open marriage and sometimes we play together.

Experimental, as Ken said. How many are they? Am I one of the few who has yet to evolve?

Me: Whose idea was that?

Chris: Mutual decision. We've been married for a while.
Chris: Are you married?

Me: No. Never been.

Chris: Ever had a threesome?

Me: Neither.

Chris: Are you up for it?

Me: I'm not into that.

Chris: Then what are you into?

Me: Traditional date.

Chris: I still do that. Then perhaps later on I can introduce you to my wife and experience a more explosive sex.

Me: I don't mean it in that context.

Chris: Oh, you mean just plain meeting over coffee and like that?

Me: Yeah.

Chris: I suppose we can, yes. It's been a while that I had a normal date anyway.

Their marital arrangement is not for the faint of heart. I'd rather go through divorce proceedings. Chris, at 55, is well aware that his prospects for a brand new love are slim, so he'd rather enjoy his remaining years of agility before time binds him to old age. His wife, at 50, shares this thought. I'm internally horrified listening to him as he shares their experiences. The thought of his wife with other men, or watching her with them, excites him. I swallow hard, imagining the scenario in my head.

"I watch porn and I pleasure myself when I do. I have seen threesomes and orgies, and whatever else there is to see. But I never for once dreamt of actualizing any of it in my own life."

"Sometimes, all it takes is the right partner. We can guide you through it. We'll go slowly."

"Hard pass, Chris."

"I understand."

McGettigan in DWTC has underground parking. Once we're down there, Chris pushes me gently against the side of his jeep and feels my sex from behind. All I can do is moan as his fingers invade my privacy.

"Why do you deny the desires of your body?"

His aroused voice heats me up even more. I try to move away, but he pins me harder to the car, and his other hand starts to roam on my body.

"Chris, I can't do this. Not right now. Not here."

He seems deaf to my pleading. He continues to rub his crotch against my ass.

"Chris, please. Stop!"

He releases me after a deep kiss on the neck. After a minute, I help myself into the passenger seat.

"Where's your panty?"

"I don't wear one when I don't have my period."

Without preamble, his tongue finds its way inside my mouth, and his hand slides between my legs. I gasp when his fingertips make contact with my wet sex. Just as I'm coming up to his fingers, three men enter the parking area and are heading in our direction. He pulls away and licks his fingers as he starts the engine. I can't believe what just happened. But I'm excited.

"You taste so good."

What's the right response for that? I'm not prepared for what happened, more so for what might come after. I opt not to say anything back but smile.

Once we're outside my building, he presses his invitation again.

"Will you think about it? If you're awkward to have my wife around, we can do it just us."

"Okay. I'll think about it."

A quick smack on the lips, and I almost jump out of his car.

I head straight into the shower upon reaching my bedroom. My body is shocked by the cold water.

There's a missed call from an unknown number showing on my lock screen. I press call back, and a thick Aussie accent greets me from the other line.

"Hi! I missed a call from this number. I'm Hanna."

"Hi, Hanna! I'm Barry. We connected on Tinder."

"Ah, yes. How are you?"

"Quite busy today. I was meaning to call much earlier."

"It's alright. What is it that you do?"

"I'm a banker. What about you?"

"Internal office affairs. Administration. Have you been here long?"

I cannot give straight answers whenever I'm asked this because, frankly, my role has evolved so much through the years that to say I'm an office manager feels like a gross understatement.

"Ten years in two months."

"Wow. That's a long time."

"Agree. I've been married and divorced during that period. Are you married, by the way?"

"No, never been."

"Nice. I don't want to keep this conversation long. I'd rather sit down with you and talk over some good food."

"I like that too."

"Are you free tomorrow?"

"I would be for you."

"That's more I like it. Is 7:30 PM okay?"

"Suits me just fine."

"See you then."

I check his pictures on Tinder. Tanned and muscular. He's not exactly my type, but my goodness, he's hot! Ashley's knocks halt my thoughts from escalating.

"Come in, babe."

"What's up, woman? We're not seeing each other often enough."

I raise my phone to her face level.

"Oh wow! He's a god, babe."

"I'll have dinner with him tomorrow."

"You must tell me how it goes after."

"Of course."

I show her my navy blue lace mini dress.

"What do you think?"

"Sexy. I think that's perfect for tomorrow."

"I thought so, too."

"Were you out tonight as well?"

"Yup. British, married guy."

Ashley makes a face.

"I know."

"What about this guy?"

"He's divorced."

"You're so busy. You seem to be enjoying going out a lot now."

"It does offer relief."

"Oh yeah? Then that's good, isn't it?"

"As a distraction, yes. Nice way to keep one's mind off things that once hurt or sadden you. But I've been to over 40 dates, and yet I haven't met one I can go on steady dates with."

"What about Ken?"

"He's a friend. I don't fancy him in any other way than that."

"Well, good luck tomorrow. He seems like a good catch, if ever."

What Ashley has said gets me thinking. How does a fisherman catch fish? It might help me to employ the same tactic.

**

The explosive temper of my boss gives me a headache. It's only 10:00 AM and I feel spent already. Ice cream is a good choice right now.

I walk to the nearest grocery store from our office. I take a Magnum from the freezer and start on it right away before reaching the cashier. Halfway through it, while browsing the latest Hollywood gossip by the magazine stand, a voice cuts my concentration. I look at him with surprise. He's our crush in our office building!

"Isn't it too early for ice cream?"

"You're as guilty as I am."

"Coke relaxes me, and right now I especially need it. What's your excuse?"

"Stops me from blowing up."

"Rough morning, huh?"

"I just survived a tornado."

"And yet here you are, looking pretty as always."

As always? So it means he notices me all along?

"Thanks. Stress seems to suit you well too."

He chuckles.

Oh, he has dimples too!

"I'm Will, 11th floor."

"Hanna, 28th."

"But you also have another office on the same floor as ours, yeah?"

"You're a keen observant."

"Hard to miss you."

That works up my cheeks.

"I oftentimes feel unseen. A white rose among the sea of other colorful flowers."

"I've always favored simple beauty."

One more word and I might just kiss this guy.

"Nice pickup lines. I've never heard those before."

"I'm not trying to make a pass at you. But if truth be told, I've had a crush on you for some time now."

I feel a sensation down at my sex.

"That's nice to hear on a day like today. Thank you."

It's not necessary, totally uncalled for, but before he steps out of the elevator, I kiss him on one cheek. I love the surprise look on his face.

"Enjoy the rest of the day."

His smile makes me giggle while going up to our office floor.

**

The day ends with no more drama. I'm able to leave on time and prepare well for my dinner date with Barry.

His tan becomes more pronounced because of the crisp white buttoned-down shirt he's wearing. He's a big guy standing at 190 cm. He scoops me up for a big hug when I approach our table.

"You are a lovely little doll, aren't you?"

"You're not bad yourself."

"Thanks, love. Let's order now and get going with our convo after. I'm really excited matching with you."

The look on his face and his demeanor match the enthusiasm in his voice. Barry, or Baron, is a banker originally from Sydney. From his stories, I can surmise that he has a wild taste in women. Which makes me wonder what his thoughts must be about me.

"You, however, I can't reconcile your look with the kind of personality that I think you have. And I think you're smart. I feel you are. You have a strong presence."

I'm not expecting any of this. I'm left speechless and yet pleasantly surprised. And as always, I just smile when I don't know what to say.

"There's a certain innocence in your eyes, almost like that of a child. You beguiled me. I must admit, you're not the type that I would usually go for. You seem too proper for me. And you're Asian. No offense meant, but I prefer the Eastern Europeans. Yet there's something about that photo you have on Tinder that I find arresting."

"It was a very sexy photo, yes. And red is a strong, powerful color."

"A lot of guys must have swiped right for you. I'm sure of that."

No point affirming the truth. It's speaking loudly in front of me.

"I wonder why you're single."

"Well, I don't want to be single anymore. I'm searching. Hence, Tinder."

"Have you met anyone well worth a try?"

"I wouldn't be sitting in front of you now if that was the case."

"What are you looking for?"

I should have a ready answer for this, having been asked the same over and over again. But the question always clamps my lips.

"If you're looking for Mr. Perfect, high time you realize that he doesn't exist."

When you don't answer, the world always seems to have a ready response for you.

"Pain has a way of changing our perspectives. It makes us more cautious."

"Where's the fun in that?"

"Love is fun with the right person."

"And who is that?"

"I'm still looking."

"How would you know that you found him?"

"The heart will know when it's finally home."

"See! That! That is the innocence I was talking about. You're a lover. A romantic. You have high ideals about love. You want a fairy tale."

"Every girl does."

"I don't think so. Nowadays, many girls prefer more money than real love."

"Maybe because you men muddled the dream for some of us."

"Maybe. But you, you surprised me with your… How could you stay this clean given how dirty the world has become?"

"I don't follow you."

"I've been here ten years. I've seen what's there to see. Love has a price in this place."

"Looks like you paid a great deal."

"Both my heart and wallet were emptied after three years."

"Have you loved again after that?"

"You said it yourself. Pain changes our perspectives. It completely altered mine."

"Did you try adopting a different outlook?"

"What's the point? Love is spelled differently now. It's capital M-O-N-E-Y. Nothing else matters more."

"But what about you? What matters to you?"

"I've been with women – lots. But never for once had anyone asked me that. I'm glad I swiped right for you."

"So do I."

"Oh yeah? You're not put off by my love drama?"

"Not one bit."

"Will we see each other again?"

"We can. But I'm afraid that we cannot date."

"Why is that? I was hoping that I could try something different with you."

"You're rough on the edges. The last thing I want is to be hurt again while I'm still recovering from my own painful story."

"I understand. But I hope from time to time you will let me see you. I like talking to you, Hanna. My mind's working with you."

"I don't see any problem with that. It doesn't mean because I'm wounded that I cannot attend to someone else's wound and help try to patch it up."

"Wow! That's amazing. And so are you. I'm really pleased to have met you. I hope I can change your mind about us."

"I believe every woman is just as amazing, if only we're loved properly. But a woman becomes a man's constant headache if he doesn't know how to take care of her."

"I can't believe he didn't fight for you, for your relationship."

"Love doesn't always have to win. Peace, family, religion – they matter too. I don't see the point in giving that all up if there's another choice."

"Where were you ten years ago when I was looking for love?"

I don't believe that Barry is an isolated story. On the contrary, I believe that men want love as much as we women do. But somewhere along the way, our choices created situations where it's not conducive for love to blossom.

**

I hate being late, but some days are just longer than usual. Even though his back is on me, his tattoos easily distinguish him from others.

"Hi Christophe!"

"Hanna!"

Three kisses on the cheeks and a brief hug. French people are more physical than others. Not that I mind. They always smell so good.

"I'm sorry I'm late."

"It's okay. I just got here myself. So, what are you in the mood to eat?"

"Do you mind eating at the food court? There's something there that I am craving for."

"I have no issues at all."

During my period, my appetite is just abnormal. Today, I'm salivating for Manchurian Chicken. And I only want it from the Chinese stall in the food court of the Mall of the Emirates.

"When did you have your first tattoo?"

"19. During my college days."

He points to a small Japanese character on his left wrist.

"What does it mean?"

"It's the initial of my name."

"Why did you decide to be tattooed?"

"My parents are tattooed. My dad has his entire back and a full arm covered. My mom has our portraits and her favorite Bible quote on her back. I took it a bit further. I have my entire body covered."

"Your entire body?"

"Yes. With the exception of my ass and cock, of course."

He opens his phone and shows me photos of his tattoos while we're on the escalator.

"So you have no space for me if ever?"

I say jokingly.

He points at his heart.

"Empty space."

"How come?"

"Sometimes, things don't work out. My last girlfriend just asked for space. But she never came back."

"And you never ask her?"

"You know when something has run its course."

After placing our orders at my favorite Chinese stall, we chose a table that was far from the crowd and out of people's way.

"Why are you on Tinder?"

"It's the easiest way to meet people."

"How do you find it so far?"

"I'm not very active on it. I think the last match I had was over a month ago. I'm surprised you swiped right for me."

"Why do you say that?"

"Many girls are put off by tattoos. They easily equate tattoos to bad behavior, drugs, alcohol, and what have you. I met someone from your country who refused to see me again because she said her parents warned her about tattooed men. After that, I changed all my pictures on Tinder, except for one that's showing my face. I thought that it was better beforehand that a girl knows I'm heavily inked."

"It's actually my reason for swiping right for you. I'm intrigued."

"Oh yeah? Do you have any of your own?"

"None. I'm not sure if I would get any. But I'm curious when I see one who has, and in your case, a lot. I know there's a story behind each one."

"You belong to a small minority with an open mind."

"Live and let live."

He nods in agreement.

"Do you follow a theme, or is it anything goes? Like whatever you fancy?"

"Japan has fascinated me from an early age. I've been obsessed with the samurai. There are two crisscrossing my back and two small ones with the blades meeting at the center of my chest."

He hands me his phone for me to see the photos in it.

"They're beautiful. Which hurts more between your back and chest?"

"Neither, but those on the back of my thighs did. And I think it would hurt to have it on my neck."

"What would you have on it?"

"A snake eating its own tail all around, and it meets right here at the base."

"I think it would look really nice if it's going to be colored."

"Oh yes, I intend to have it that way. Definitely."

"When do you plan to have it?"

"When I visit Berlin again next year. I have it all done there."

Christophe is an open book, but one must leap into his pages in order to know him. He draws a lot of attention to himself because of his tattoos, though he gives none to anyone. He will, however, reward your curiosity with stories from his adventurous travels and colorful life inked on his skin if you initiate contact.

On the love front, however, the shade is of a lesser, almost fading hue. We all have someone in the past. In Christophe's case, it's different; he is still in the past.

A metal chain corrodes with time and becomes malleable, enabling a prisoner to free oneself. Pain, on the other hand, sometimes intensifies with the ticking of the clock. It's got a strong hold on him.

I fear sharing his reality.

**

"You're not operating a charity clinic for broken men. Don't get carried away by their drama. Their problem is not yours to solve."

We're having breakfast at Paul's outside the seating area in JBR. Lourdes is my emotional police. I don't always agree with her, but neither are her views contemptuous enough for me to react to.

"Maybe I should. Might be another great way to meet more interesting men."

"And end up as damaged as, or worse, than them?"

"I think *damaged* is such a harsh word. *Blemished* is perhaps a better way to describe them."

"Whatever you say. Just don't get involved. You're looking for love, not problems."

"But to you, those are synonymous."

"I've run my race. You still have time."

"Fate seems to be against me."

"Fate favors only the few. You're not being punished on purpose."

Am I not? Because it surely feels that way to me. My temerity in choosing to love someone who's meant for someone else disturbed the order of things arranged by some cosmic powers. I'm surprised lightning has not struck me dead yet.

"What makes you swipe right for someone?"

"Pictures, of course. Then I check their bio. Many barely write anything in their accounts. So I engage them in chats and phone calls after matching."

"And then you meet them?"

"If I feel good while talking to them, then yes."

"Have you met anyone of them again after the first time?"

"None so far. There had been messages exchanged with a few of them for a second date, but either they or I wouldn't be available when the day came. And no follow-up after that because I have other matches to meet."

"Is there anyone who has made more impact than the others?"

"I've made really good connections with a few of them. However, no one stood out from the rest. I need more time."

"Okay."

She doesn't look convinced despite her affirmative response. I don't dare probe.

I may not be able to influence time, but I will not allow myself to be rushed by any circumstances. I'm the one who'll deal with the aftermath of my decisions after all.

**

"50? Five zero?"

To say that he's surprised is gravely inaccurate. If his jaw could fall, it might have fallen.

"Yes. I've met 50 Egyptian men already."

"So I'm 51st. Tell me, who are you looking for? I'm serious. I might be able to help you. I know a lot of them here."

"I'm not looking for anyone, Mohamad. I just happened to be matching mostly with you guys. Sometimes, I'd match with a guy thinking that he's from another country, only for me to find out once we met that he's actually Egyptian."

"I hope they were pleasant meetings."

"Yes. Nothing untoward happened in any of it. But if I can be very upfront with you, it seems that your country has a high divorce rate, especially involving those who are working here."

"Maybe. I cannot refute that. All of my friends are divorced. But I cannot take it against the men, too. We have

238

a different way of life. Sometimes, the better chance comes to us quite late. If you know what I mean."

"I don't want to assume that I understand you. But we don't have to talk about it any further if it will put you off. It's not a subject to be discussed in dates like this anyway."

"But you want to know. I can sense that strongly from you."

"I've always been the curious type."

"I think it's more than curiosity for you. You seem to have a genuine interest in understanding."

"I don't want to be just a passive participant in life. Understanding fosters better relationships with people."

"True. Yet many others simply don't care."

"But I do. I always do."

He smiles at me before he continues.

"The family unit has a central significance in Egyptian lifestyle. And since premarital sex is haram in Islam, we marry sooner than we should. As young as 20 years old is considered an ideal age for marriage."

"Do we factor in any way for your broken marriages or the infidelities of some?"

"Yes and no. Yes, because what we see here is not something we have at home. It is a natural human tendency to become attracted to those unfamiliar to you. And sometimes those attraction goes out of hand. We also have needs. Sometimes we want those needs to be met now."

"And why did you say no?"

"There's always a choice. I don't believe that at any point in time, regardless of the situation, where an alternative choice apart from the obvious isn't present. But I hold no judgment against any of them who engage in such affairs."

Contrary to what has been said, not every Mohamad has the same story. Not every Mohamad thinks the same and makes the same choices. This Mohamad is different. He untangles the web of confusion in my mind from my first 50 dates.

**

"Then stop. But before you do so, think of what benefit such an action will generate."

Robert compounds my confusion. He's a handsome, wide-eyed military contractor from Maryland, USA. He's visiting me from Qatar this weekend.

"Of course, people will be surprised, or even be shocked, to know that you've met this many men from a dating app. But so what? It's not a crime."

"It may not be, but I'm starting to think that I might just be wasting my time."

"And this disposition is based on what?"

"I've met more than 80 men, Rob. Eight zero. I've not seen anyone of them again. Who am I looking for? What am I looking for?"

"Love."

One short word, but it has the power to silence all the voices in my head.

"We live in a time when it's not that easy to find it anymore."

He has a point, and a strong one too.

We've made breakthroughs in medicine, communications, and transportation. We've advanced in Science & Technology. We live in a more modern world, and yet the single most essential of all human needs seems to have become a scarcity. Before learning the alphabet, we have been taught love through the tender kisses and caring gestures of our families. It has been an integral part of our sustenance growing up, along with food and education. Becoming an adult and acquiring experiences, knowledge, and better judgment, how has our capacity to love diminished?

"We learned something else apart from love: power."

I'm taken aback by it. I sip my beer slowly, savoring its taste and feeling its coldness run down my throat while my eyes stay fixed on his.

"I was deeply in love with a girl once. I did everything and gave everything she asked, because I thought that's how it should be when you love someone. I lost myself in that relationship. I was *overpowered*."

Raw, jagged emotions register on his face.

I reach out and caress his cheek. I can see how my touch ignites his carnal desires.

Power.

**

Just after our used plates have been collected, Youssef opens a square mahogany box, and in it is a necklace with ethnic designs typical of Jordan.

"It's pure copper, handcrafted by a Bedouin woman."

"It's beautiful. I've never received a gift from my Tinder dates before."

"Can you put it on? I'd love to see how it would look on your neck."

"I don't think that's possible right now with this dress."

I'm wearing my favorite chiffon Japanese printed dress with long sleeves and a high turtleneck. In his Tinder profile, he describes himself as a doctor with conservative manners. Given his reputable profession, he prefers his dates to be modest in appearance.

"How would you like to do so up in my apartment?"

"That means I have to take my dress off."

"I don't see why that's a bad idea. And I can reward you with more if you will."

His face displays the confidence of someone who has intellect and money.

"It has been a nice evening until this minute."

I abruptly stand and walk towards the ladies' room. My heart's pulsating with rage for his insolence. My mind's shouting curses, wants to avenge my insulted pride.

And like pouring vinegar on a wound, he's standing outside the door. I ignore him and walk straight to the elevator platform.

"I'm sorry. I did not mean to offend you."

"What were you expecting a lady would feel from such a proposition?"

"I'm sorry I mistook you for—"

"You mistook me for what?"

My Chinese eyes are blazing at his big, round browns.

"Look at me carefully. Do I resemble someone who would go to a stranger's apartment just to try on a necklace and get paid for it? I can report you to the police for solicitation of prostitution!"

He freezes, and his eyes convey dread and alarm. I'm silently pleased as I walk into the elevator.

"So much for your fake conservatism."

I'm still able to spit that out while the elevator doors are closing.

The bed magnetizes me to it upon reaching home. It's one of those meetups where I feel tired after.

Another Hollywood blockbuster moment.

I'm close to falling asleep when my phone vibrates. It's a WhatsApp message from another pilot I connected with on Tinder. He's a good catch, if ever. Intelligence is my weakness. Match a handsome face to that and I'll start getting wet. However, when I look at his second photo again, the alarm in my mind starts blinking red. I open YouTube. My annoyance is heightened. Another potential movie plot.

Me: You're a famous YouTuber.

He's typing, then stops. Starts typing again and stops again. He's probably thinking of what to say back to me, good enough to keep up the façade.

Me: Today is Friday. It's off day for most of the GCC. You can't be having simulations today at an Oman aviation school. You're not a real captain. You're an impostor, probably from Nigeria, who uses other people's identity to lure victims.

He read my message, then blocked me after. He was convincing enough. But even the most well-guised devil can be stupid sometimes.

**

I don't need someone with the eloquence of a politician, but I'm quite particular about how someone talks.

My mind is okay to fill in some missing words or auto-correct the crooked English of many of those I have met. As long as the essence is expressed clearly, I can fill in all the gaps in between. This native from Birmingham, though, has a different peculiarity. He says the word *mate* so frequently that after half an hour, it's the only word I can hear from him. My ears grow deaf to everything else he says.

"It's still quite early, mate. Do you really need to go now, mate?"

"Yes. I'm beginning to have a headache."

"Alright, mate. Will we see each other again, mate?"

I might pull your tongue out next time.

"Let's see about that."

I hail the approaching taxi.

"Thanks for dinner."

Quick peck on the cheeks, and I almost jump inside.

**

He kisses me full on the lips the moment I get in. I want to pull away, but his breath smells so good and his lips taste sweet. I look around as we slowly drive out of the cluster.

"You seem anxious."

"You're not the first one who picked me up here. I don't want my male colleagues to tease me, if ever."

"Have you dated anyone of them?"

"I don't play in my own backyard."

"So where do you play?"

"In the car."

I'm not sure how that slips out of my mouth so fast. His reaction is equally swift. His right hand is already caressing my left thigh underneath my dress. Again, I want to resist, but his touch has the opposite effect. It's making my legs part a bit wider, letting his fingers access a private road leading to a more private location.

Bora is an architect from Turkey. He's almost finished with his project here in Dubai and will soon be off to France for another assignment. He has relaxed ideals and a mind that I'd like to explore more. He's like Hosni, my favorite Lebanese. They've both stimulated my sex with their tongues, sans the actual contact.

Once we're in the underground parking of JBR, I allow his fingers to finally penetrate me while his tongue is busy with mine. When he pulls out his fingers, they are drenched.

"Wow."

"Thank you."

My cheeks are red and hot. My heart is throbbing madly from excitement.

**

"I meant no disrespect, but you don't look Italian to me. You seem to be from Pakistan or Afghanistan."

"What made you say that?"

His eyes are bright and curious.

"Your eyes."

"What about them?"

"We have a National Geographic magazine at home, and on its cover was a girl with piercing green eyes looking directly into the photographer's lens. Later on, I learned she's an Afghan. You have the same piercing gaze. Apart from that, I don't know why I suddenly thought of her while looking at you."

Aaqil looks at me for what seems like a minute before speaking again.

"I'm an Afghan, but was born and buttered in Italy. I do have a framed copy of that magazine in my place."

"Are you related to her?"

"No. I do love that photograph, though. It's a haunting image of a home I've never been to, of someone I could have loved had I been given the chance."

I sense a sentiment in his words, an almost tangible loneliness.

"Do you have plans to visit Afghanistan?"

"I will not hurt myself in that way."

His words baffle me. He reads the confusion on my face.

"There are stories that started long before we were born. Stories that are painful and can be damaging to our souls if we choose to involve ourselves in them. Sometimes we need to love from a distance so that that same love cannot destroy us."

My emotions are getting riled up with those words. Why does it seem so easy for others to ignore the promptings of their hearts, while mine can paralyze me?

"I think I'm reminding you of a story where you have been written off by destiny."

"Don't you long to be a part of something that made you *you*?"

"I'm a product of choices – those of my parents and mine. Afghanistan is in my blood. Italy is home. Italy raised me."

Who am I?

**

"I don't know who I am. One of the caretakers in the orphanage I grew up in found me outside their door one July morning. Hence, the name July. I don't like it, but it's the only thing that ties me to a life I was born into."

His story can bag an award at Cannes. It's one thing to doubt oneself. It's another not to know your identity. I'm speechless, now of all times when words can offer some comfort.

"But you've made something of yourself. You're the head of a big foreign company here in Dubai."

That sounds empty to me. I'm still opening drawers in my mind, looking for the right words.

"One's position at work does not give one an identity."

"I know. What I'm trying to say is that you did not let your past deter you from having the life you now have."

"My adaptive parents made this life possible. They took me home to Luxembourg from Iraq and helped me mold an identity."

"Some stories may not start right, but develop into a happy ending because of love."

"That's a nice way to put it. What about you? What's your story?"

Should I tell him? What harm can it do? Where to start?

"Your reluctance makes me more curious."

"I'm sure it's something you're all too familiar with by now."

"Perhaps. But everyone tells their story differently."

"I fell in love with an Egyptian, but religion could not allow it to blossom."

Silence. I have to look away. The intensity of his hazel brown eyes makes me conscious. My heart's starting to pulsate faster. I'm not sure why.

"Are you over him?"

I cannot answer because I do not know what answer to give.

"Do you want to come with me to Luxembourg? I can give you a good life there. A new place can help you forget, and maybe even heal."

What's the right response to a proposal like that? Sure, Luxembourg sounds like a rich experience. But am I ready to leave Dubai and be a different woman from what Zaki helped me become?

"You don't have to give me an answer now. Think about it."

I lightly squeeze his hand back in acknowledgement. My heart has left my body, though, running home fast.

**

"You're a long way from home."

It's a known fact that many Japanese prefer to live and work in their own country.

"So are you."

His tone is earnest. Hiroto is a Japanese businessman who flies constantly between Dubai and Tokyo to oversee their operations.

"What brought you here?"

"I was just really bored back home in the Philippines."

It's one of my go-to answers when I can't find the right words or don't want to expound myself.

"There are other countries closer to your home. Why here?"

"There are birds that sometimes fly further away from the nest they grew up in. I'm one of them."

"Speaking of flying, my name Hiroto means soaring or flying far."

"That explains well why you're here too."

We toast to our shared plight.

"Do you like your life here?"

His question surprised me. No one has ever asked me that.

"I can't complain. What made you ask?"

"Curiosity. Genuine curiosity."

"What about you? Are you not perturbed by the atmosphere and different sounds here?"

"Every tree in the forest is different. Every wise bird knows that."

"Have you met some interesting *birds*?"

"Quite a few, and a handful with *clipped* wings. Dubai is very fascinating to me. If you want to learn about life and people, then this is the place to be."

His words intrigue me.

"Care to share what you've learned so far?"

"Every woman is the same, regardless of how you do your makeup or what color of lipstick you prefer. You all want love, but consider money as not a bad substitute."

"Give and take. Sounds fair to me."

"You've wised up."

He raises his glass to me and empties its contents.

"We've always been wise. Nowadays, we're learning to be more *adaptive*."

I raise my glass too and pour all its contents down my receptive throat.

I love conversations like this where you forget about the time or your phone. Conversations that expand your mind are somehow better than how school or books can.

**

"I'm meeting someone tomorrow. He's asking me what I want him to bring for me."

"Tell him nothing because you're not going to his place after."

"Is that what it means?"

Lana nods as she takes the last bite of the macaroon in her hand.

"Where's that guy from?"

"Lebanon."

"Can I see his photo? He might be the same guy I met once who brought me a good wine from Lebanon and expected sex after dinner."

"Oh, wow!"

"It's Tinder, girl. That's their common thinking. Here. No, it's not him."

After months of being active on the app, I'm still learning something new in connection with it.

"You've been using it for some time now. But no one has stirred your heart again?"

I answer with a head motion as I sip my tea.

"Well, just keep dating. Eventually, who knows? It's fun anyway."

"Lana, have you watched a movie with a date?"

"Yeah, a few times."

"And?"

"There were fondling and kissing here and there, but that's it."

"I see."

"Don't agree to go if you're not comfortable with the idea, or you don't like the guy that much."

"Noted. Do you keep in touch with any of them?"

"Yes, few. We've become friends. Men also get lonely as much as we do."

Who does Zaki talk to when he's lonely?

"What do you talk about when you're out with them?"

"Many things, but mostly about their relationships. I think many of them are really dissatisfied with their marriages. Those I've met were either divorced or separated. The single ones do not want commitment."

Would Zaki suffer the same plight?

"What do you think could be the reasons for it?"

I'm not just keeping the conversation going. There's a nagging voice inside my head.

"I don't think it's just one issue or the other. I think it's a mix of many things, and money seems to be one of the top reasons."

Money. Money. Money. Am I one of the very few who is perpetually preoccupied only with thoughts of love?

"What are you thinking about?"

Lana notices me thinking and probes me.

"Money, women, men, relationships. They seem to have a direct correlation with each other, though I cannot connect the dots in my head."

"I've been thinking of the same. Hearing about it from my dates again and again, it is impossible not to."

"It's a given that men will foot the bill on dates and in relationships. Material gifts and financial support between couples are accepted and expected gestures. But what of women who ask for money from those they've just met or are casually dating? What do we make of that?"

"Getting even with men?"

"Or *adaptation*."

Lana's eyes narrow at me as she tries to make sense of what I just said.

"Think about it carefully. Why do we go on dates? To meet someone to hopefully build a relationship with. Love is our ultimate aim. But what if it's not attainable? What are we willing to settle for in exchange for that?"

Her eyes brighten up as she begins to see the outline of my thoughts. I press on, deliberate to complete the puzzle.

"If two people want to keep seeing each other, but the guy is not ready for commitment, what do you think are the tactics he might think of employing in order to keep the girl? If I'm a guy, and I have the financial resources to spare, I wouldn't think twice about spending some portion of it for her, to keep her company."

"No money, no honey."

She's aligned with my thoughts now.

"Many guys think in a linear fashion. If an issue can be resolved with money, they'll readily open their wallets instead of their minds.

"Now let's admit it. Dubai is not a cheap place. In order to survive here, one needs a stable job that pays decently. But if there's an easy alternative source, with little effort expected from our end, who wouldn't like that? It may not be love that we're getting, but we're still getting something from them. So somehow, it's not a complete waste of our time."

"We *adapt* to the situation."

She suddenly becomes excited as she's able to see a clearer picture of the reality in her mind.

"And many become *adept* at it."

I say so, matching her enthusiasm.

"Adapt and adept."

She's tossing the words like balls in the air.

"Play and profit."

I add again, with more conviction now.

"But what about us?"

"What about us? Lana, we're principled and educated. Why do we need to settle for mediocrity?"

**

100? I've met that many men?

I count again. Indeed, I've met 100 men already. And I have not seen a single one of them again. Lying back on the bed, I think of those 100 encounters I have had. Have I missed my chance in love again without realizing it?

It has been said that what's rightly ours cannot be taken from us, nor would it pass us by. I just wound by with several of my meet-ups. Could I have been the one who passed my chance and not know it?

I line them all in my mind, and one by one, I cross out those I don't want to see again. Out of those who are left – and there's just 15 of them – only five are going to advance, *possibly* on to the second date. Two Germans – the pilot and the aviation engineer, the Spanish teacher, one Egyptian, and the Emirati.

As I make up my mind about them, my fingers start typing away. I need to initiate the second dates, and this time around, I will see it through. Then I will take a rest from Tinder. I want to explore whatever chance there might be from those five connections.

As I'm about to put my phone down on the bedside table, it lights up again to Ken's call.

"Hi, stranger."

"I sent you messages 15 minutes ago to go for dinner. You haven't answered, but I can see that you're online."

"I was composing messages. I'm asking some of my previous Tinder meetups for a second date."

"What? Why?"

"I want to further explore the connection."

"They should have reached out to you again if they were interested in more than a mere hookup."

"What if it was me who didn't show enough interest then, so they thought I wasn't, and it discouraged them from pursuing me?"

"Hanna, men are born hunters. We hunt differently, yes, but if we want something – or someone – we'd go after it. Desire is a very strong catalyst."

Ken is a sensible guy whose mind is always where the money is, so to speak.

"You're forgetting that there are so many of us here. We are looking, and so are you guys. I could be someone's, or some men's, viable option. But if I don't help them in a way to consider me further, then I could lose my *slot* and *slip* down their *list*. Thus, possibly losing my chance."

"You're treating this like a game. Love is not a game, Hanna."

"In some ways, it is. Besides, what's the harm in my inviting them for the second date?"

"You seem bent on this idea. I rest my case then."

Ken's argument echoes sentiments from a time gone by. I think many men, through time, have grown tired of pursuing and learns to enjoy options that are readily available to them. And why shouldn't they? It's not only a logical choice, but economical too. I believe all men will agree with me in saying that we are not working only so we can afford to have love in our lives. If a few solid strokes will not do it, they'll paint a different reality for themselves, one that will not require them to exhaust their resources: their time and money. And this is the picture that's fast becoming clear to me here in Dubai. Even if they think I'm worth pursuing, if I don't show interest, they'll abandon the chase, thinking that I might be a futile hunt.

Cinderella attended the ball to meet the Prince even though she was prohibited by her stepmother from going. Ken, or anyone of my friends, cannot stop me.

I will party!

**

"Aren't you going to check them?"

I should've left my phone on my desk. I think the constant vibration is annoying Kaycee.

"I'm sorry."

I pick up my vibrating gadget off the table and place it on my lap.

"It might be important."

"Nah. Their notifications from Tinder."

"Then they are important."

We both laugh at that.

"I am thinking of taking a break from it."

"Why?"

"I've met 100 men, and nothing materialized from those connections."

"Nothing yet, but who knows? Perhaps from those new matches, something will."

Thank God for friends who extend your hope when you're running short of it.

"I want to explore the connections I have with those I've met. Maybe there's something there."

"Okay. But I don't see the harm in you continuing to meet new people while you do that."

"I don't want to miss my chance because I'm not focused enough."

"Any of those you've met so far who present even a glimmer of potential?"

That makes me think harder. Why do I want to see some of them again? Because they offer possibilities. But is it really there, or am I imagining it because I want my time with them to matter?

"Chance is like the wind. You must feel it around you and on you. Otherwise, it's just an illusion created by our minds."

Kaycee has the maturity that I appreciate.

"Perhaps you're right. If I can be openly frank with you, I'm not 100% sold out on the idea of seeing again any of those I've met before."

"Then carry on forward. If any of them really wants to be with you, they'll catch up."

She echoes Ken's views, but with a more friendly undertone. As I think about it, indeed, it seems like a better option for me going forward. If they really want more than sex, then they'll find a way to reach out to me. On with the show then.

**

I'm not one who usually asks my matches where they're from. I like our conversations to either suggest or disclose that – be it in chat, on the phone, or in person.

Janis looks European, but speaks with an accent that seems to be a combination of Russian and other countries around the Baltic area. He has friendly blue eyes, a sweet smile, and a warm aura about him.

"I have never been to the Philippines, but I hear so much about it from my colleagues. Have you been to Latvia?"

"Not yet, but I do want to see that country and the surrounding ones."

"If we still know each other by the time of your visit, I'd show you around. It's a quaint, charming old country that speaks of history everywhere."

I know what he means. Connections through Tinder are usually fickle. It's meet and forget.

"Are you open to friendship in case the meetup does not pan out romantically?"

I have to ask. I like him, but I can sense this early that I will not fall in love with him. Though I think he'd be great as a friend.

"I actually prefer everything to start in that way. I've never been the kind who jumps into a relationship just because I like someone."

"I like that. No pressures, less expectations, and everything grows naturally."

"Or *organically* – free of everything and just allows something to grow on its own."

"To our organic beginning."

We clink beer bottles and continue our talk right down to midnight.

**

"There are buses going to RAK from the Union Metro station. If you have nothing planned this weekend, feel free to come over. I'll drive you back tomorrow."

We have been chatting and exchanging photos on WhatsApp for over a month now. Our schedules couldn't align in our previous attempts to meet here in Dubai. I find Loren's invitation very tempting and, oddly enough, my mind's not protesting against the idea.

I pace inside my room with both excitement and concern. I've never travelled outside of Dubai alone, more so to do it to meet a guy.

"Let me check for a hotel close to your place."

"No need. You can stay with me. I have private access to the beach."

Loren knows I love swimming in the sea, especially on the weekends. And a private access to it? That means that there will be very less people. Something I really love.

"Can we swim tonight?"

"Absolutely."

I don't need more convincing. I immediately pack, have a quick shower, and run off to the Metro station.

"I'm on my way. In the Metro now. It will take me about 40 minutes to reach Union Station."

"Okay. Get off at the mall once you're in RAK. It'll stop there. I'll be there waiting for you."

I usually fall asleep during long drives. Today, my heart is beating madly inside my chest, preventing me from napping. I want to send Lana a message, but I'm worried that her reaction might affect my mood. I just play Fishdom to pass the time. Half an hour into the trip, my eyes feel heavy. I'm certain that sleep is imminent.

"Hi! I'm Hanna. It's my first time going to RAK. I'm really sleepy and I might doze off any minute now. Please wake me up once we reach the mall."

"I'm Lucy. Okay. No worries. I'm getting off there as well."

Just my luck!

"Thank you."

Her friendly presence beside me helps usher in sleep. And true to her word, she wakes me up at the bus stop opposite the mall.

"Where are you staying here?"

"I'm visiting someone. I don't know where he lives. But he said he's just 15 minutes away from the mall."

"He'll be picking you up here?"

"Yes."

"Do you want me to stay with you until he arrives?"

She doesn't sound alarmed, but her words quicken my heartbeat. I've put aside security concerns over my excitement about this excursion.

"You wouldn't mind doing that for me?"

"Not at all."

I am hardly at ease around strangers. But Lucy has a calming effect on me. There's no awkwardness between us, and no invisible wall that separates people from each other. I'm taking this as a positive sign.

And as if it's divinely designed, Loren is delayed, affording us more time to talk and share little things about each other.

"Are you hungry, by any chance?"

"I am, yes. But I'll just wait for him."

"Here. You can have this. Fifteen minutes is a long time for someone who's hungry."

She hands me a burger from Jollibee. The smell of it defeats my will to refuse.

"Thank you. This is so nice of you. Let's share this."

"I'm still full. I ate before I left Dubai."

Fifteen minutes – and a burger – is all it takes for friendship to develop between us.

Loren is a huge chunk of meat for a guy. The top of my head reaches just his shoulders. But he has a non-threatening boyish appeal about him.

"Finally!"

My initial worry dissipates as his arms cage me inside it. Genuine kindness cannot be faked, even by strangers.

"Let's get you home now."

His studio apartment holds the bare minimum: a table for two, an Ikea armchair, a cabinet, and a bed. The kitchen area only has the fridge and microwave oven. Loren is a vegetarian.

"How was the trip over here?"

"I was asleep for the most part."

"You mentioned a girl you met on the bus."

"Yes. Her name's Lucy. She's from my country as well."

"You met her in your sleep while you're dreaming?"

"Before that."

Our laughter fills the empty spaces of his apartment while it also dissolves our invisible walls around each other.

"It's a bit hot right now. But if you want to see the beach, we can take a short walk outside."

"Let's!"

The sand quality is not the same as JBR's, and the shore is rocky and muddled with seaweeds. But the water is just as beautiful. I'd love to immerse myself in it now, but the heat's discouraging.

"Late in the afternoon should be a good time."

We pass the hours talking. I love an intelligent mind. We seamlessly flow through topics from plants to aliens. But I guess to talk about love is innate in all of us.

"Do you think that true love is really as elusive as many thought it is?"

"Are you one of those many?"

"I've met 100 men so far. Nothing came of it."

"That's interesting. Were you hoping to fall in love with each meeting?"

"Not exactly, but I'd prefer to spend my energy and time in the discovery of one, rather than the search for many."

"Hardly anyone has it that easy. But that's the fun of it. You learn more about yourself as you get to know more people. That's an invaluable experience, I have to say."

"Agreed, but it's a tiring endeavor. It can get disheartening."

"And yet here you are."

"Some men are worth the effort. And of course, you have private access to a beach. Perhaps I can finally realize my dream to swim naked."

"We'll have to go out at an unlikely hour, then, to do that."

"Are there cameras?"

"Good question. I have not noticed any. Perhaps we can check later. If none, then we go back to the waters very late at night."

"You're seriously considering my crazy idea?"

"It's worth indulging in."

I playfully throw a piece of a chip at him.

"I don't want you to be evicted from here, or for us to end up in jail for indecency."

"Thanks for the consideration. But how did your idea of night swimming morph into skinny dipping?"

"Don't we all, at one point, want to do something prohibited?"

"Agreed. But we are in a very different world. Almost everything here has a different meaning than what you and I may have been more accustomed to."

"Love included."

"We may have to agree to disagree on that subject."

I eye him questioningly.

"Didn't you know of their customs and traditions?"

"I thought love was above it all."

"That's only in the movies, Hanna. We coexist with each other, but there are things we cannot do together."

"Ain't that sad."

"Maybe. But there are many others who you can be happy with. However, I guess that's one of those things that differentiates us men from you women. We can approach the matter of love from a mental perspective."

"How can I adopt the same practice?"

"You're a woman. You're born with your emotions."

"You say it like it's a disease that we can never be cured from."

"I'm sorry. I don't mean it that way. All I'm saying is that you try to balance it with your intellect next time. There are plenty of people to love, but who presents the highest potential to make you happy without causing you to sacrifice so much of yourself?"

His simple logic quiets my usually argumentative mind. It's well worth a try. I'm a deeply emotional and intense woman. But my mind and thought processing can go to the same depths as my feelings. The balancing of both can be a challenge, however.

At 6:30 PM, though the humidity is still somewhat high, the temperature outside is relatively better. The water is temperate. The tide is even. It's a good time to swim.

Loren displays no reaction seeing me in a swimsuit, despite an ample amount of my breasts being exposed with its deep V-cut front stitching. I'm pleased. My voluptuous figure always makes me self-conscious.

Hardly any conversation passes between us while in the water. I prefer it that way. When my fingers begin to wrinkle, I start swimming back for the shore. Loren follows my lead. We thought it best to head straight back to his apartment and shower off.

He has a movie ready on his laptop when I join him back at the table. We move to the bed when he's out of the shower. Before the movie ends, I'm asleep. I feel him move shortly after, perhaps to position himself better. I move slightly to my side of the bed, and sleep wins over once more. He's up earlier than I the following day.

"Good morning, giant."

"Morning, dwarf."

"How did the movie end?"

"They continued on their journey. You hardly missed much, believe me. It didn't take long to finish after you fell asleep."

"The swim wore me out."

"I thought so too, little mermaid."

There's a ready grin on his face.

"I love being in the sea. It's when I'm most calm, my breathing more even, and I'm fully aware of my body, even feeling my muscles tense with each stroke. I'm fully alive while swimming."

"Do you feel different when you're out of the water?"

"Our world drains me. It pulls me in many different directions, sapping my energy in the process."

"I know what you mean. Moving here was one decision I'll never regret, even if I have to drive a little over an hour twice every day to go to work. The peace this place affords me is well worth it."

"Our world is so noisy."

"Yet many hardly make any sense."

"I'm so glad I came. Can I come back?"

"Any time you want."

I'm sure to come back. Loren has offered me something no man has dared to before – a haven for my tired heart. He's free of malice or judgment. The simplicity with which he lives and his humble virtues easily endear him to me. I have fallen in love with his character overnight. But it is not the kind of love that couples normally feel for each other. And I think he feels the same.

**

A young and really good-looking guy is waiting for the elevator I'm just walking out of. He's sporting a malicious smirk on his face.

"Hanna, baby! Come in!"

Lourdes seems to be in a very good mood. She smells different, too. I look at her bed.

270

"You cunning bitch! He's a boy!"

"He has a cock, nonetheless."

She winks at me as she pours me a glass of wine.

"Judging from the state of your bed, seemed like he knew how to use his boy toy."

"He was a good workout."

"Where did you find him?"

"Abercrombie and Fitch. Mall of the Emirates."

My Chinese eyes widen in disbelief. If there's a ladies' man, there's also Lourdes. Deeply tanned and fit, she looks more like a Mexican femme fatale than a timid Filipina. I shouldn't be surprised.

"Hands down to your lethal magnetism."

I empty my glass as a salute.

"I have one now and again. But you – over 100! That's record-breaking!"

"Believe me, I did not have as much fun as you did."

"That's because you refused to."

"I have been tempted a few times. I just couldn't go all the way. The desire wasn't there, or at least not enough."

"Because you're still tied to a dead memory."

Even without malice, Lourdes' words always sting.

"Well, it's not like I'm not trying."

"Can you not at least have one on the side? Maybe the pleasures of sex can help you forget."

And she renders my logic completely defenseless. I remain quiet.

"Are you afraid to be judged? This place is a paradise, but not for the saints!"

"You wicked bitch with tits and wits!"

We clink our glasses and satisfy our throats with their contents.

**

It's one of those days when I wish I could pick up an axe and chop in half whatever's in sight. I'm methodical and time-conscious. I get highly irritated when things do not align with my expectations.

As I'm about to dial one of our vendors' numbers, my mobile phone lights up with an incoming call. It's Zayed.

"Your call saved someone's ear from burning."

"Oh, bad day, huh?"

"One of our vendors has been testing the limit of my patience. I like standards and everything executed in a timely manner. And it annoys me to no end when they don't respect my schedule."

"I also hate it when things don't get done as I specified. What can I do to take you out of this rotten mood?"

"It's the middle of the day. I doubt it's possible."

"Why? What do you have in mind?"

"A kiss, perhaps. A long, passionate one."

I say it in such a way that I'm sure to elicit a reaction from him.

"Are you sure?"

"Very."

Never ever dare the devil. He takes jokes rather seriously. As I'm having a heated discussion with a contracted vendor on my desk phone, my mobile lights up once more to a call from Zayed. After replacing the receiver, I hastily redial his number. He picks up in one ring and answers not in his usual way.

"Get down to the ground floor right now."

As if hypnotized by some power stronger than my mind, I find myself almost running out of the office and into the elevators.

Upon reaching the ground floor, I immediately see his car in front of my building entrance with the passenger window opened.

"Where are we going? I cannot be out for a long time."

"We won't be."

After a complete roundabout of the JLT block, we are now descending to the underground parking of Cluster O. There are hardly any cars on the second basement level at this hour. He opens our windows halfway down and switches off the engine.

"I'm happy and ready to oblige your wish."

I smile giddily at him and lean forward to receive his lips. He hungrily launches at me with his tongue, eagerly searching for mine. His full lips are equal parts firm and supple. I'm getting aroused by his kisses.

After a few minutes, we slow down to mere smooches. I smiled at him when we parted lips.

"I'd really be careful when making jokes with you next time."

A look of surprise registers on his face.

"I do want to kiss you again, but I wasn't expecting that you'd take my word for it. Weren't you in the office when we were talking earlier?"

"I was. That's one of the perks of being the boss."

"Well, I'm not the boss, so you'd better get me back to the office."

He makes no protest. He fires up the engine and eases us out of isolation and secrecy.

"You own an apartment here?"

"Yes. It's an old one. I'm leasing it. It's vacant right now. You can stay there if you want. It's fully furnished."

"I have an apartment. I'm sharing it with a friend."

"You'd rather pay than stay at one that's rent-free?"

"That's thoughtful and generous of you."

"However, you cannot accept."

How can you serve rejection sans the sting? If only it were possible to keep seeing each other without falling in love. I opt not to respond. It's not like he doesn't know how futile it is for us to even try.

"I want to kiss you again soon."

I cannot let his sexy Emirati accent glue me to the passenger seat. I kiss my fingers and press them on his lips. Then I step out of his car and walk straight into my office building with purposeful strides.

**

"There are questions that can only be answered by love."

Another day, another guy, another Egyptian. By now, I can tell Arabs apart and distinguish European men from each other based on their accents. After over 100 dates, I'm still on Tinder because I don't know how else to fill my time. It feels good to be liked by so many men. It's such a boost to my ego. But the void inside me keeps growing deeper and larger. I'm hungrier and lonelier by the day. I wonder, out of the hundreds of thousands of men here in Dubai, if there's one who isn't afraid to go deep into a woman's heart.

"And until we find love, we live with the questions."

I say with some resignation.

"We can speed up the waiting. We can search for it."

"Is that why you are on Tinder?"

"Among other reasons, yes. What about you?"

"I'm looking for the one."

He must have been taken aback by my answer. He's been quiet for some time. His tone is tentative when he finds his voice again.

"Do you believe in that?"

It's my turn to be silent. There's love, hope, and then there's me. My connection to either one is not a solid straight line at the moment.

"If only I could understand what your eyes are saying."

"I am confused."

"About love?"

"That's one of it."

"They say love is only confusing to those who try to define it."

"I'm afraid I don't follow you."

"Perhaps because our perceptions of love are different."

"Put that in perspective for me."

"Many women go about searching for the one. You're set in your minds on what kind of man he should be, enough so that you hardly consider deviations. We, men, on the other hand, consider someone who has the most potential to offer in a relationship. We get to know her, and eventually she turns out to be the one for us."

I remember Loren saying the same thing.

Why wasn't I born a man?

**

"Have you ever wished sometimes that you were a man?"

"No, but had I been one, I'd definitely have more sex than I'm having now."

"How can you be so casual about it?"

"Sex is sex. Why do you need to be so serious about it?"

Perceptions.

Now their point is beginning to be clearer to me. But I'm a Scorpio, a fixed sign. How can I be what I do not believe?

"I think sex can do you good. It can loosen you up."

As outrageous as her thoughts are, Lourdes always means me well.

A Rough Awakening to Reality

"Another Egyptian? Haven't you had enough of them yet?"

If men can hear us talk sometimes, I think some of them would be livid. Gee, aren't we nasty at times!

"I didn't know he was Egyptian until we spoke on the phone."

"Are you meeting him?"

"I'd like to hear you try to dissuade my mind from going."

"Hanna, there are other men out there. I hope this is not because—"

"Lana, I'm not looking for another Zaki."

"And yet here you are to meet another one of his kind."

"His kind? They're not from another genome of species. Besides, I go for personality and intelligence. He sort of fit the bill."

She's eyeing me incredulously.

"What?"

"I think you need a vacation."

"I was in India not long ago."

"That was last year. Go for another trip, regardless of how short. I think it would help freshen up your perspective."

Or help me gain one. I have been wandering aimlessly for some time now. Today, she makes the thought more pressing in my mind.

**

"According to our great-great-grandfather, we descended from the family of Ramses II. I don't know how much of the story is true, given the length of time between him and us, but neither am I keen to dig into the past to confirm so."

Ramsee is explaining the origin of his name.

"Are you not curious, at least?"

"What can I benefit from my curiosity? And let's say that I may have been from his bloodline, what then?"

"Perhaps your blood can shed light on the study of your ancestors."

"How?"

His big, bold, and deep brown eyes rimmed with thick and long lashes challenge my raven pair. He is the most handsome Egyptian out of the 66 others that I have met. He's tall, muscular, and has natural caramel-colored skin. His thick, reddish lips make me conjure malicious sexual thoughts.

"I'm not sure, but perhaps…"

"I can understand the fascination of the world with our ancient past. It was incredible. But I'm a man with a mind for the future. I'd rather concentrate my energy on what I can make happen tomorrow. The past cannot be undone anyway."

"But it can be rewritten."

"Yeah, sure. But again, how will it benefit me?"

I like my intellect being challenged. He, however, is mocking my common sense at the moment. And it sucks more.

"The past is important, but not as much as now and tomorrow."

Why do I seem to be the only person who's so attached to my past?

"I'm sorry."

His voice is gentler, almost soothing. His composure softens a bit.

"For what?"

"I think I hit a sensitive nerve inside you. I don't mean to offend you in any way. I thought we were just having a conversation—"

"I'm taking no offense. Please, continue to speak freely."

He clears his plate before speaking again, thus allowing me to refocus my thoughts.

"It seems that your heart has not yet close the book of a past story that it no longer belongs to."

Am I really that easy to read?

"Somehow the pain has not dulled yet."

"When I was a kid, I had the nasty habit of peeling the scab off my wounds. Not only did it hurt, but it made the wound deeper and took longer to heal."

He's looking at me knowingly.

Am I guilty of the same?

"Do you drink?"

I nod in affirmation.

"Looks like you need some."

We decided to go to Barasti. Inside the car, our conversation is much lighter, to my relief. He's telling me about his most recent dates. As we're slowing down to ease right to E34 on Sheikh Zayed Road, a car slams hard behind us, causing us to hit the car in front of us. Everything happened so fast. My mind, which never stops thinking, is suddenly blank. Despite all the noise, I can't hear anything for a few seconds until the accident registers in my consciousness.

"Hanna, are you alright?"

His deep brown eyes are blazing with worry, and his voice thundering with anger.

"Hanna?"

I can only nod. When I try to unbuckle myself, the seatbelt is jammed. I look at him in horror. What my lips can't say, my eyes manage to. He slams his big fist against it, and it gives way.

A stranger opens my door and tries to help me out. I collapse on his arms when I make the attempt to walk. My left leg has no strength! Terror overwhelms me. I start crying. Then all the pain starts to manifest. My right jaw hurts so much. My upper body does too, my back in particular. People are talking to me, but I cannot hear my own voice in response. I'm in so much pain.

Zaki.

"Hanna? Hanna? Talk to me, Hanna!"

I can't keep my eyes open.

Zaki.

**

My mobile phone is screaming by the bedside table. It's slightly out of my reach, given how my bed is angled. I press the button to call for the nurse.

"Good afternoon, Miss Hanna. How are you feeling?"

Her tone is alert and urgent.

"Sore."

I say dryly.

"You were in an accident last night. Do you remember?"

"Yes."

How can anyone forget such an experience? How can I forget?

"Is there any part that hurts more? The results of your X-ray are already with the doctor. He will discuss them with you. Let me call him now."

"Can you please hand me my phone first?"

She leaves almost in a run after handing me my mobile phone.

Lana is not picking up. Lourdes accepts my call in one ring.

"Hey, bitch."

"I'm in the hospital. I was in a car accident last night. Can you come?"

"Oh, fuck! Are you alright?"

"I think I'll live."

"Which hospital?"

She does not disappoint. At 20 minutes flat, she's by my bedside with a dress, magazines, a newspaper, chocolates, plus a silver canister with white wine in it. She hands it to me, and I readily take a sip, thinking it is tea.

"I'm on medications, you bitch!"

"Before everything, there was just alcohol. Tell me what happened?"

"A car slammed into us from behind. We hit the one in front of us because of the impact. I lost consciousness while still out there on the road."

"Who was with you?"

"I was on a date."

"Where is he?"

"Good question. I woke up and he's not here."

And just then, in walks Ramsee, a towering figure of a hot god. I love the look on Lourdes' face upon seeing him.

"Hanna! Thank goodness you're awake! How are you feeling?"

"Like I've been in an accident. And you look as though you were not in the car with me."

"I'm good. Alhamdulillah! Just a minor bruise around my belly area. The doctor said it's from the seatbelt. How are you? Where does it hurt more?"

"Everything hurts. And why do I have a neck brace? Did I hurt my neck?"

"No. But your jaw is swelling. Probably from the seatbelt when we were thrust forward because of the impact from behind."

No wonder I find it a bit difficult to talk.

"Where is that fucking idiot?"

"He was fined by the police."

That's all? While I languish here in pain?

He looks at Lourdes and extends his hand.

"I'm Ramsee."

"Lourdes."

"How long am I going to be here?"

"I don't know. Depends on your progress, I think."

"Do you mind asking the nurse? She said she'd inform the doctor that I'm awake."

"Okay."

Lourdes' eyes follow him to the door.

"I'm on a hospital bed and you're thinking of doing my date?"

"He's a hot specimen. Where is he from?"

"You can't tell?"

"Is he an Arab?"

"Egyptian."

"Really? A pharaoh in the flesh."

My sides hurt when I laugh.

I have not sustained any serious injuries. I opted to go home and rest there. Back in the apartment, Ashley is pale with worry.

"You should have called me, babe. I thought you might still be sleeping earlier because I knew you were out last night, so I didn't come to your room."

"I passed out. I woke up only this afternoon. I thought of calling you after Lourdes, but the happenings at the hospital occupied me."

Our conversation is interrupted by the ring of the doorbell.

"I think that's Lana."

"Okay, babe, I'll check on you later again."

Ashley leaves my room to receive Lana at the door.

"Girl, I'm sorry. I was taking a nap earlier. How are you? What happened?"

My jaw still hurts, but there's no escaping Lana.

"We had an accident on Sheikh Zayed Road. We were heading for Barasti."

"We? Who's with you?"

"I was on a date. It's with the Egyptian you didn't want me to go out with. After dinner at Mövenpick in Ibn Battuta, we thought of having drinks at Barasti."

"Perhaps it's a sign, girl. No more Egyptians."

"Lana, it was an accident not of our own making."

"Still. What did your doctor say?"

"I have swollen ribs, a big bruise on my stomach, and my left lower leg should be rested for at least three days. My jaw should be okay right about the same time."

"And your head? Did you have a scan?"

"Yes. No damage there."

"Do you want to eat anything? I'll cook for you."

"Now, that's music to my ears! Can you prepare *Sinigang na Hipon* (shrimp in sour soup)?"

"Okay. I'll go home now and see if I have the ingredients for it. I'll come back at dinner."

My lids have been heavy since waking up in the hospital earlier. Now that I'm in my room all by myself, I allow the tears to come out. Apart from physical pain, there's sadness weighing heavily in my heart. I've never felt so alone.

Ramsee's call cut through my self-pity. I opt not to answer. I'm tired. I close my eyes, and sleep knocks me off.

Upon waking up, I'm inundated with calls and messages from my friends in the office.

"Thanks, Kaycee. I appreciate the call. Roshie is calling now. I need to speak with her regarding my duties. See you next week."

Roshie drops out as I'm about to answer her call. She picks up in one ring when I dial back.

"Hi, Hanna! How are you? I informed our boss about what happened to you. He's extending his regards. He's staying in France for a few more days. I'll take care of everything in the office while you're away. Don't worry about anything."

"Thanks, Roshie. I appreciate that. I have one more request, please."

"Sure. Anything."

"Please don't let Zaki know."

She's been quiet for some time.

"You haven't told him yet, have you?"

"No. I just told our boss. I'll tell Joan not to tell her manager, too. But will you tell him?"

"I'm not sure. Should I? Does he have to know?"

"Think about it. Whatever you decide on, we're with you on that."

"I'm embarrassed to tell him who I was with, or what I was doing, should he ask."

"Why? I know it's awkward, but he knows at some point you have to move on and start seeing other men."

Other men. Oh, how he'll flip over if he finds out that I have been out with 123 other men!

**

A week of complete bed rest has done the job. I'm fully recovered and well on my feet again. Ramsee has asked me out once more, but I politely refused. I just don't feel right about seeing him again.

Towards the end of the month, one Sunday morning, while at work, Lana's suggestion of a quick trip somewhere comes to my mind again. It's more appealing this time. The urge is strong, too.

I check my calendar. Our auditors from the head office will be here in the middle of next month. Our boss is already on his annual leave. He'll only be back two days before the auditors arrive.

I'm actually free!

I open Google. I click on maps. I'm reading the names of the countries on the screen in front of me.

Where to go?

I close my eyes and point my index finger at the screen.

Nepal.

A short vacation should be fine. Easier to plan as well. I searched about Nepal.

Not bad at all.

"Roshie, will you be alright if I take Wednesday and Thursday off this week?"

"Yes, sure."

"Nice! Thanks a lot!"

After putting the receiver down, I start planning for my trip.

**

The airport is one of the busiest places in the world. Different personalities walk endlessly on its carpeted floors.

Today is another such day. Not a single table or seat is vacant. I walk around close to my terminal – nothing. However, on my second turn, a couple stood from a table in the middle of the small food court, fronting the fast-food chains. I walk towards it and reach it at the same time as the cute curly-haired guy.

"Can we share?"

"Sure. We got here at the same time."

And his smile can make any girl's day.

"Where is that?"

I ask while pointing at his Starbucks coffee.

"From there, turn right."

He points at my terminal.

"Okay. Don't let another girl take my seat."

"Depends. If she's also cute or pretty…"

I playfully raise one eyebrow at him. And there's that smile again. Four minutes later, the same smile welcomes me back to the table.

"Glad I still have the seat."

"I'm a gentleman."

"Sure."

And we both lightly laugh.

"Where are you going?"

"Lebanon. You?"

"Nepal. Is Lebanon home?"

"Yes. What are you going to do in Nepal?"

"I'm in search of the *elixir of happiness*."

"Then why trouble yourself going there, when you can just *take a tour within you*?"

He's cute and smart. And if he can walk on two hands, I'll give him a standing ovation.

"We're not made up of the same thing, you and I, sadly."

"Maybe. But I don't think we are that different from each other, either."

"No?"

"I, too, am not as happy as I wish to be right now."

"So you're escaping to home?"

"Home is where happiness started."

"Do you think it's too late for me to change my tickets?"

We laugh from the sadness of our hearts.

"I'm Hanna."

"Majid."

We fist bump.

"So, what's your story? If you don't mind me asking."

"Forbidden love."

"Oh. He's married?"

"No. He's a Muslim."

"Yeah, that's hard. But why did you allow yourself to fall for him when you knew that he was one?"

"I didn't realize prior to that it would be a problem."

"Where is he from?"

"Egypt."

"That figures. They still observe arranged marriages. And many of them are devout Muslims. They don't usually marry outside of their faith. They'll carry relations with other women temporarily, but would build a family only with their own people."

"What about you? Where is she?"

"At her place, still sleeping. I was just there. I walked out of there with a satisfied ego, in a manner of speaking. But with a confused heart."

Amazing how a man's cock functions independently regardless.

"What's with the confusion?"

"We really like each other. We have been going out for a little over three months. Then, recently, she broke up with me because I'm younger than her. But we are still sleeping together now and again."

"How old is she?"

"32."

"And you?"

"27."

"That's a mere five years. Is her age sabotaging her looks?"

"No. Well, at least I don't think so. But she's so conscious about it."

I'm a Scorpio. I don't like grey areas like this. If someone's confused about me, I'll take myself out of the equation and see how that sums up for him.

"Would you like to hear my mind about this matter?"

"Please. A woman's perspective is sometimes better than ours."

He's definitely wiser than most guys his age.

"Don't let the confusion of others confuse you, too."

"So I'll just ignore her next time?"

"No. But square the situation with her. You deserve more than to be lusted for. If she, or you, wants sex, there's plenty to go around. Don't drag your heart where your cock plays. You erode your capacity to love that way."

He's quiet, but I can see my logic kicking his back into gear. His eyes display comprehension. One less confused heart is better than two.

The announcement for my flight cuts the silence between us.

"That's mine. So, see you next time."

I stand and extend my hand.

"Nice sharing the table with you. Can we keep in touch?"

"I don't see why not."

After exchanging numbers, I walk towards my terminal.

Nepal

We may think that we are the ones choosing our destinations, but I also believe that sometimes our destinations are chosen for us. There are certain truths that we stumble upon only at certain places.

I'm standing in the middle of Durbar Square in Kathmandu. The 2015 earthquake has left long-lasting reminders. Many of the stone statues have either collapsed or been severely damaged. Some historical houses are supported by big, long woods to keep them from falling completely. The place is dying, but the people are forcing it to stay alive. They're clinging to a past that nature is asking them to let go. They want to keep the story that does not belong to them anymore. Just like me.

But unlike me, Nepal is a country, a cradle for nearly 30 million people. It needs its past because it is its foundation. Mine, my past with Zaki, is just a chapter, not even an entire book. And yet…

Enough.

I willed to keep inside the tears threatening to escape from my eyes.

Time for a new story.

**

It gets dark here early. It's not wise for me to continue roaming alone. Good thing that the hotel I'm staying at is in the city center. A few of the tourist spots to see, including Durbar Square, are within walking distance. There are also shops and restaurants littering the area.

A shop selling scarves and shawls is directly below where I'm billeted. The nice displays outside it draw me in. As I'm inspecting a blue-green silk shawl with a floral design, a voice startles me from behind.

"The lady has exquisite taste."

I turn around and am surprised to see a man who has facial features that are atypical of this place.

"Nepal rears silkworms, which this material may be made of, but I highly doubt it produced you."

"I'm Persian, and everything you see here is from there. Welcome to my shop! I'm Imtyaz."

"I'm Hanna. Quite a shop you have here."

"Thank you. Anything is half price for you. My first-visit shop policy. And a cup of Persian tea, of course."

"A warm reception and a warm tea. How very nice."

When he hands me the cup, I place it down on the table and continue examining the silky shawl in my hand. It is just a pretense, though, as I wait for him to take a sip from his own cup. As a Scorpio, I'm highly doubtful of people, and I'm a solo traveler. It does not hurt to be extra cautious.

"I'm curious. You don't sound Chinese to me, but you do look like one. Indulge me, please."

"I have Chinese blood. I'm from the Philippines."

"Ah, a Filipino. I've met a few through the years. Nice people, bought a lot of gifts from here when they visited. They're working in the UAE."

"So am I."

I smile and take another sip of my tea.

"This is stronger than what I'm usually served. Also tastes a little sweet. You added honey to it?"

"Yes. I usually add it while boiling the tea, not after. That way, it integrates well with the tea. And a few mint leaves."

"And you don't leave the bag in."

He motions his head to mean no.

"That takes away the somewhat bitter aftertaste. Very nice."

"I'm glad you like it."

He raises his cup to me and empties it.

"So, are you settled with that?"

"Yes. I like this one."

He folds it neatly in a string pouch and puts it in a plastic bag.

"Do you know a good restaurant where I can have dinner?"

"Yes. I'll take you there. Let me just close the shop."

"You don't need to do that. Just guide me to go there."

"I don't think you'll be able to find it on your own. Besides, there are hardly shoppers now at this hour. And I need to eat too."

He's right. I'd take an entire night to get to the restaurant he wants us to dine at if I walk alone going there. At just 7:30 PM, the sky's darker. There are a lot of people – tourists and locals alike – still milling on the streets, though.

Once we're seating, he extends his indulgence and throws in more questions my way.

"So, what brought you to Nepal?"

He's a stranger. I may not see him again. I can make up a story or tell him *my* story. But that will only further strengthen the old narrative that I want – *and need* – to leave behind.

"I need a break, but I don't have much time. So, Nepal."

"How long are you staying?"

"Just four days. I fly back on Saturday."

"Very short. Do you have a planned itinerary?"

"Actually, no. This was kind of a very last-minute decision."

"May I suggest a place?"

"Yes, please."

"Nagarkot. It's less than an hour's drive from here. I can help arrange transportation for you. My friend drives tourists around anywhere they wish to go. He's a trustworthy guy."

"What's in Nagarkot?"

"The hotels there, or cottages as they're mainly called, offer their guests an experience to watch the sun rise from the foot of the Himalaya Mountains. I think it's something that you don't want to miss."

"Wow! Yes, please!"

As Imtyaz speaks to his friend, I scout for a place to stay in Nagarkot. After confirming it with him, I made the booking.

Our food arrived shortly after. Everything smells and looks like Indian food. Being one of Nepal's biggest neighbors, this is not surprising.

After dinner, we moved to a café where we shared a table with two German ladies for some more tea. They're a jolly pair. Our night stretches on, and by 10 PM, we're having beers at a local bar.

"We were together for 15 years. Then one morning, three months ago, she told me that she wanted to leave. I was too shocked to stop her. So I just said 'okay,' and off she went."

Alcohol has a way of unmasking people. Or making some mute, such as in my case.

Ida's story is heartbreaking. Here's a woman who shared more than a decade of her life with another, only to be left behind with nothing that can constitute an explanation. My own heartache suddenly seems petty.

"And you know what's worse? I'm almost 50. If it's difficult to have a heterosexual relationship at this age, imagine what more for us lesbians."

All this time, I have not felt past my own emotions. I've been too caught up with my own pain until now. Straight, gay, or whatever else, the heart feels pain in the same way. I have no words of consolation to offer. I don't think there's anything anyone can say anymore. I hug her instead.

At quarter to midnight, Imtyaz escorts us out of the bar. We drop the sisters at their hotel, and we walk back to mine.

"I feel so sad for Ida."

"Same here."

Now I find my voice again, but I still can't say enough.

"How old are you, Hanna?"

"35."

"You're not married?"

"No. You?"

"Neither."

I'm waiting for him to continue. Nothing follows it. I opt not to probe. The reason of one heart is unique to its own, and it's no one's obligation to explain it to the world.

The silence of the night hurts my ears and makes me feel sad. I open the conversation after about ten minutes.

"Are you happy here, Imtyaz?"

"What is happiness?"

Now, why did I ask him that?

He offers no answer. Neither do I want to dare. No more words pass between us until we reach my hotel.

"Thank you for tonight. It has been a wonderful evening."

"Indeed. Come to my shop tomorrow after you check out. My friend will pick you up there."

I nod in acknowledgement.

"Good night, Hanna."

"Good night, Imtyaz."

**

Nagarkot has a countryside appeal. The cottage I'm booked at offers a fantastic view of the Himalayan Mountain Ranges. It sits atop a luscious green valley.

It's quiet here – a soothing place for weary souls like me. I sit for an hour on the rooftop, contemplating the plight of my heart. I want to stay longer, but the cold is becoming unbearable for me.

Back in my room, located in the annex, a kettle of hot tea is sitting on the table by the window. The staff has opened my curtains to a view of tall pine trees. I take the book by

Elon Musk from my backpack and walk over to the tea table. After an hour of reading, my lids feel heavy.

It's only 5 PM. It's too late for a nap but too early for bedtime. I unpack my hula hoop and put the pieces together. I struggle for the first minutes, because despite the heater and downing one kettle of hot tea, I still feel cold. I pressed on, however, and after 45 minutes, I achieved a good sweat.

A dinner of hot lentil soup, scrambled eggs, and bread toasts ready me for bed. I need to get up at 4:30 AM tomorrow. It will take an hour to get to the area near the base of the foothill of the Himalayas to watch the sunrise.

**

The staff driver is at my door as scheduled. It's very cold and dark.

"Wait. I need to go back in to get my eye drops. I'm wearing contact lenses. This cold will dry my eyes fast."

He just nods. I quickly go in and grab my asthma inhaler and ballpen on the bedside table.

I hope I'll never have to use either one.

All the lights around the cottage are a stark contrast to the thick darkness that surrounds us. My breathing quickens, but I remain composed.

"Good morning, Miss Hanna! Ahupathi, your driver, will wait for you until the sun has fully risen. Then you come back here for breakfast."

"Thank you, Taral. I appreciate your help in making this arrangement."

"Enjoy yourself out there, Miss Hanna. You'll love it."

His friendly manner eases my fear somehow. But once we commence on the journey, the uneven dirt road and dense trees serve only to intensify my anxiousness. Throughout the hour-long drive, I have my inhaler in my left hand and the ballpen in the right. I opt not to use the seatbelt, for my ease of movement, if ever.

My waking nightmare ends when we arrive at the hilltop. There are other tourists already walking around the viewing deck. I exhale in relief upon stepping out of the car and almost run towards them.

A short while after, a collective silence falls upon us. The very top of the sun is now visible on the horizon. No one's talking, but everyone's mobile phones and cameras are focused in one direction. What an astonishing sight it is to behold the majesty of the sky ascends to its throne. A new day is beginning, and I'm awash with its light.

"Good morning!"

The wind pushes his voice in my direction. But I make no effort to respond.

"It's very beautiful, isn't it?"

He comes closer to me now.

So he's actually talking to me.

He's sporting a ready smile when I look up at him.

"Indeed."

I smile back at him.

"I wish you a good day!"

Then I walk in the direction of the parking area to rejoin my driver. My heart is beating with excitement.

My god, he looks good!

And as fate would have it, as I'm checking out at the front desk four hours later, Mr. Handsome walks right in.

"Hey! It's you again."

He looks genuinely happy to see me again.

"So, we're staying in the same cottage. But what took you so long to come back?"

"I just walked and got distracted along the way."

"I see. Well, it's nice to see you again."

"Are you leaving?"

"Yes. I'm heading back to Kathmandu."

"I'm going back there, too. But I'm not packed yet."

"Do you want me to wait for you? I have arranged transportation."

"Are you sure? I have not had breakfast either."

"Taral, is it possible for him to have his breakfast on the go?"

"I think I can arrange that."

"Very well. Off you go to your room!"

He immediately turns to leave, then stops.

"Wait! What's your name? I'm Felipe."

A big smile decorates his face while extending his hand.

"I'm Hanna. Your hand is very cold!"

And we laugh like silly teenagers.

"Go now!"

After ten minutes, he rejoins me at the lobby, and we bid Taral goodbye.

Felipe is from Spain. He's been travelling for the last six months, and along with his luggage is a heavy heart.

"I really thought we were in love."

Those words come with deep pain.

"I wish she didn't have to lie. More than anything, it's what hurts more."

"I guess it's not easy for some people to tell the truth."

"I can understand that, but why lead someone on? Why make them believe in something that is not real when you know it can potentially hurt them?"

"Yes, that's just plain cruelty."

"And selfish."

He finishes his omelet sandwich before proceeding.

"Aren't we all looking for love? So why do we have to hurt each other if we cannot help one another in that quest?"

Why indeed?

"I'm sorry. I think I'm boring you with my love drama."

"Not at all. And I don't consider it as such, otherwise all of life's a drama then."

"What about you?"

"I've not experienced the same, though I've been played by fate."

"Fate fucks us all. None of us can do anything about it. But us hurting each other, that's entirely *optional* to us."

I unbuckle myself and move closer to him. He copies my movement and wraps his left arm around my shoulders.

"We'll both heal in time. For now, let's enjoy Nepal."

"Yes, ma'am."

And he kisses me on the forehead.

A small accident delays us by 30 minutes in reaching the city proper. But it's still early in the afternoon, so we have plenty of time to see some sights.

There's a temple close to his hotel that arouses both our curiosity. The guards deny us entry, though. It's a site for their burial ceremonies. Only members of their faith are allowed in. I feel crossed, and I think so does he.

"Come on. Let's find another way in."

I'm not one to break the law, especially as a tourist. But his invitation infuses me with excitement.

After a few minutes, he asks, "What do you think?" He's pointing at an alley littered with rubble and trash.

"Do you think it leads inside the temple?"

"The temple stretches until the end of this street. Notice how those walls look alike?"

"Yes, they do look the same. So perhaps the next alley is more passable?"

"Let's check."

I am right, but there's a gate. Felipe pushes it, and it opens. Monkeys roam the place like bosses. There are so many of them. Some people are feeding them, while the majority ignore them. There are also vendors selling food and knick-knacks.

An area on the edge of the waters has people pooling around it. We follow their lead. There's a cremation ceremony underway. Out in the open! I'm silently shocked by it. Felipe wants to come closer to see the going on better. I stay behind him, burying my face on his back. I can't look. I don't have the mind or the stomach for it. Halfway through, when the smell of burning flesh intensifies, I pull Felipe away from the scene.

"I can't take it anymore. I'm going to puke."

I start coughing. I feel a heaving sensation in my stomach.

"I never thought that this is how they do it. I know they throw the ashes of their dead into the water, but it never occurred to me that it's done this way."

I can't respond, for I'm still trying to wrap my head around it. I release his hand only when we're some distance away.

"Are you okay?"

I nod as I take a sip from the bottled mineral water in my hand. I pass it to him after.

"Let's continue roaming."

With no direction or planning, we just walk until we reach Patan Durbar Square. Like in Kathmandu Durbar Square, this place also bears the devastating temper of nature, though to a lesser degree.

Felipe is busy taking pictures. I've taken a few myself. I'm not one who takes too many shots of the same subject. I have steady hands. I precise each shot before I click. I observe the people instead while waiting for him.

How many of them who are here are walking with a broken heart right now? What struggles are their hearts silently fighting with?

I don't think we can ever capture an image of what pain really looks like.

"You don't look very good. Do you want us to go to the hotel now and perhaps rest a bit?"

"I'm okay. Can you just please hold me?"

We embrace in the middle of the square, amidst hundreds of other strangers who might be longing for the same genuine touch of love.

"Is something wrong?"

Is there anything right in my life right now?

"Hanna?"

"Memories. They're haunting me like ghosts."

"Perhaps because you have not buried them yet."

How can you bury something that has not died yet?

"Come on. Let's go to the hotel. I think a nap would do us both good."

We walk in relative silence on the way. A heart that has known pain can understand the suffering of another.

When my body hits the bed, sleep wins over. I'm too tired and sleepy to react when he takes his place beside me. I feel his face behind my head as he snakes one arm around my waist. It surprisingly feels good. A wounded heart sure knows how to touch another hurting one.

Our nap extends until 7 PM. The gentle kisses he plants on my neck pull me out of a dreamless sleep.

"I'm hungry."

He mumbles. His warm breath is arousing me.

"Should we order room service or do we go out?"

"Perhaps we should first check what the temperature is outside."

I'm asthmatic. I like the cold, but too much can trigger an attack.

"Ten degrees Celsius."

"Oh my. Are you okay with room service?"

"Suits me just fine."

While waiting for our room service, I take a warm shower, and he checks for a place for us to visit tomorrow. Then we discuss it over dinner.

"Dhulikhel seems nice. Almost the same views as in Nagarkot. Check this."

"Very scenic, yes. And it's just over an hour from here. Should I go ahead and make the hotel booking?"

He nods as he sips his soup. Upon completing the reservation, I resume eating. Momentarily, he lays his mobile phone on the table, showing a photo of me in the square. I look so lost in it. It pains me to see myself in that state.

"I'm ready to listen if you want to talk."

"I'm not sure where to begin."

"Okay. How about you telling me how you feel right now?"

"I'm not really sure about that, either. I'm a bag of emotions, in varying shades and intensities."

"What happened to you, Hanna?"

"I loved and lost."

"As do we all. But I sense that there's so much more to your story than the usual."

"I feel things more deeply and stronger than other people. I think that's what amplifies the pain. He was an extraordinary man, too."

"Wow. I wish someone would think that way about me as well."

"I'm sure you are, too, Felipe, in your own right. It just takes a certain woman to see that."

"I wonder where she is."

I cannot answer that. We are all searching for love. But I think it looks different for each of us. So I'd rather leave it to time, or life, to answer him.

By 9 PM, the temperature drops to seven degrees Celsius, making it all the more impossible for us to go out and stroll. So I head back to bed after brushing my teeth. He follows my actions. He lays flat on his back and invites me to snuggle. It feels like the most natural thing to do. He's drawing circles on my shoulder. I'm doing the same on his chest. I can feel the inevitable.

By the end of the hour, I hit a milestone in my sexuality. If the bed swallows me whole while sleeping tonight, I'll be going with a smile.

The following morning, his alarm is an intrusion on my dream. But he makes up for it by repeating last night's passion. Then he goes out for a short run while I stay in bed thinking of it. Oddly enough, I don't have any untoward feelings about the experience. In fact, I want more. Half an hour after he left, I started touching myself to satisfy my urge, but the ringing of the telephone on the bedside table halted me from continuing.

He's calling to inform me that he's circling back to the hotel, and asks if I want breakfast in bed.

"How cold is it outside right now?"

"17 degrees Celsius. It's refreshing, actually. The sun is out."

"Alright. I'll get dress then."

"Okay. I'll meet you down at the restaurant."

Breakfast in bed sounds more romantic and more to my liking. But we've been holed up in here since arriving yesterday afternoon. So, if the sun is out, we should be too.

He kisses me full on the lips before sitting down. His curly dark blonde hair is damp from sweat, and his cheeks are red from the cold.

We plan our itinerary for today while enjoying our breakfast.

"You're okay to take public transportation going to Dhulikhel?"

"Sure. It would be an experience."

The elevator is too small to accommodate more than three people at most. So we let the other couple go ahead of us. When we're in the lift shortly after, our lips reunite the moment the doors closed - and they hardly part even when we're in the shower.

We walk out of the hotel holding hands. We don't know each other's last names. Tomorrow, I fly back to Dubai while he continues on with his journey. Whether we'll see each other again or not, today we're holding hands on the way to the bus station.

Any religion can pass its judgment. But no law will convict me for choosing to move on.

**

Dhulikhel is a quiet town. There are no skyscrapers here, just tall trees. The inn I've booked for us is actually a three-storey family house. We are the only guests today. We are assigned to one of the rooms on the third floor with an unobstructed view of their charming town and the Himalayan Mountain Ranges. After dropping our backpacks, we stroll around the surrounding area.

The ground is not cemented. It's pure earth naturally flattened by human foot traffic. As we walk down the hill, the way becomes steeper, and it's a deep drop from where we are. What I find most incredible are the trees. They are very tall! From where we are, I can only see the middle part of the trunks. The rest of them still go high up.

We continue our descent. Wildflowers and tall grasses dot our pathway. On a flat clearing, facing the valley, sits a small hut. Smoke is emanating from it; seems like someone's cooking inside.

Felipe's walking in front of me, blocking my view of whatever's ahead. So I'm surprised when he suddenly speaks.

A little boy is playing with his football barefoot. It's the middle of winter!

"Where are your shoes?"

I fail to minimize the panic in my voice.

"No shoes. I use it for school."

We look at each other in disbelief.

"You're not feeling the coldness of the ground?"

He only smiles, which further compounds my shock.

"Where do you live?"

Felipe asks him. He points to the small hut.

"Can we go to your house?"

He nods and runs ahead of us.

When we are standing outside their house, his father, carrying his young daughter on his back, comes out to greet us.

"Namaste!"

He slightly bows his head with his two hands clasp in a prayer position. We return the greeting in the same gesture.

"Tourists? Welcome!"

"Thank you."

We say in chorus.

"Come inside."

We look at each other. Felipe shrugs his shoulders. I motion with my hand for him to go ahead.

Inside is a room with a large wooden bed with scattered pillows and blankets on top of it. Their clothes are hanging from hooks lining the walls. Outside their bedroom, there is a wooden table, made from the same material as the bed, which can seat four people. There's a small island for their plates and cooking pans. And on the ground, something is being boiled in a pot directly above the fire. I cannot escape noticing the absence of a bathroom. I want to ask about it, but I thought better not to.

"Thank you for letting us into your home."

"Stay! We eat together. My wife is coming."

His genuine kindness makes its way into my heart as fast as the air that I inhale. They don't have much, and yet his open willingness to share with us mere strangers what little they have is truly touching.

"Thank you so much. But our food is also being prepared up there in the inn."

"Tashidelek?"

"Yes, that's where we are staying."

I give a hinting look at Felipe.

"Thank you for being so nice to us and welcoming us into your home. We will leave now so you can continue cooking your dinner."

We both bow our heads to the father, then Felipe lightly touches the boy's head before taking our leave.

On the way back to the inn, he is in a melancholic mood.

"They're such wonderful people."

"They've not been corrupted by the filth in this world."

"I wish to go back in time when my life was that simple."

"When was that?"

"Before I knew love."

"You wouldn't have known happiness as well by then, if ever."

"Happiness is fleeting. And in its stead is pain. Nothing seems to last longer than pain."

Don't I know that too damn well?

The hot water is very relaxing, so I take my time in the shower. He's lightly snoring when I join him in bed. He's on his belly, facing my side. I look at him for a moment. He's a beautiful man. He has a friendly countenance. I want to love him, if only our situation were different. And sleep takes me away with this thought.

At 7:30 AM, we wake up to one of the most beautiful views I've ever laid eyes on. Just outside our window are the Himalayan Mountain Ranges, and at some distance yet clearly visible, the majestic Mount Everest. The best part yet? We don't need to leave the bed. We prop the pillows and sit upright, quietly looking out at what's in front of us.

"What would you like to do today?"

"Well, we have the town to discover. However, please don't forget that I'm flying back to Dubai later this afternoon."

"So this dream ends today."

"But not the fun just yet."

I pull my shirt off, and my naked body shivers in the morning cold. I straddle him. My breasts, with their erect nipples, are glaring at him straight in the face. He hungrily sucks them. That ups my arousal. When one of his hands reaches for my sex from behind, I'm in delirium. He pushes me down gently on the bed and spreads my legs apart. As his tongue runs on the outline of my legs and inner thighs, my floodgates are opened. My initial cum further moistens my entry point. He delays my satisfaction for a minute or two.

"Felipe…"

He hears the agony and deep longing in my voice. He leaves the cave between my legs and kisses me full on the lips. And without preamble, he conquers me once more. The wooden bed creaks with the combined intensity of our desires. His moans mirror the rapid beating of his heart. I, on the other hand, am an unbridled wildness exploding with his every thrust.

For nearly an hour, the world outside our room, regardless of how captivatingly beautiful, only serves as a background to a memory that our bodies are creating.

Our breakfast is served on the rooftop. It's past 9 AM, but the whole village still seems to be asleep. It's so quiet, except for the sound the prayer flags and the leaves of the trees make as they sway to the wind.

He thought some soft music might be good. He opens the music player on his phone. We listen in silence for a few minutes. When his favorite one starts playing, he stands and lays out his right hand to me. I oblige; after all, we are alone. There's no one else who can see that I dance like a penguin.

I don't know the song. I've not heard it before. But I like its melody. And the lyrics, it's beginning to move me, the chorus in particular.

If I never see you again
Then think of me now and then
Though it hurts so sweetly
They say all good things come to an end, hmm
You've changed my life completely
I'm touched by your love
Even if I never see you again

I look up at him. His eyes are closed. I don't want to close mine. I want to commit his face to my memory. Chances like this don't come to me even seldom enough. I wish I could lengthen, even just a little bit more, our time together. But wishes are child's play. In reality, life never gives a fuck about anyone's feelings. And time, it respects no one.

It's now 11 AM local time. Two hours seems like just two minutes. At 12:30 PM, we need to leave. Our fairytale is coming to a conclusion. My heart aches a little over this thought.

"Do you really need to go back today?"

I cannot answer because I have none to give. I like him a lot. But I have a life to go back to in Dubai. It's not the reality that I'd like to resume living, but it is real. The last three days we shared together are not a mere fantasy. But what we have, this, is a dream vacation – literally – which at some point I need to wake up from. And it's today.

Felipe is a good catch. However, like me, he has a heart that needs healing. We can take the road to recovery together. But is he heading that way? I cannot stay on the same bus he's on, so to speak, not knowing where its destination is.

He's been quiet since we checked out of the inn. I don't think there's anything I can say that can lift his mood. So I keep my silence as we walk side by side around the village. At an intersection, there's a small stupa that's surrounded by thick vegetation and prayer flags. I allow him to meditate as I inspect the lovely wildflowers strewn about in the area.

Nepal is a sweet and charming little country. It's a dreamy destination for urban dwellers. There's green everywhere. So many scenic views. The cold weather makes you fall in love and crave the warmth of a human companion. That's what it has done to us. This place has pulled us to each other. Sex opens the door for love, or at least the possibility for it. And he wants love. So do I. But how do we do it? We are not in the same place in our lives. We're not even living in the same country.

At the airport, our farewell is brief. He's in a more serious mood now. I'm flattered to think that he likes me back enough to be sad about our parting. But I still wish that our ending had been different. Although I think somehow it's better this way. It's easier to let go and move on because there's nothing holding you back.

The Heart Never Forgets

My phone runs out of battery. So, immediately upon reaching home, I plug it in. After taking a shower and unpacking my backpack, I switched it back on. I added a password as an additional layer of security. I type in that password – or what I think it is - but it turns out to be an incorrect one. I make several attempts until I have two tries left. Panic grips my mind. I put the phone on the bedside table, and I try to calm myself down.

An hour later, I still cannot recall what my password is. I open my laptop. I can't remember my password for it, either.

Oh my fucking goat…

I go over the loose papers on my study table. It's not my habit to write down my passwords anywhere. I'm just hoping against hope that I might have done so, at least for my phone. The laptop can be taken care of by our IT guy tomorrow.

Our main door opens, and I rush out to greet Ashley.

"Hi, babe!"

"Hey! Welcome back!"

"Thank you. So, how were things while I was away?"

"Same. Nothing out of the usual. What time did you arrive?"

"I walked in a little over an hour ago. Babe, do you know how I can open my phone if I forget the password?"

"I have no idea. I just used my fingerprint on mine."

"Alright. I'll go rest. Hopefully, later, I might be able to remember what it is."

**

Sunday morning, and I'm going through my emails while sipping my tea.

"Welcome back, Hanna. I was calling you. Your phone's off."

"Good morning, Assad. I can't open my phone. I can't remember my password yet."

"I need tickets for Iran."

"Send me an email and I'll work on it."

The biometric machine pings three times in succession as my other colleagues pile in, one after the other.

"Hanna, good morning. Don't forget to order the cake before lunch."

"Cake? For what?"

"For whom. It's Bilal's birthday today. I sent you a message on WhatsApp last night."

"Sorry, Roshie. I can't open my phone. I can't recall what password I used for it. I have two attempts left, and I'd be forced to do a factory reset just to open it again."

"Oh my. Our IT can't do anything about it?"

"I asked him already. I'll check now what cake to get for later."

I'm not too attached to my phone. But it is an integral part of my day-to-day life. It feels odd not to be able to use it.

After three hours of sorting and answering emails, and securing the cake for Bilal, I thought it might be a good idea to check what's for lunch at the nearest convenience store to us.

While in line at the counter, a voice interrupts my concentration.

"Hey, you! I've not seen you in a while."

He looks familiar to me. But I cannot remember his name. My eyes are fixed on his face. My brain is searching for his identity.

Who is this guy?

"Oh my god. You don't remember me?"

There's a hint of insult in his voice.

"I just came back from vacation and I dove straight into my emails upon arriving this morning. My mind's just loaded with work stuff right now. And I'm hungry. I'm sorry. I kissed you in the elevator."

And my cheeks instantly flush at that recollection.

"You remember that, but not my name."

"I also cannot remember the password to my phone or my laptop. And yesterday I missed my apartment by two floors."

"Wow! Where did you go? I sure would love to forget a few things myself."

"Sure, but not important details like passwords. It's annoying. I can't use my phone still."

"Yeah, that sucks. Did you back up its contents? You might need to factory reset it."

"Will it affect the photos that are on my memory card?"

"No, but those on your phone, yes."

"Hmm."

We reach our building. Neither of us pressed the up button.

"You really can't remember my name? You just said it."

"You're on the 11th floor."

"And?"

I look at him blankly. There's really nothing else I can remember about him right now.

"Something's wrong with my mind. I hardly forget. Ever."

"I believe you."

He extends his right hand.

"Will."

"Yes! Will. That sounds about right."

It's so easy to remember. In another context, it's a word that I use in my daily communications.

"I'm Hanna."

"I remember who you are. White rose."

I smile at that. Then he goes out to his floor.

Will.

**

"Hi! It's Hanna. Where is the food court again?"

"On the ground level, close to Carrefour. I'm already here in front of the Chinese food stall that you like."

Sheila is a good friend of mine. We met through a mutual friend who, by now, has become our mutual enemy. Time is a good judge of people's character.

"So, how's Nepal?"

"Serene. It's a cheap option for those who wish to leave the noise of the urban jungle for a little while."

"How long were you there? By the way, I already ordered."

"Just four days. I came back yesterday. What did you order for me?"

"Shanghai Rolls and Manchurian Chicken. Did you change your number?"

"No. I can't open my phone. I can't remember the password. I never changed it since getting the phone last year."

"Whose phone were you using just now?"

"That's my work phone. Do you think if we go to Samsung here, they'll be able to help?"

"It's a password issue. I'm not sure. We can try after dinner."

Samsung cannot help. The problem with man's memory is currently one of the limits of technology.

Since we are here in the Mall of the Emirates, we thought we might as well go to Carrefour. And here my memory is once more tested.

"Hanna! How are you?"

At least 20 people within our proximity learned my name because of his loudness. But it's not what unsettles me. I cannot remember him. Another one!

What is happening to me?

"Hi! I'm sorry…"

"Aaqil."

Aaqil. I'm rummaging through my memory, but no information comes up on the screen of my mind.

Who is he?

"Afghanistan. It's been some time. I did not hear from you again after our first date. So I can understand why you cannot remember me."

"Ah, yes. How are you?"

I'm tensed, confused, and fast becoming scared as the reality of my situation is becoming clearer to me.

"I'm good. Alhamdulillah. You? Why did you never message me again?"

"I just got really busy with everything."

"I understand completely. Everybody is all work here. But I hope we can catch up soon."

"Sure. Let's see about that."

Sheila notices my uneasiness. She wheels our cart faster than we normally do.

"He's one of the 123 men I have met so far. I know it's not easy to keep track of people we've met, but I have a good memory. Before I went on vacation, I remember them all."

"Someone had too much fun in Nepal."

I ignore her. There's a thought that's beginning to take a solid form in my mind. As Sheila is scouring the raw meat section, I make the call to Saudi German Hospital.

"Good evening. I'm a patient of Dr. Khalil El Din, a neurosurgeon. Can you please check if he has a clinic tomorrow after 5 PM?"

******

"How are you, Hanna? Are you experiencing headaches since the accident?"

"No, doc. But there's something I want to ask you related to the accident."

"I'm listening."

"You said there's nothing abnormal in my CT scan. Are there any other tests we can do to ascertain that my head, my brain in particular, has not been affected by the impact during the accident?"

"We can, yes. There are tests that we can perform to check you further. But I cannot just make such a recommendation without concrete reasons. Are you feeling any kind of discomfort? Any pain anywhere in your head?"

"I'm forgetting things. I don't forget things."

"There are a few reasons why the mind is not able to recollect some information at any given time. And I know that can be frustrating. But explain to me exactly what is going on."

"I forgot the passwords to my phone and my work laptop. The other day, I went up to a different floor from where my apartment is located. I didn't just press the button by mistake, but I remember being uncertain which floor to press. And I'm forgetting people whom I have just met."

"Stress can be a strong element that can rigor the mind. Tell me about your activities of late."

"Nothing extraneous. I rested for a week as you have suggested. I flew to Nepal recently. Just for a very short break."

"Did you experience any headaches during or after the flight?"

"None."

"Dizziness? Blurry vision?"

I motion my head to mean no.

"Is it possible to lose part of one's memory after an accident?"

"It is. There are different types of amnesia that patients may suffer from after a crash. I think yours is Retrograde Amnesia. It is when patients cannot remember, or have difficulty remembering, events that occurred before the accident. But this does not mean complete loss of memory. Usually, just the most recent ones."

That feels right. Certainly, it does. The pain of the past is still weighing heavy inside me. I still remember everyone I ever hated. So my long-term memory is intact. Everything new or recent, especially those base and boring ones, is lost in oblivion inside the labyrinth of my mind.

"Do I have anything to worry about it?"

"No. But observe yourself. You may keep a journal if you want. Then we can refer to it when we meet again."

"Will I be able to recover those memories that I might have lost because of the accident?"

"Perhaps with the help of your family and friends, and activities geared in that direction. This type of amnesia is brief. Come back after a month. Let's see if there will be changes."

******

I'm surprised to see Ken comfortably seated on our couch beside Ashley.

"Ken!"

"Hey! I had to come. I couldn't reach your phone."

"I still can't remember my password."

"There's Samsung in the Mall of the Emirates, babe. Perhaps they can help?"

"I tried already. It's a password issue. I might need to factory reset my phone just to be able to use it again."

"Did you back up your photos and files?"

"Yes, except those I recently took while in Nepal."

"Cloud?"

"I don't know that. Anyway, I have already posted the photos on my Facebook. Maybe I can just grab them from there and go back to my phone."

"Yeah. Good idea. Anyway, I'll leave you two now. I need to iron what I'll be wearing tomorrow to work. Nice to see you again, Ken."

"Same here, Ashley. Have a good night."

Once she's in her room, I motion for Ken to follow me to my bedroom.

"Feel at home. Do you want a glass of wine? Have you had dinner?"

"Not yet. I came over thinking of inviting you."

"Can we just have something delivered for you? I just had dinner. And I'm not really in the mood to sit outside of my room right now."

"Something is up with you. Tell me."

"I went to see my neurologist today. I'm forgetting things. He confirmed my suspicion."

"What's that?"

Ken looks like Kenny Loggins, the famous American singer, sans the hair. He is sporting a clean military cut and has a sweet countenance, which has drawn me to him since that late afternoon we met in JBR. Tonight, his baby blue eyes are alert and focused on me.

"I might be suffering from what is called Retrograde Amnesia. It's when people forget their most recent memories due to trauma. He said I have nothing to worry about, that this could be just for a short time."

"Okay. So why do you seem sadder than you should be?"

"The accident took away the wrong portion of my memory."

He chuckles. I cannot stifle a laugh as well.

"Looks like the Nepal trip helped. You seem different."

"I had a nice time there. That sunrise experience was amazing."

"I could tell just from the photos you sent me."

"More than that, I had time out to reflect. And I think I'm better now. Really. I feel lighter inside."

"That is wonderful! Seriously, I'm happy to know that."

"I hope I can stay on this new course moving forward."

"It's a challenge, I know. Being a soldier once, even though I have not really been involved in any heavy combat, seeing the aftermath of previous encounters, especially in Iraq, was heavy for my mind and my psyche. There are things that I cannot forget. It was a real struggle for me to have normal days when I first came back."

"I don't know what a normal day is."

"Because we lived realities where pain was constant. And while we're at the heart of it, we thought it's where we should be. It felt natural. Then I was made to understand an alternative truth, and that's when I decided to walk away."

"I feel naked, Ken."

"You shed the old skin, so to speak. That's understandable."

"And confused, if I may add."

"Letting go of what's familiar is always confusing."

"Frankly, I'm double-minded about the current state of my memory. I wish I could forget even half of the pain of losing him."

"But wouldn't that mean being just half of what you've become, too, because of it?"

He has a point. Sometimes it's easy to wish away parts of our lives that we don't like, without realizing that it's usually at those moments when our character is being built up. I feel guilty in an instant. Zaki was an important part of my life.

"When you're done talking to yourself, there's something I'd like to tell you."

"I'm sorry, Ken. That's one habit that I'm still struggling with."

"No issues. But I thought you should know that I'm going back to the States. I've decided to resign from my work here. HR is already looking for my replacement."

This is one reason why I like talking to myself. Sometimes I don't like what the world tells me.

"Say something, Hanna."

"How long before you go?"

"Once they find a new guy, my notice will officially start. One or two months more. Maximum of three, maybe."

"That's so soon, Ken."

There's no hiding my shock now. I don't like changes, especially those unplanned. It shakes me really good inside.

"The idea has been playing in my head for some time now. I tried to make a life here. It's not working for me."

He's not the only one. Loren feels the same. He will not be renewing his work contract at the end of this school term. Two colleagues at work will permanently relocate back to France. Other people can just leave when they want to. How come I can't do the same?

Ken joins me on my bed. He cajoles me into his arms.

"You're welcome to visit me in N.C."

**

It's salary week. I must complete the payroll summary report today. I usually don't entertain calls at this time, but a local number is calling me for the third time now.

"Hello. This is Hanna."

"Hello? Is this Miss Hanna?"

"Yes, it is I. Who's calling, please?"

"I'm Christopher. I'm a nurse here at Al-Zahra Hospital. Your friend Baron had an accident. We need you to come over here at once."

Baron? I repeat his name a few times in my mind. *Who is Baron?*

"Hello? Miss Hanna?"

"I'm still here. What happened to him?"

"We'll explain it to you here. Please come now. It's extremely urgent."

How can I identify him in the hospital when I cannot recall who he is?

Upon reaching the ER, my steps are tentative and timid. I cannot remember him. How do you look for someone you don't know?

"Excuse me, nurse. My name is Hanna. I received a call about my friend Baron. I was told he had an accident."

"Right here, Ms. Hanna. I'm Christopher. I was the one who called you."

"Can you explain to me what happened, please?"

My head hurts imagining how his head hit his kitchen countertop. That's solid stone.

"And according to one of the rescue paramedics, he mentioned your name a few times before he completely passed out. He was also mindful enough to open his phone so we could contact you."

"Is it serious?"

"We don't know at this point. But he was bleeding heavily when the paramedics arrived at his place. I called you in case he needs to be operated on. Do you know if he's depressed?"

"No, I don't. Why do you ask that?"

"He was intoxicated when he was found. Can you stay for a little while? We might have some more questions for you."

I nod. I'm sure I have no answers for whatever else they might ask me, but my initial shock has not worn out yet. And now, finding out what happened to him, my confusion is compounded. It nailed me to this cold bench.

Within the following hour, I'm informed that he'll be moved to a room on another floor.

"Is he awake?"

"Perhaps, but maybe not lucid."

I'm in the same state. I'm swimming in my confusion. I gained a small recollection about his identity through our Tinder conversation. From the bits of information in that limited chat, I surmised that he's Aussie, a banker, and divorced. I'm sure we've talked about that last piece, but I cannot recall how it went.

A heavy bandage covers his head. There's a contusion on his right eye. He still looks good, though. But what happened today would surely leave a mark on his forehead. And I hope in his memory too. The next time could be lethal.

I'm going through my emails on my phone. I fail to notice that he's already awake.

"Hanna."

"Hi, you."

I touch his arm lightly, unsure which other parts of him might be hurting.

"I knew you'd come."

"Not the type of call I'd like to receive, to be frank. You got me really worried. What happened?"

"I hit my head against the kitchen counter."

"That I already know. They told me they smelled alcohol on your breath."

"I was let go at work."

No judgment there. Alcohol may never help anyone get a new job, but it certainly can be a liberating ally when one needs to temporarily forget.

"I'm glad you're here."

"How did you know that I'd come?"

"You believe in love."

"Be serious, Baron."

"I am. You have a heart, Hanna."

"Don't we all?"

"Yeah, but yours understands better. You understand pain better than anyone I know."

"Thank you. That's flattering to hear. By the way, the doctor told me that though the wound is big, the cut is not as deep. And there's no serious damage to your skull and brain. You're lucky."

"I don't feel that way."

"Regardless, be thankful that you didn't hurt yourself worse over what happened."

"I think I have."

I'm beginning to realize what he's actually meaning. I'm just not sure it's the conversation I'd like to have now when I'm struggling to remember him. But he's right. I understand pain, because despite the state of my memory, the heart never forgets.

Searching for Superman

After over 100 dates, one might expect that I don't feel jitters anymore when going out for another meetup. While that may be true to a certain extent, today, however, I am anxious. I'm meeting a Saudi national – my first! But something about the way he sounds on the phone unsettles me.

I've been to Shimmers Restaurant once for my birthday. I love the view here. The Burj Al Arab is my favorite building here in Dubai.

He's seated at a table with a very good view of the Burj and the sea. Upon recognizing me, he stands and rewards my cheeks with kisses. He's strikingly handsome, the kind that makes people look. But at this hour, there are very few diners. Yet still, I feel so self-conscious.

"I was worried that you wouldn't show up."

"Why do you think that?"

"I know my effect on people, even on the phone. I sensed your reluctance. But I suppose that's typical with intelligent women."

He raises his glass to me.

"Riesling, as you said."

"You intrigue me."

I take a sip from mine in order to calm my nerves.

"As I supposed you'd be. And I can reward your curiosity, and eventual cooperation, very, very well."

What on earth could he possibly mean by that?

My confidence staggers before him. This man has real power. I don't know how to explain it, but I can feel it from his presence. He's studying me like a scientist examines an organism under a microscope.

I empty my glass. He attempts to refill it, but I cover it with my hand.

"It's only 4 PM. I don't want to drag my sexy ass out of this place just as it starts to peak. Let's talk. You said on the phone that you need help with something. I'm all ears."

"I need a child. Help me bear one."

The crash did not affect my hearing. I'm sure I heard him right. But it's something I never expected. The shock renders me speechless.

"I'll pay you 500,000 Dirhams. The first half you will get once we're married. The rest, after our child is born. You get a little bit more if we have a boy."

Again, I'm not hearing impaired. But I still can't talk. My shock has just compounded.

What kind of joke is this?

I pour myself another serving, then down it in one go. My heart is beating madly. After a minute more, my tongue regains its normal sting.

"What kind of drugs are you on?"

"My dear, in my country, you can get punished for being insolent."

"Am I not glad that I'm not from there?"

"I'm offering you an opportunity to become rich. Sleep over it. Let's meet again tomorrow for breakfast."

"500K does not make anyone rich."

"So you want more? How much do you want? A million? I'm willing to negotiate."

His eyes convey a dead serious intention.

"Do you realize how ridiculous this is? You're asking a complete stranger to marry you and give you a child! Who, in their right mind, would make such a proposition to their date that he's meeting for the first time?"

"Me."

Suave, sure, and strong. Who is this man?

"Aren't you guys usually arranged with someone in marriage?"

"None fair well to my liking. And if I am to bring a child into this world, I want to be the one to choose my bride."

"Did others turn you down, so now you're pitching this to me?"

"You're the only one I've asked so far. And I want you to consider my proposal carefully."

"I don't even know your last name. I know nothing about you. I cannot be expected to get into a bus when I am not certain of its destination."

"Fair point. That's quite a strong argument, too, I must admit. You're proving to be a very good choice by the minute."

"But I'm not on the menu for the type of dish you wish to be served. And I will not be forced into it, especially not over money."

"Consider it a gift."

"Not the kind that I prefer."

I try to put enough strength on that last statement. But I think I fail to make an impact, for he has remained stoic, but looking resolute as ever.

"I'm gay."

Holy mother fox. That sure stitches my lips to silence.

"We will divorce after six months. But I will keep the child, or my parents will. Then you are free to live your life once more – as a millionaire. And you will never hear from me again."

I want him to stop talking now. I cannot afford to hear anything more of this nonsense. This severe assault on my logic is paralyzing my brain. I cannot think beyond this moment, and I so desperately want to leave it.

"I don't want to take any part in this madness."

"Madness?"

His tone takes on a different shade. There's an emotion visible on his face now. His deep-set eyes are beginning to burn me.

"How else can you explain this?"

"There are many gays in your country."

"Your point is?"

"Why do you seem so shocked by my confession? There are gays who have families and kids. It's perfectly normal—"

"There's nothing normal about what you're proposing to me!"

My voice slightly goes up. I'm so riled up inside. I stand and ready myself to leave.

"Hanna."

"I'm sorry. I cannot do it."

I kiss him on the forehead and then walk away without looking back. I do not want to play even a cameo part in somebody else's story with a plot similar to his, even for a million Dirhams or more.

**

Days after meeting the Saudi guy, I'm still reeling from the experience. Even remembering it feels surreal.

"But I have to give it to them. It's very challenging to be gay in this region. They have a very masculine definition of a man."

"So he wanted to use me as a front. His reality is not an accepted truth."

"He might be desperate. For many of them, death is better than shame."

I know what desperation feels like. But you cannot make it go away with a lie.

"Seriously, though, between us, you never gave his offer a second thought?"

"What's there to consider?"

"I mean, it's a million Dirhams—"

"Lourdes!"

"Alright. I'm sorry. Just trying to lighten the conversation. You're so tense. I've not seen you like this since Zaki."

"Well, it's not every day that you get proposed to in that way. And this whole dating experience has got me thinking."

"What about exactly?"

"Is there still a man out there who isn't afraid to go deep into a woman's heart?"

"My darling friend, you're asking for Superman. He isn't real."

Maybe. But my man is out there. Somewhere. Perhaps with someone he shouldn't be with, but he hasn't realized it yet.

******

He has an unusual name on Tinder: Relat. Or could it be a short version of a word?

I've met many sorts of unusual people since embarking on this journey. I can let his name slide. I swiped right. It's a match!

Wow.

I'm still thinking of a witty way to say hi, and his message pops in.

Relat: Hi! I'm Bob.

Bob. Hmmm.

Me: Hello Bob.

Relat: How are you today?

Me: Apart from being confused over your name here, I'm good. You?

Relat: I can explain it to you over the phone, if you'll share your number with me.

Smooth operator. I'm fact-hungry, so I give in. Five minutes and my phone's vibrating to his call.

"Hello."

"Hi, beautiful."

I know better than to be thrilled by mere words. I remain non-reactive.

"Are you familiar with Einstein's Relativity Theory?"

"Why don't you refresh my memory?"

"Do you know Isaac Newton?"

Do I really want to talk with this guy right now?

"Yes. Gravity guy."

"That's him, yes. According to him, the planets in our solar system rotate around the sun because of gravity. Albert Einstein came up with another perspective on the matter, or added to it, as others would put it. Space-Time Curvature. Simply put, we are attracted to the sun because of the indentation in space that its mass created. We got lured into its path."

"Okay, but why do I feel like it's an incomplete explanation?"

"Because I'm not done yet."

Thought so too. Now, why did I bother to ask?

"If we use the same context in life, people are not merely pulled to each other by attraction. But we meet certain people in this world because we are meant to share paths at some point."

I'm sure Einstein did not mean for his study to be used as a pick-up line or a means to entice a girl towards a guy. But I think this one will be able to get away with it.

"Your silence means you disagree with me."

"Are you expecting me to be in agreement with you on it?"

"Don't you think the comparison makes sense?"

"I prefer to keep science out of the love sphere."

"Fair enough. How about dinner to make up for this boring talk?"

"You're paying."

"Deal."

Bob is half-Lebanese, half-Spanish. He's a physical masterpiece, with a mind to match it. But like a sculpture, he's made of stone. I've sat across more than a hundred men and have seen emotions in their eyes in varying shades and intensities. Bob is almost void of any. Perhaps his divorce dried up his emotional well. Or that's why it happened – the well does not have enough water to start with.

I will not risk getting to a dangerously low level myself in order to pour some on another. I have my own race to run.

**

I barely have time to eat today. It's been so busy at the office. I'm happy with my French date's choice of restaurant, though I'm not happy with him for company.

An impasse comes to every relationship. But I don't believe it's a strong enough reason for two people to give up on each other, or more so, to cheat on our partner.

"As a doctor in Psychology, there's nothing in the book that you can use to help you both get past this situation?"

"Not every life dilemma has an answer that can be found in a book, Hanna. Sadly, especially for relationships."

"But how does meeting other people help you with it?"

"It's a matter of perspective, I guess."

"I'm listening."

And I regret hearing him talk. As a psychologist, it's his job to explain his patients' ailments. He's been in practice for more than a decade. Of course, he has become adept at explaining the maladies of the mind, including his own. This blabbing nonsense is a sad excuse for a man.

**

Another day, another guy. Another Emirati. And my oh my, his eyes are making me wet. His luscious lips are so enticing. I can't stop thinking about how it might feel for him to kiss me down there.

"It's not always that easy to get out of a relationship, especially if you've been with someone for a long time."

His accent. Damn it! I'm not wearing panties right now. I'm struggling to focus. I cannot afford to look stupid before this demi-god.

"But how does staying in it is in any way easier?"

"It's not, either. So, after some time, it has become a balancing act for me, ensuring my actions do not make even a ripple."

"But that's not living. It's a life of compromises where you're at a disadvantage."

"And today is one of those days when I wish I had held out just a wee bit longer until I could meet someone with your maturity and openness."

Now's one of those instances when I think I'm lucky for being single still. I may not have someone checking on me every day, but I also don't have that problem where I answer to someone for it.

Choices. A simple enough word that carries with it a profoundness that shapes our lives and our world.

"Can you not get a divorce?"

"We're not in the USA. We don't just toss that word out here and not worry about the serious repercussions that follow it."

"I understand. I'm sorry for my innocuous question. Please don't think I'm suggesting it."

"I know you're not. And don't worry, I don't take offense easily. Besides, it's normal to look for the exit in a tight situation like mine. But again, there are factors that cannot be ignored when considering divorce here in the UAE. And my children…"

His countenance turns very serious at the mere thought of his kids. I reach out for his hand. Muscular but soft, typical hands of people with money.

"I'm sorry, Khalid. No good heart deserves this trouble."

In the days that we have been communicating on WhatsApp and through phone calls, I have come to know him to be a sweetheart. I sincerely wish that I could love this man. But I do not see myself as the other woman, regardless of whether I'm the one he loves.

**

"I think an affair is a necessary evil in a marriage. At least in mine, I strongly believe that it helps. I'm able to look at my wife differently and appreciate her more now with my dalliances on the side."

Some of my dates are as fucked up as this. I feel like banging my head on the table so his words will make sense to me. Or perhaps I should bang his head on this table to knock some sense back into him?

What am I doing here?

I stand abruptly and walk in the direction of the main door. His shock disables his English tongue from uttering a word.

Nothing personal, mate.

**

I'm wearing a little black dress with grey flower embroidery on the sides. The fabric hugs my body right without taking away the decent appeal I'm going for. And because I'm running late, I opt for a pair of black ballerina flats.

He greets me with open arms upon seeing me descend the stairs. We are at UBK in the Mövenpick Hotel in JLT Cluster A. Most of my dates are always well within my comfort zone. And since lately I've developed the propensity of walking away from them, it's getting closer and closer to home.

"I'm sorry I'm late. Tight day at the office."

"No worries. You're here now. And I'm glad to finally meet you."

"Same here. I thought we'd never meet."

"I know. 75% of my job requires me to travel around the region. It sucks, to be honest, because I cannot cultivate a relationship. So it's kiss and go all the time with me."

"What a hectic life you have."

"That's why I make the most of my chances whenever I'm presented with one."

He rests a hand on my lower back. My senses are alerted. I might be the one to kiss and go tonight.

This big pharma guy has a big ego hiding underneath his plain appearance. His preference for white shirts is a façade to a more colorful character who's dying to have an audience. Perhaps once I have my fill, I can run out of here under my usual pretense of going to the ladies' room. I'd rather be thought of as a jerk for a woman than suffer him longer.

"Why don't you just excuse yourself nicely?"

"In many of my dates, I was conversing with their ego. It does not have ears."

"Then why did you go out with them in the first place?"

"It's not always easy to tell what a guy is like over chats and phone calls. And I think when you're searching for love, you should not exclude anyone."

"Right you are. But when do you park? When do you realize that the search is futile?"

"When has the search for love been an unworthy endeavor?"

"That's not what I mean. And I know that I will not be able to dissuade you. All I'm saying is, why don't you give it a rest? Let it find you instead."

Let Cupid deliver love to me? That's a scary thought, especially since I always thought of Cupid as Casper. He's a friendly ghost, yes, but a ghost nonetheless!

"I prefer to have an active role in the matter than to allow chance to just give me the option."

"Have it your way. But how many more times are you going to run here after another disappointing date? Not that I mind, really. But I'm thinking about your heart. We can also break it over our own disillusion."

This is why I love coming to her place and have come to respect her more through the years. Lourdes offers logic sometimes stronger than self-help books do.

**

Koi no yokan [ko-ee no yo-kan] Japanese

(n.) The extraordinary sense upon first meeting someone that you will one day fall in love.

I have met some admirable gentlemen since I started "Tinder-dating." Seeing this word today in a pin on Pinterest, however, brings one particular man to mind: my 129th date.

Friday last week, a date (no. 128) from Lebanon walked out on me over lunch because I flat out refused to go home with him "for coffee" afterwards. Upon returning to my apartment, I remember telling Mr. 129th about it over on WhatsApp. The guy has the same name as he does. Mr. 129th and I have not met yet by then, but we have been corresponding over on WhatsApp for two weeks already. He proposed a quick meetup on the same afternoon in order for him to "redeem his name," as he jokingly said.

He's warmer in person and as friendly with his words as he is online. He seems really smart too, for he doesn't get lost during our conversation, even though I talk fast. We've kept in touch since, something which I, intentionally, avoid doing with almost everyone else. Why? I don't know. I'm so hungry for a genuine connection that one might think foolish of me for not exploring those earlier ones I've had. But my heart is like a cat. It has a mind and temperament of its own. No matter how seemingly amusing someone is for "other cats," if I don't think it so, I walk away.

However, it's not the case with Mr. 129th. He constantly sends me messages. Mundane they may be, but it feels so good to be thought of by someone.

Mr. 129th: Hello

Mr. 129th: How are you today?

I can feel his genuine concern even in his simplest of messages. His boy-next-door appeal seems authentic. And I think he's a really sweet guy, too. His easy manners allow me to put my guard down – another first for me with him. Our exchanges do not feel forced or fake, and are never boring. In fact, I've never met a guy who's as talkative as I am. Ken and I have become very close, but we don't talk the way Mr. 129th and I do. Even flirting with him feels natural. Should things continue to progress between us, I'd stop meeting men from Tinder and concentrate my attention on building a stronger friendship with him.

******

"I want to drink and eat to drown my frustration in their delicious menu."

Lana is a cool head. She's a Scorpio born in October. They're usually more mellow and even-tempered compared to us November babies. Today, however, her stinger is out and ready to strike anyone whom she might deem unsightly.

"I can feel the heat coming from the flames inside you. What happened?"

"I went to Omar's apartment with breakfast, thinking of surprising him. A girl opened the door and she's wearing his shirt!"

I open my mouth, but not a word escapes my lips. I think I'm a bit more shock than I appear.

"Fuck! Fuck! Fuck!"

The dragon is not only awake. She's also searing with anger.

"I need two glasses of Riesling now."

I almost shout in an urgent tone to a passing crew. Then I switch to a friendlier one when addressing her.

"Could she be just a friend who slept over for the night?"

Seconds after it dawns on me how stupid that idea is.

"I don't think so, girl. I don't think so."

Never refute a dragon on its claim. Or you'll turn to ashes from its flame.

Never meant for that to rhyme, given the dragon is out of rhythm. I stay quiet.

"How could I not have known?"

"There are people who deserve an Oscar even though they're not actors."

"I'm usually good with this. We are. Scorpios are the hardest to fool. How could he have pulled this one on me?"

"Your guard is down because you started to develop feelings for him."

"Motherfucker!"

"Did he see you?"

"Yes. I slammed the breakfast I brought into his face!"

I clink with her glass and pour the chilled alcohol down my throat. My empty stomach felt the impact of it. I'm glad the service is fast. My body's clamoring for food. After some time, I open the conversation again.

"Where is the girl from?"

"She's a Filipina too."

"Seems like he has a thing for us."

"Or we could be the only ones he could fool."

"How long have you been going out?"

"Three months."

"Was there an agreement between you two that you're exclusively dating already?"

"That has to be elaborated? We're together twice during the week and almost every weekend. So what's there to discuss? Our picture is even his home screen wallpaper!"

No one can see the home screen unless the phone is unlocked. I've not seen any of my previous dates open their phone in front of me. Ah, men! And the lengths some would go through just to have and keep a girl!

Incredible.

She signals to a crew for a refill. Alcohol can constrain the dragon's agility, but it can never douse the fire inside her.

The queen may cry, but after the tears, there comes fire.

"I think it's cheaper for us to be drunk at my place. I just restacked my cabinet."

"Did you keep the empty bottles?"

"No. Why?"

"I could use them on his head."

That's a real Scorpio woman talking. If the devil sidesteps when we're angry, every guy should as well. Or better yet, they should run!

"Well, time to activate your Tinder again."

"I never deactivated it. I was just not active while we were dating."

"This change in your situation now permits you again to be so."

"Definitely! I need new dresses for my new matches."

We clink glasses to toast to the idea.

**

Mr. 129th: Do you do the same?

I'm chatting again with Mr.129th on WhatsApp.
Yes, that's his name I saved in my contacts.

Me: No. I don't go to that extent. But I do prepare myself when I'm meeting guys.

Mr. 129th: What do you do then?

Me: I go over our chat on Tinder and I try to recall the conversation I shared with them on the phone. That way we have something to talk about when we meet.

Mr. 129th: You seem serious about this.

Me: I'm spending time and energy on it. I think it's just right that I am clear about my own intentions, even if many of them are not.

Mr. 129th: I agree. Any new meetups recently?

Me: Yeah, there were. I met four guys this week. Needless to expound.

Mr. 129th: It was that bad, huh?

Me: More like frustrating because we don't like the same thing. And it seems that regardless of what I wear, they're more interested to use their mouths on my boobs than to talk to me.

I can imagine him laughing through the emoji he sends through his message.

Mr. 129th: I can't blame them. I could barely keep my eyes on your face when we met.

Me: I know. I noticed it. And I think it was sexy.

Mr. 129th: Oh, yeah?

Me: Yes. Definitely.

Mr. 129th: Will I see more next time?

Me: Maybe.

I don't feel ashamed of carrying on a conversation like this with him. In fact, I'm enjoying it and more of his company.

**

"How many?"

"144 so far."

Sultan's shock is real. I can see a concoction of emotions in his eyes, both confusing and exciting his mind.

"Clearly, you have certain standards. But may I be bold enough to ask what you are looking for?"

"Someone who is not afraid to love."

"Now I understand. Many of us got easily disqualified."

"Are you afraid to love?"

"What man isn't?"

"But why are you afraid to love?"

"Well, for me, it's not really fear. I think it has more to do with our differing understanding of love, or how it should be."

I give him a questioning look.

"Think of a puzzle. In order to complete it, you must fit all the pieces together. Human relations are the same. If your pieces do not fit, then perhaps you both belong to different puzzles, and got mixed up together by life. Sadly, even if we try different ways to make things fit, it simply won't if they're not meant to be."

"Isn't that what communication is for?"

"Yes, but then again, how one person communicates to another is one extra layer that can compound the story. We all communicate differently because we all think differently."

Love is an action word. It's not a noun to be defined, nor a matter to be weighed. But Sultan is right. Unless two people share – or endeavor to have - the same understanding of what love is, their pieces will not fit. The puzzle can never be completed then.

Being in a country that's a melting pot of so many people from around the world, how can we find a common ground where we can both decide how love will be for us?

"Looks like I infected you with my skepticism over the matter."

Sultan jokingly throws that at me, but his eyes are like those of a judge, serious and focused on me.

"On the contrary, in fact. I'm wondering if I have been too critical of everyone I met. You know, not knowing their pieces well enough. And in the process, unknowingly denied myself a chance to build something with someone."

"We have a saying in Arabic that what's for you will never be given to another, and what's not for you will be removed from your life so you will not be harmed by it."

And yet here I am, barely whole without Zaki.

"Hanna?"

"I'm reminded of an old memory with what you said. Sometimes it persists in my consciousness. I'm sorry."

"Don't give so much power to a memory enough to hurt you again."

I feel naked right now. And embarrassed. My past has no place in this table, yet I'm allowing it to spill over like this.

"Sometimes it's still hard for me."

"That's perhaps because back then, you did not see what was wrong in your situation. You do now, but still you cannot accept it."

"I felt betrayed by fate."

"You're not the only one."

"Why are you still single, Sultan?"

"Like in your story, fate has its hand on mine too."

"It seems that there's no way to escape it."

"I'm afraid not."

"What would you have done differently, if you could?"

"To be frank, I don't know. That's why perhaps sometimes fate has to intervene. We are not always sure of what we have to do."

But what about for us who do? We were ready. We were sure. Why did fate intervene in our story?

"You impressed me as one who has a renegade heart. What would you have done if you could change anything?"

"I wish the circumstances surrounding our love back then had been different. Everything else could have stayed the same as they were."

"We create the circumstances in our lives. I strongly believe that we determine our choices on our own."

Choices coerced by fate.

I take another mouthful of the Arabic dish Sultan has ordered for me. I realized just now that this is the only way that I can ever hope to experience intimately the Arabs or their way of life. But his invitation offers another possibility.

Sultan drives us home to his place after our sumptuous meal. I have had the same invitation more than a hundred times. Today I accepted. His quiet charm and sweet demeanor towards me make me relent easily. Something about his presence makes me feel at home. So when he leans in for a kiss, I readily open to his invasion. My lips hungrily reciprocate his advances. My body is very welcoming to his touch. When he feels my sex, he's surprised at the amount of moisture that pools around my opening.

"You're not wearing panties?"

I giggle at his remark, intensifying the heat I feel on my cheeks.

"I don't wear one when I don't have my period."

His eyes widen in disbelief and lust. I pull him to me for another kiss. He's game and becomes more sexually charged. I don't know what will happen tomorrow, whether we will still see each other again or not. But today, right now, right this minute, nothing feels better than him, his kisses, and his touch. I feel a sense of liberation as he undresses me. I loosened my chastity belt in Nepal. Today, Sultan has taken it off completely.

**

"Allelujah!"

Lourdes excitedly fills my glass.

"I know you're timid with information. So just tell me: how was it?"

"Well, you're right. It's a freeing experience. I felt like something in me had been unlocked."

"Your sexuality, no less! It's part of who we are. I don't understand why so many women are afraid to own up to that side of their personality."

"I'm not sure that fear is the right word. Though I suppose you're right that it is one factor that contributes to others being coy about it. But I think it's more to do with the guy. I mean, who wants to be just taken in and be done with?"

"Sometimes that feels good."

She gives me a wicked wink.

"There's an animalistic element to it. You'll see one time."

"Sounds exciting, but then again, I think who the guy is matters."

"Whatever."

She finishes her drink.

"Oh, just one more Q please?"

Her hands, clasping her wine glass, are in a prayer position, as her eyes plead to me.

"You want to know where he's from."

She nods enthusiastically.

"Local."

"You cunning bitch! The moment you got the chance, you gunned for the top choice!"

I cannot hold my laughter. Lourdes can be a clown at times when she's not dispensing life lessons.

"Are you going to see each other again?"

"I don't know. And believe it or not, I'm not entirely hooked on that idea. I'm happy right now, and I just want to stay in this mood."

"That's the attitude, babe!"

And we toast to my newfound sexual freedom.

I'm at an all-time high for weeks. I've not been out on another Tinder date after the Emirati. Even though I hardly heard back from him, Mr. 129th has kept me occupied. We have been exchanging messages on WhatsApp almost every day. We've gone out twice more since, and it has just been awesome. We're two very talkative people who seem to have loads and loads of stuff in our minds. He has electrified me back to my old self which I've been eager to be again.

Today, however, I am tangled inside in my own emotions. The truth isn't just stranger than fiction; it's far scarier, too.

Melka's face displays worry that only serves to amplify my own. I embrace her tightly and longer than I usually do when she reaches our table.

"I've seen you very sad. But this look on your face now, I do not know what to make of it. What happened, woman?"

How do you start talking about the truth when you're still trying to comprehend it yourself?

"Mr. 129th is Anna's ex-boyfriend."

"What? Are you sure?"

"I wish it wasn't so, but yes."

Anna used to be Melka's flatmate in International City. They have a "shallow" friendship, as Melka would say, and have been out together to scout guys in the bars around town. I've met her a few times. She's like an audiobook that plays on itself, trying to regale us with stories of her own Tinder dates. I've always been a passive attendant in conversations that do not interest me. However, she arrested my attention when she started talking about him, Mr. 129th. When she mentioned his name for the first time, I felt something inside me move. From then on, I listened to her with willful intent. And I fell in love with him in the privacy of my mind.

"Do you remember that afternoon we were having tea by the beach and she joined us?"

She looks relieved that I opened the conversation again. I can see how the shock is melting her makeup. She's been profusely patting her face.

"Yeah. The same afternoon that they broke up."

"You wished that you could meet someone like him."

"And you wished that you were the one who met him."

"I have been in love with him all this time, Melka, even though I didn't know who he was."

She lost her tongue in the astonishment of my admission. I, too, cannot proceed beyond it. After some minutes, she manages to force some words out of her mouth.

"Did you tell him?"

"Told him what?"

"About knowing Anna."

"No. And I don't think I can, ever. I saw the pain in his eyes when he shared with me their story. Your friend is a liar. What she told us that afternoon was her version of what happened, not the truth."

"Hanna, that's their business. Don't get wrapped up in their story. Stay out of it."

How? How can I not be involved when my heart has made it its business to be involved with him?

"Hanna?"

"There was a full moon that night. I told the moon more secrets than I ever did to another soul. That night, I asked the moon to look after him until we meet. That night, I promised the moon that I'd search for him, and that if it would help me, once I'd find him, I vowed to love him with all of me."

My tears come gushing out, heavy with the emotions barraging my heart inside. Melka reaches out for my hand.

"Now I understand why you've gone out on all those dates. You were searching for him. You're giving me goosebumps, woman. Why can't you just have a normal love story?"

Her hearty laugh is infectious.

"So what now?"

"I asked for this, didn't I? So I'll see to it that I will not disappoint with the chance I have been given."

Melka is quietly contemplating my words. With gentleness, she dispenses her counsel.

"You knew what happened to him. A broken heart can hurt another heart. You need to be careful with his broken edges, babe."

Am I ready for this? Can I really love again while I'm still nursing my own broken heart? Love sometimes comes without an announcement. My heart may still be limping, but I'm certain that I cannot let this chance pass me by.

"I don't know how I can help you in this. But if you need me, you know I'm just here."

"I know. Thank you, babe."

A seemingly meaningless meeting turns out to be an answered prayer, a granted wish I cast out to the universe some time back in the past. I'm thrilled at this realization. But do I have the upper hand in knowing his past?

**

For days on end, I've been beset with thoughts of him.

Should I tell him that I know? But what good will that do?

I'm all for honesty and transparent communication. But this is about the past that nearly shattered him. What is the better route to take moving forward?

"First and foremost, it's not your story to meddle with. You knew the story, but you were not a part of it then.

So don't be a part of it now. Write a new one with him instead."

And with that, Lourdes empties her glass of Merlot.

"I agree. Use the information you know to love him better."

Lana is enjoying our brunch well enough that she's mostly been agreeing to what Lourdes is saying.

"This seems to me a straight shot case. Why do you look daunted with guilt?"

Spot on. There's a shadow hovering over my consciousness since finding out who he is.

"Should I talk to him about what I know?"

"How will that help?"

That question has been pounding my mind for days now, robbing me of essential sleep.

"There's nothing that you could have done, even if you knew him before. And there's nothing you can do about his past now, except to heal him from it."

Be it about sex or a more serious matter, Lourdes beats all self-help books.

"Can the love from one broken heart be enough to heal another broken one?"

"Time alone can tell, Hanna."

Lana has caught up in the seriousness of the discussion.

"There are chances that come to us only once. Don't waste this time because of your fears of non-existent issues."

That's a solid case. I have no arguments left strong enough to counter that.

"Why does knowing his past bug you so much? It's not like you went out of your way to find out about it. On the contrary, it was volunteered to you."

Lourdes pours the remaining Merlot into her glass.

"Oh!"

Lana suddenly bursts.

"Serendipity! You're perhaps meant to know his past because you're going to play an important part in his future."

I get goosebumps hearing Lana's words.

"Think about it carefully," she continues. "Of all people, you came to know about what happened to him through the one he used to be with. You didn't seek her out. Life introduced her to you. Fate, universe, or whatever you want to call it, gave you a private viewing of what transpired in his life before you. Why? Because you are the continuation of his story. You might be his happy ending."

Her thoughts are stirring my mind. I've always held strong opinions about the occult and mysticism. It never occurred to me, though, that my life would become a platform for it one day.

"We've always been cautioned to be careful what we wish for. Something heard you that day. Your words echoed into the consciousness of the vast universe. They heard your heart's plea."

Lana is starting to tear up. I slightly shiver at the thought. Deep within me, I believe her. My mind rushes to my consciousness the memory of that night when I cried before the full moon and made a solemn promise of love to a man I hadn't even met yet. I've never done that for any man. I've seriously considered a few I've met along my journey, but I've esteemed no one to that level – not even Zaki. A quiet stillness comes upon me. I'm no longer in control here. Something else, a higher and greater force, has come along to direct this next stage of my life. With him.

Redemption.

The universe wants to make up for the betrayal he has suffered from his last girlfriend by introducing me to the story. I am to be his repayment in kind, so to speak. Realizing this makes me understand my overwhelming anxiousness. I'm not afraid that I'd fail. I'm afraid to disappoint the universe. Will I forever be doomed if I fall short of its expectations?

Am I enough for him?

"Hanna, don't overthink this. Enjoy the chance and have some great sex."

Lourdes raises her glass to me. We three toast to my new beginning with Mr. 129th, who could very well turn out to be *the one*.

What if the last time you try

turns out to be

the best chance

you've ever taken?

**

Han Birondo